Chasing Destiney

Chasing Destiney

Sweet Destiney Book 1

Vivienne Paul

Hibiscus Tea Publishing

For my husband.

*You've held my heart since I was twenty, and our love is a dream
I could never have imagined.*

Cherished readers,

Thank you for diving into the pages of this story!

I can never express enough gratitude for your support.

I truly appreciate it.

This book marks my very first published work, and I'm deeply honored to share this story.

This is a friends-to-lovers, slow-burn romance. Please be patient with Destiney and Micah on their journey to loving each other. Some love stories are worth the wait.

Fear not; spicy moments await!

xoxo,

Vivienne Paul

P.S. This story ends with a cliffhanger, and you'll need to read book two, *Destiney Fulfilled* for the complete story of Destiney and Micah.

Preface

In seventh grade, I began writing a story about a girl named Destiney, who was also in seventh grade. It was a coming-of-age story highlighting the struggles that we Black girls often face during those awkward years: challenges at school, friendship drama, boyfriend troubles, and family issues. I wrote on notebook paper wherever I could and kept those pages in a three-ring binder. My sisters eagerly read everything I wrote, acting as my first beta readers. I worked on the story on and off for a few years but never finished it. Yes, I still have it. I packed it when I moved into my first apartment and held onto it over the years, getting married, attending college, moving to two more apartments, and buying our first home. Over the years, my sisters have asked about Destiney, encouraging me to finish her story.

While the story has evolved, the character of Destiney reflects the young woman that seventh-grade Destiney has become.

Vivienne Paul

one

DESTINEY

"It has got to be the most *epic* wedding kiss! Have you seen it yet?"

"Yes! Just watched it for the thousandth time."

"That's so sweet! Can you imagine a man adoring you that much?"

My sister, Daijah, and my best friend, India, were gushing over a viral wedding clip.

I watched it earlier, getting the feels myself.

The clip had millions of views.

Definitely swoon-worthy.

The clip was less than a minute long and began just as the pastor pronounced the lovely couple husband and wife. When he tells the groom he may kiss his bride, the groom immediately performs several push-ups effortlessly. Wedding guests found it hilarious, and so did his bride. I did, too.

But when he finally kisses her, it's the most passionate kiss I've ever seen. The love and adoration they held for one another was palpable.

Intensely romantic. And beautiful.

How fortunate they were.

As with most viral clips, I watched it several times. Then, I fell into the rabbit hole of watching other wedding clips that were just as passionate.

And I kept watching them.

One after another. I guess I couldn't help myself. I'm a hopeless romantic.

I loved seeing those brides being loved on like that. I figured it has to be an incredible feeling.

"Des, will you come out already?!" Daijah was at the doorway of my ensuite bathroom. *"Yassss Sissy!* Turn around and show us all that ass!" I guess that clip was long forgotten. Daijah held up her phone, recording as I modeled the white lace jumpsuit timidly. Strappy nude wedge sandals completed the look. *"You better werk, Sis!"* Daijah had the confidence of ten women, and right about now, it was contagious. I slowly spun, examining my final look in the full body mirror on my closet door.

The jumpsuit was a sheer lace at the top, with capped sleeves and a high waist, enhancing my modest curves and hugging me like a second skin. I wasn't voluptuous by a long shot, but the splicing shorts put my thick thighs on full display. A big ass wasn't something I was blessed with either, but there was a little something back there I could work.

Stepping towards the mirror, I examined my hair a little closer. Daijah had styled the top half of my locs in a high bun, and the back hung freely. I didn't style my locs a lot these days because they'd grown so long. Ridiculously long, but Daijah wouldn't take no for an answer. She said *"we were on birthday behavior and weren't doing anything ordinary tonight."* The bun sitting high on my head, along with the wedge heels, gave my short ass at least three inches in height.

"Come out here, let me see!" India harped. She was sitting on my bed, eagerly anticipating my emergence. *"Destiney!* Oh my gosh! You look stunning! You did *damn good* Day!"

Daijah hand-selected everything I wore tonight, down to the delicate jewelry adorning my ears, neck, and wrists. As great as I looked, I admit I wouldn't have picked any of this for myself—especially this white jumpsuit.

It was absolutely sexy, and I felt sexy in it. But I would have gone with a black one. Hell, maybe even a red one.

I rarely ever wore white.

Daijah and I had tastes and styles that were as different as night and day. Black was my go-to color for pretty much everything. And as much as I tried to object, Daijah wouldn't hear any of that. Anyway, just like I knew it would, everything came together nicely. My baby sister had an eye for great fashion, that was for sure.

"Thank you boo! Come on, let's get a few ussies before we get out of here," Daijah said, taking a place on my right and India joining us on the other side of me. It was my twenty-seventh birthday, and we were headed out to celebrate. I wasn't thrilled about this initially, but these two ladies, as dear as they were, persevered. Honestly, I didn't mind a lounge on the occasion I had the energy, which I did have tonight. Thankfully. The best part was that I'd be spending time with my two very favorite people in the entire world. So, they eventually won me over. I was excited and I planned to enjoy myself.

Daijah and India busied themselves taking pictures for the book, the gram, and snap.

"Oh my gosh, this one is *sooo cute!*" Daijah gushed. "I'm sending it to Julian!"

"Let me see!" I turned toward Daijah, "*Oooh, that is cute!* Send me that one."

"I just sent it to both of y'all."

"Girl, Julian is gonna wonder where the hell you're going with your legs and titties all out!" India jested playfully.

"He knows where we're going and won't mind." Daijah cackled. "He'll probably try to come get me and crash our party."

"He better not!" India declared through a chuckle of her own.

"Right. I love Julian, but it's just us ladies for the next couple of days," I said.

"Hell yeah it is, and I am so excited!" Daijah squealed.

I was, too. It had been a long time coming, and I was beyond ready to relax and enjoy the low-key festivities planned. These two knew exactly how I wanted to spend the weekend. Tonight, after the lounge, we'd watch movies, binge on junk food, and have a sleepover. Tomorrow, after we sleep in, we'd have brunch, a spa day, and a little shopping if we got around to it.

Several pictures later, we headed downstairs to wait for our ride. We looked damn good, like a girl group stepping out for a night on the town. The sun had gone down, but it was a moderately warm evening for mid-April, so we had arms and legs out, each showing off shades of melanin.

India was gorgeous as usual, wearing a spaghetti-strap tiered bodice dress with a v-neckline. It was cute and flirty, stopping mid-thigh, and her slim figure was perfect for it. I loved the back; it was a deep scoop open back stopping at her waist. The rich marigold color perfectly complements India's smooth cinnamon skin. Her long black hair was pulled into a sleek low bun with a fresh sunflower tucked behind her ear.

My sister was as beautiful as ever, giving me life in her burnt orange with golden polka dots satin cocktail dress. It embodied Daijah's feminine style with a vintage flair. She'd begun a loc journey with sister locs that were thriving and now shoulder-length. Tonight, she had them styled in two French braids tucked into a side bun. I loved my locs, but I had to admit how much I missed them short. Shoulder length was my favorite phase, and I'd contemplated cutting mine shorter multiple times.

"Indie, you want another shot? The Uber is a few minutes away." Daijah had just tossed one back herself before offering India one.

"Hell yeah."

The girls were pregaming while I was getting ready, and they were already feeling it by the looks of things. I didn't drink often at all—nothing dark and never anything straight. I planned to have my one drink for the night when we got to the lounge. We chilled a bit longer and took a few more pictures, and once the Uber arrived, we were on our way.

***

We entered Torch, a hookah bar and lounge, immediately consumed by the sweet, smoky ambiance. I was a big fan of hookah, and I've been to various hookah bars all over Sacramento.

Torch was absolutely one of my favorites. Black owned, has the chillest vibe, superb hookah flavors, and a bar and restaurant. I love the food here. They have your typical bar food, plus featured menu items you can't get anywhere else. There was a sushi burrito with many build-your-own options, which was pretty good. Then they had *Cajun with Asian fusion* items. That gave me pause at first. But I ordered some Ragin'Cajun fries one day, and my mind was blown. They're tossed in a medley of Cajun and Asian spices. The fries are so damn good, I get them every time we come here. They had a house sauce too that was so bomb you could eat the sauce on damn near anything. Daijah loves their Ragin'Cajun meatballs and wings.

I took in my surroundings as we headed toward the back of the lounge. It wasn't too crowded for a Friday. The lights were low, and the walls were vibrating with sound. Tonight, the music was on point. The DJ was playing hits from the nineties and early two-thousands. I grooved with my girls on the moderate-sized dance floor, and after a few songs, I returned to our section. I got comfortable on the couch, vibing with the music. Daijah and India stayed on the dance floor, returning soon after. Our hostess set us up with our hookah, and we put in food and drink orders.

Daijah and India ordered a platter of Ragin'Cajun wings and fries.

I ordered a basket of Ragin'Cajun fries. Extra spice. Extra sauce.

"Are you having a good time, Best?" India asked. The music wasn't super loud, and it was nice that we didn't need to yell to hear each other.

"I absolutely am." I smiled. "Thanks for being here."

"Of course!"

"Do I really get to have you for the next two days?" I asked India gingerly.

"I really hope so Best."

I gave her a quick side-hug and decided to leave it at that. India had a lot going on at home, and the last thing I wanted to do was ruin our good vibe.

Our drinks came out first, and I took a few sips, smiling in delight. I loved it. It was a pretty drink—guava-colored with an orange slice in the rim, topped with fresh cherries, pineapple wedges, and fresh mint. The flavor was vibrant and tropical and had banana, pineapple, and coconut.

"A birthday girl in the house tonight?" My face grew warm, but I smiled anyway. I gave Daijah a knowing expression, and she was wearing a sheepish grin. Daijah knew exactly what she was doing, insisting I wear the "Happy Birthday" sash, conveniently surprising me with it once we got out of the Uber. Attention was inevitable. "Happy birthday, beautiful," The same voice said in my ear. He walked around to the other side of our section. Now facing me, he stooped low resting his forearms on the back of the couch, "*And I do mean beautiful.*"

"Thank you," I returned sweetly.

"What you drinking, mama?" The mystery man asked me. The surrounding tables had a mix of men and women, but I hadn't noticed him before.

Not that I was looking anyway.

I shrugged. "My sister ordered it for me." I looked at Daijah, taking another sip. I wasn't as versed in this area since I didn't drink much.

"No idea. I just asked our server for something sweet," Daijah chimed in.

He peered at the contents of my glass intently. Whoever he was. Meanwhile, I canvassed him. I figured I might as well; he was front and center.

And he was handsome, that was for sure.

Likely in his late thirties.

Smooth as hell too.

And he smelled good. I got a whiff of whatever he was wearing as he walked by me a moment ago.

"Hawaiian Screwdriver," he stated matter-of-factly, "I'll get you another one. And another round for these lovely ladies."

"Yes, please!" India chirped.

He chuckled, nodding, "Sure thing."

"Thank you," we all said in unison.

"You're welcome. Enjoy."

Just before Mystery Man turned to leave, he slid me a business card. "That's my cell. Call me birthday girl. I'd love to see you again."

India grabbed the black business card from my hand. "Tyler McBride. Torch Hookah Bar and Lounge…*oh my gosh! Destiney! He owns this place!*"

My eyes grew wide, "Damn for real?" I muttered.

"Yes, for real!" India placed the card on the table, pushing it back toward me.

Daijah picked it up, having a look of her own, *"Birthday girl, he wants to see you again!"* she said in a singing voice, raising her eyebrows, "Ooh Girl!"

"So it seems," I said absently. I didn't have anything substantial to add.

The girls didn't either because moments later, our server returned with our food, and we dug in immediately. We didn't talk for a while, just let the food fill our mouths. Not long after, our server returned with our second round of drinks.

"You planning to call him?" Daijah segued, taking a long pull from the hookah pipe. I knew she'd make her way back to this.

I had just taken a pull myself, and I loved the flavor. We tried a new one tonight. Royal Raspberry Muffin. It tasted like a mix of vanilla and freshly picked raspberries, perfectly smooth with a balance of sweetness and faint tartness.

I shrugged, somewhat dismissively. "Maybe."

"Oh sissy…" Daijah began, passing back to me, "You get all the cat calls. Yet you never entertain any of these men."

I smirked, my brows knitted. "You guys get hit on too."

Daijah waved that off. "We aren't talking about us right now. You my dear sissy are single as fuck."

After my turn, I huffed my annoyance and passed to India as she chimed in.

"Right! He's handsome. He's polite. Nothing is repulsing about him at all from where I'm sitting."

"Live a little for once," Daijah said.

"I don't do one-night stands."

"Destiney! Who said anything about a one-night stand?" That was India.

"I don't know…he just gives me that vibe. He didn't even ask my name." That screams an indifferent lack of regard. To me. "What if that's all he wants?"

"You don't know that." Daijah said, sipping her drink, "Maybe he's keeping it casual and will ask all the vital questions once you talk more." Daijah would say something like that because she didn't know what was out here. Daijah had Julian. Been had Julian. "Call him. Get to know him."

"He may be the perfect gentleman," India chimed in.

Yep. India had a man, too.

I signed audibly. They seemed positive and hopeful and…

I'm no cynic. I swear I'm not.

Taking another pull from the hookah, I gave this more thought.

Meanwhile, my girls were on to the next topic of discussion just that quickly, and I tuned them out. Aside from our lack of a formal introduction, Tyler seemed nice enough to talk to again.

Maybe he was different.

There was only one way to find out.

I nodded, agreeing silently.

I could call him.

two

DESTINEY

So, I called him.

I even saw him again.

In fact, we hung out a total of three times.

Unfortunately for him, it was over before it started.

Pretty much right away it was clear he wanted nothing more than to screw me. I am keenly aware of how many women are moving out here, so I didn't hold it against him initially. He just needed some course correction.

The thing is, I always tell men up front that I would not be having sex with them. Not anytime soon. I informed Tyler of the same. And he told me he was cool with that. But he was lying through his teeth. Tyler saw me as a conquest; he was right back to it days later.

Also, he *constantly* bragged about the money he had. And he had plenty of it.

I'd imagine he could get just about any woman he wanted with that kind of money. There are women galore out here looking for a come-up.

Also, unfortunately for him, I am not one of them.

You cannot buy me.

Grandiose gestures from the wrong person turn me off. A man pursuing me need not lead with his wallet, especially if we just met and are in the building stages.

But say we've been together for some time, and it's just because of our anniversary or my birthday. Feel free to take me on a helicopter ride or some shit. I really would love that. But please don't pull out a bunch of stops when you haven't bothered to learn my middle name or my favorite color. Because meanwhile, I am making it a point to know yours and everything else about you.

I'm not a grand gesture type of girl when I get to know someone new.

I love sweet gestures, though, and Tyler did not seem to know the difference. He would have figured that out had he been paying attention. Thoughtfulness and simplicity are the way to my heart. And for the record, I like the finer things just as much as the next girl. But it's all in the intent. Buying me something just because you have the means doesn't impress me.

Tyler McBride took issue with the reality that I was unimpressed with his money when really, I was unimpressed with *him*. He never bothered to get to know me. He was dead set on taking me out, wining and dining me, and tossing me lavish gifts with the assumption that I'd give him the panties.

Once, he called his bank on speaker so that I could hear his account balance. He had a few hundred thousand and was sure to mention that he had more money in multiple accounts. That was the last time we hung out.

But he kept calling me.

Even after weeks went by, he continued calling me. But I kept it moving.

I should have told him to move along, but whatever. I realize now that my handling of that was immature.

About a month after I'd last hung out with Tyler, Daijah and I hosted a girl's night at our place.

Daijah's best friends came. Twins Veronica and Victoria. India came by, and my friend Neeka. On the weekend of my birthday festivities, Neeka met Daijah, India, and me at the spa the following afternoon. India gushed about the owner of Torch giving me his number. When Neeka came to girls' night, she asked how things had been going with Tyler and me.

I told Neeka that I stopped seeing him and why.

Neeka went on and on, criticizing me for unceremoniously tossing him aside. Giving me the third degree, "Girl! Pass him over here if you don't want him!" She was dead serious, too. Informing me she would have gladly taken him off my hands. Daijah rolled her eyes so hard I thought they would pop out of her head.

I didn't care one way or the other. Neeka could have Tyler. Dude was barking up the wrong tree, plain and simple.

The funny thing about it, from what I'd gathered about Tyler and knowing Neeka, that arrangement wouldn't have lasted past a simple *fuck*.

Neeka absolutely would have wanted to attach herself to Tyler, marry him, and everything else, but he wouldn't have been remotely interested in anything more than sex with her.

three

MICAH

"Come on ref!"

"You can't be missing them travels, man!"

The worst part about this was the nagging parents. I didn't mind officiating games, but they were all convinced their child was the next Lebron. Half were trying to overcoach from the stands, and the other half were yelling obscenities about all the calls we *were* or *weren't* making.

The crazy thing about it is that these players were eight-year-olds.

Meanwhile, my partner was trickling off and missing a bunch of calls. Since I was on my shit, it seemed I was calling every little thing. There were a few cuties in attendance, but Terrence needed to chill. I rolled my eyes every time we were paired up. Terrence was the homie, but he stayed flirting with these women.

I was a referee for youth basketball at the Salvation Army in my spare time. They had a recreational league for ages five to fourteen. I coached on occasion as well. I did it for fun more than anything. I got the opportunity to work with kids, which I enjoyed. It kept me in shape, and it was something to do. Most importantly, it was a terrific way to give back. My brother and I grew up playing basketball here, so it was a great feeling to return and pay it forward. I believed in their ministry, and my values aligned with everything they tried to do for the youth and the community. They paid officials a small stipend for each game, but I refused to take the money; I claimed it as a charitable contribution each year. I was glad to volunteer my time because the funds returned to the program.

I blew my whistle for one of the coaches requesting a time out.

"T, man… You need to keep your head in this game," I sighed in frustration, glancing at the scoreboard. "We got about six more minutes. You think you can handle that?" There were many single women at these games each week, but now wasn't the time for Terrence to exercise his many options.

Terrance chuckled, "Man, don't worry about all that. They ain't coming back, no way. This game is about over."

I shook my head. There was more than a thirty-point lead. The guest team was getting hammered, I had to admit. Just the same, Terrance needed to focus on the task. He'd have plenty of time to get at whoever the hell his flavor of the week was. But that was T. not taking things seriously. Well, aside from entertaining the women, that is.

A beat later, Terrence blew his whistle, ending the timeout. "You can chill on all the calls you're making. That way, nobody else can get mad at me," he cracked up, taking off behind the ball as the kids made a fast break.

All I could do was shake my head.

***

About two hours later, I pulled my bag over my shoulder and headed out through the gym's double doors. I'd just finished two back-to-back games and needed a hot shower. The referees ran just as much as the players, especially the older kids.

You could almost stay at half-court with the little ones and still see everything since they're so small. But since the younger kids were still learning to handle and control the ball, things could go all over the place, and we had to stay with it.

When officiating teenagers and adults, the game was more controlled, but we still ran up and down the court. Plenty. Those back and forth and high intensity moments could get to be exhausting. I stayed in decent shape, which helped tremendously, but I was glad to be done for today.

Walking through the vestibule, I waved at Carlos, the site supervisor who hung out at the front desk. Most of the crowd in the lobby had cleared out except for the spectators standing around watching the next game through the oversized windows. I was near the doors leading out to the parking lot when I heard someone calling after me.

"Hey, excuse me!" Her voice was soft and meek, and as I turned around, I saw that it fit her petite stature perfectly. She was bending over to retrieve something, and as she stood to her feet, I realized it was my sweaty towel. It must have fallen from my neck as I approached the exit.

"Oh goodness, you don't want to touch this." I gently took it off her hands. "I just wiped my sweat with it." She was chocolate with a beautiful smile, and I smiled right back at her.

"No harm done." She shrugged. "Just making sure you don't leave it behind."

By now, I was taking in her features. I counted one dimple when she smiled.

Her face was soft and pretty.

No resting bitch face in sight.

I didn't know when that happened, but it would be a great day once that fad was gone. I didn't find anything about that shit attractive.

"Excuse us," A woman with a few children passed me. I hadn't realized I was standing in the doorway. Apologizing, I quickly moved aside. As eager as I was to head out just moments before, I wasn't ready to go yet.

Before I got too carried away, though, I needed to establish protocol.

"Thank you so much," I told the chocolate cutie. She had since turned back toward the glass windows.

"Sure," She tossed over her shoulder.

Her hands were in the pockets of her hoodie, and I couldn't recall if she had a ring on her finger.

Taking the few steps toward her, I held my hand, "I'm Micah. I'd love to thank you properly. Would you be okay with giving me your name?"

"Sarina. But really, it was no big deal."

"Sarina," I nodded, "Thank you, Sarina. You're very pretty, by the way."

Smiling, she brought her hands out, a bright gold band with a shiny diamond sat snuggly on her ring finger. It was a lovely ring. I don't know how I missed it.

"Thank you," she glanced at me quickly with that smile again. And you're welcome, Micah."

After shaking quickly, her hands returned to her pockets, and her eyes were back on the game.

Meanwhile, I mused for a moment.

I'd heard some unmarried women wore a ring on their ring finger to ward men off, something akin to mosquito repellant. That cracked me up, and I suppose that is a thing for the more conventionally attractive women.

Then there are the men who will pursue a woman regardless. Wedding ring be damned.

That's another conversation entirely.

Anyway, as a gentleman and a straight shooter, there was only one way I could know for sure.

"Forgive me if this is forward, Sarina. Are you married?"

"I am married," She returned with a confident smile. This time, she kept her eyes on the game.

I nodded in understanding, turning toward the game myself. "You have one out there?"

"Yes, my nephew."

"Indeed," I returned, stepping back, "Have a great evening."

"Thanks, you too."

I quickly made my way out of the gym and toward the parking lot.

She was pretty with a kind spirit.

Of course, she was married.

In my experience, women like that didn't stay on the market long.

I was never the type to operate from a scarcity mindset; however, occasional abstractions from the dark side got into my head.

Like right now.

But I kept them in check—most of the time.

I'm a hopeful person.

Perpetually optimistic.

I tossed my bag in the trunk, and as I climbed into my Mercedes, I reminded myself that I wasn't there for that anyway. Before cranking up, I checked my phone for any notifications. Shortly after, I was merging onto Highway 99 South, headed toward home. Traffic was moderately light for an early Saturday afternoon.

The Salvation Army was in the Oak Park area of South Sacramento, and I lived in Elk Grove just about twenty minutes away. As I cruised down the highway, I considered what I would do with the rest of my day.

I needed to restock my fridge. Today was the second Saturday of the month, so I could go to the farmer's market. As convenient as it was to go to a supermarket, I tried to shop small as often as possible. Mentally, I ran over what I needed when a call came in over my Bluetooth. I quickly glanced at my screen, seeing Malachi's name.

"Brother."

"Baby Brother. What's happenin' man."

"Just leaving Salvation Army. Had two games this morning."

"That's was'sup. It's hardly noon. Must have been the little ones."

"Yup. Eight and under."

Mal whistled, "Bet them rugrat's ran yo' old ass ragged."

"Old? Mal, we're the same age."

Malachi cackled, "You have a partner today?" Occasionally, we were on our own, and that was a lot more work. It was always nice having another official. Malachi understood the concept well since he also officiated every blue moon.

"Yeah. T."

"Oh yeah? Bet he had a good time," Mal cracked up all over again, and I couldn't help but join him.

"Man, I swear."

"I'll see you at the Blue House tomorrow, but I wanted to make sure we have you all set for next week."

"I appreciate you, but we gone be straight dude."

"No doubt. Ella wanted to be sure. This is the longest they'll be staying over at your place."

"Well, they aren't babies. And we can drop by your house anytime we need to." I had a key to Malachi's home, and he had a key to mine.

"True."

"You and my sis just go enjoy yourselves. We'll be fine."

"Sure plan too. Got all sorts of ideas. Bout to have a good time rediscovering…"

"Mal, really?" I had to stop him because I already knew where this was going.

Malachi's hearty laughter flowed through my speakers. "We grown man, stop it," he said once he calmed down.

I shook my head. "Anyway. That all you wanted?"

Mal paused for a beat. "Yeah. What you got planned for the rest of the day?"

I preferred the early games because I could still make plans in the afternoons and evenings, like date plans, even though I haven't been dating much lately.

"Shit. Gone hit the shower, get this gym smell off me. Grab some groceries. Nothing else concrete."

"Come by. Jackson and Polsinelli are on tonight." Mal was a huge MMA fan. I enjoyed watching the fights but didn't follow the hype as much since I was no MMA fanatic. Just as well, any time with my big brother was a good time.

"Yeah, I'll come by."

"You have a standing offer to join us for dinner, too. Always."

I smiled at that. "You grilling?"

"Nah. Ella is fixing something."

I already knew whatever she made was going to hit the spot.

"What should I bring?"

"Don't worry about it. You're already doing us a solid."

"Anytime. You know it ain't nothing," and it wasn't. I loved Mal's children just like they were my own.

"Good stuff. I'll see you this evening, baby brother."

"Bet."

I made it home about fifteen minutes later and headed straight upstairs to shower. On my way back downstairs, I gathered my dirty laundry, deciding to get a cycle going when I returned from the market. Back in my kitchen, I used the last of my fresh produce to make myself a green smoothie. I sat on a barstool while I drank it, using the notes app to list everything I would need to grab. I thought over a few meal ideas for the upcoming week and added that to the list as well.

When I returned home, I decided to vacuum and clean the restrooms. My mother taught us young that maintaining the regular habit of household chores always kept your home clean and kept housework light. That was a habit I continued to practice when I went to college and still do now: making my bed each morning, cleaning behind myself as I go, dusting surfaces regularly, vacuuming high-traffic areas daily, cleaning my kitchen every night, and keeping my laundry done so it doesn't pile up.

I glanced around.

My home was tidy.

It was considerable in size.

It was quiet.

It was empty.

And… I was man enough to admit that I was lonely.

I was ready to fill this home with a family. I've been preparing for a few years now. I yearned for intimacy. Not even sex necessarily, though it had been a very long time.

Coming home to an empty house and sleeping in an empty bed was getting old.

When I had this house built five years ago, I thought I would at least have a wife and a child by now. I wanted to fill my home with a family and make memories.

Create a legacy. To make this house a home.

Beyond the basic things, I hadn't even decorated the place. The walls aren't even painted. I wanted my future wife to decide all of that. Now and then, my niece will playfully tease me about my house looking like the doctor's office with the plain off-white walls.

My cousin gave me the third degree; asking in part, *"why I built a big ass house without any prospects."*

I felt criticized and defensive as hell at the time.

Now, I'm beginning to wonder the very same thing.

four

DESTINEY

"Best."

"Hey, Indie."

"By the sound of things, you're still down for the count?"

"Yeah, still down. I hope I can return by mid-next week at the latest."

Today was Friday, and it seemed the week was going slowly. Funny, in any case. I was so disoriented just days ago that I had no idea what day it was. I'd somehow caught a cold.

"No rush. We'll be here. Rest up, and let me know if I can get you anything."

"Thank you, Indie." I placed my phone down beside me and turned to my back.

I hardly ever got sick.

I honestly couldn't even remember the last time I had a cold. And this had been a cold straight from hell. I thought it was a cold but shit, maybe it's the damn flu. It had been even longer since I had that. For the past hour, I felt a sinus headache building.

I'm an independent artist, which I love. But it sucks in the unfortunate event that I got sick. I love working for myself and the freedom it afforded me. Having the latitude to do what I wanted. Commission work, freelance. Pick up multiple gigs simultaneously, spending weekdays at one project site and weekends at another. A flexible work schedule. Taking jobs in the next town or city over. Having the choice to work as a part of a team or work independently.

I tried the corporate route, and it just wasn't my thing.

Doing what I loved and with autonomy was lovely.

Working as an independent artist had its cons, too.

Murals were my bread and butter, and although they could be indoors or outdoors, outdoor projects could be more lucrative but were less common during the winter months. Searching for work during the off-season could be stressful when gigs weren't as plentiful.

Another con was contracting out my work and dealing with difficult people. It was reminiscent of corporate America.

Then there was the shitty insurance because it's the best I can afford and that wasn't fun either.

It also meant I wasn't getting paid when I wasn't working. This cold wiped me out, and I was down so bad that I couldn't go to work if I wanted to. I was currently a featured artist working as part of a collective for a beautification project at a charter school. India was also part of the collective, and we often worked together.

Holding a paintbrush would be far too difficult with chills and body aches. I wasn't good for shit. And I appreciated India checking on me. Art was actually how we met. About eight years ago. I showed up at a volunteer opportunity for a community mural project, and she was there volunteering too. And India was the first person to speak. We sketched ideas, and she complimented me on something I'd worked on. Then, she started talking about my hair.

"Girl, oh my gosh, your locs are beautiful, by the way."

"Thank you. You are beautiful, period."

She had an exotic look I hadn't seen before. Her long black hair is what threw me—it was really long and super straight, naturally. Later, she told me about her heritage.

India and I were in college when we met, and right away, India inspired me. She'd shared that she eventually wanted to work with kids as an adaptive arts teacher or an art therapist. That came as no surprise because India embodies the word "artist". She could paint, she could draw, and she could dance. She is so talented. India always says I was the better painter, but I would fight her on that every time.

The community project lasted a couple of weeks. India and I were the only two black girls, and having India there was nice. Even on subsequent projects, there isn't much representation, which we both wanted to change. But we were fast friends, remaining in touch, and I quickly discovered that India is my twin flame. We have so much in common. And she is so much fun to be around. I love her spunky personality.

At first, Daijah was low-key jealous because she and I never made room for other friends. Daijah is my absolute best friend ever. She always will be, but that got in her head at first. Understandably. No one could get close enough to either of us. We had each other, and that's all we cared about. Anyway, she loves India now.

I sat in bed and headed down the hall toward the kitchen once I gathered the strength. I was in desperate need of something to relieve my aches and pains. Searching my cabinets was all for naught. I realized we were out of DayQuil, and no Tylenol was in sight. Sighing, I accepted the realization that if I wanted to rest tonight, I had to make a quick trip to my neighborhood Walgreens.

I went to pee in my ensuite bathroom, making a mental note also to buy more Charmin. I washed my hands, grabbed my wristlet, then pulled on my hoodie hanging by the front door. Once I locked up, I climbed into my hunter green Honda Accord.

It was still raining, and it had been all week. Seeing the heavy overcast, I was especially eager to get into bed and sleep off this cold. Gratefully, my house was less than ten minutes away; I knew I'd be in, out, and home again within twenty minutes.

I parked, headed inside, and made a beeline for the Cough, Cold, and Flu medicine. Using my manners, I squeezed past a few other patrons in the crowded aisle to peruse my options. Deciding on a twin pack of DayQuil and NyQuil, I continued to the other end of the aisle, now on my quest for toilet paper. I was so glad the store wasn't large and I wouldn't have to walk too much. I had hardly any energy, and my headache was gradually worsening.

I continued surveying the aisles, glancing from left to right, recalling the scarcity of store aisles during the COVID-19 hysteria. That shit was crazy.

"Wings or no wings?"

I halted briskly and looked to my left, regarding a tall gentleman, possessing two packages of maxi pads.

Did he just ask me that?

His voice was a deep register—my goodness.

He was absolutely handsome, dressed in a black tailored suit, with a bald head and full beard. His voice stunned me.

I returned a perplexed expression, simultaneously noticing the comfort of his warm brown eyes. I quickly scanned his tall stature. He was over six foot tall and solid, with broad shoulders and milk chocolate skin. Daijah and I would call him a teddy bear.

And dammit, was I a sucker for a teddy bear.

"My niece and nephew are spending the week with me," He explained, "And my niece had an emergency." Nervously, he looked back and forth at each package. "Just trying to ensure she's comfortable and has everything she needs for the next few days. She's twelve, in case that helps."

He smiled kindly. And I was somewhat lost in a trance, partly due to my headache but primarily because of his voice, his baritone flowing smoothly like velvet. I gave a reassuring nod and returned a warm smile of my own.

"Yes, that helps," I said, chuckling lightly. Though I wasn't feeling well, suddenly, I felt an immense calm. Seconds ago, I had been in such a hurry to get home, yet now, I wanted to be consumed in the company of this gentleman who sounded damn good and looked even better. "I'd say wings. Then she can move freely, it stays in place, and she won't have to worry about any…leaks, you know…" I gestured with my empty hand at nothing, sniffing the entire time. I stammered as he intently gazed back at me. He nodded in understanding and appeared entirely engaged in the uninteresting, unexciting subject of feminine hygiene products.

"So, wings it is." He sighed in relief and turned, placing the other package back on the shelf. "You made it so simple. I appreciate your help. Thank you…" Returning to face me, his eyebrows rose.

"Destiney." I offered, smiling widely, "I would shake, but I don't want to give you my cold." Resisting the urge, I offered a fist bump.

"I'm Micah." He returned the gesture and tucked the maxi pads with wings under his arm like a football. "Thank you for being so considerate. I must admit I was overwhelmed by all these options," he laughed.

I laughed too. "It can be overwhelming. Let's say I've had lots of trial and error, you know," I shrugged, "It happens every month after all." After a couple seconds and suddenly unsure of myself, I leisurely took a few steps, pretending to consider bandages and ointments. I felt some kind of connection. That, I was sure of. I returned my gaze, and his warm brown eyes were still regarding me, and I wondered if he felt what I did. I didn't want our exchange to end, so I added, "I'm glad I could help."

"Well, thank you again, Destiney." His smile never leaving, he held my gaze, my name rolling off his tongue as if he'd said it hundreds of times.

"You're very welcome, Micah." After a beat or two, I took a few more steps, finally rounding the corner of the aisle, already wondering so many things about him. For some reason, I was too afraid to turn around and see if he was still there. Was he wearing a wedding ring? I couldn't remember.

No way he's single, I resolved.

But wait, maybe he was. He had to be single after asking me a question like that.

With sinus pressure building, I wandered through Walgreens, all the while contemplating. Men and relationships, in general, have been an afterthought for me lately, but the immense comfort and familiarity I just felt made me want to feel it again. The million-dollar question was, did he?

I certainly couldn't have asked for his number or some shit. I mean, I'd never asked a man for his number before.

Never had to.

I glanced to my right, eyeing the rainbow of nail polishes and various mascaras. This was wild and not my style at all, but I felt a gravitation toward it and wanted to explore it. Still musing, I continued my stroll, and by now, I had passed four or five aisles.

Fuck it.

I wanted to know more.

I spun around quickly and began scanning each aisle I'd passed, hoping to spot him. He was nowhere in sight. Shit. I kept scanning; the drugstore wasn't very large. My pace increasing, I continued scanning. I returned to the aisle with all the pads and tampons. I walked a bit further then surveyed straight ahead. There were two check-out lanes open. The clerks were moving slowly through monotonous scans, and about a half dozen people were in line. He couldn't have checked out that quickly. Spotting one self-service checkout with just one person waiting, I pondered if he'd used it.

Defeated, I slowly turned again and headed back toward the rear of the store, my frequent body aches reminding me I just needed to get that damn toilet paper and take my ass home. I sighed, pissed at myself.

Maybe I'll see him again someday.

Yeah right, that shit only happened in movies and romance novels.

Strolling past more aisles, I heard the deep timbre of a once-unfamiliar voice behind me.

"Destiney."

I turned around, peering up at him.

"I'm so glad you're still here. I thought I'd missed you." His chest softly heaved. "You took off so quickly. I didn't want to seem like a creep chasing after you." His handsome face still displayed that warm smile.

Was he looking for me?

I felt a tinge of embarrassment but smiled back anyway. Unsure of what to say, I asked, "Do you need help with something else?"

"Can I have your phone number, Destiney? In case my niece has another emergency." He reasoned, reaching into his pocket.

I reached out to receive his phone and nodded slowly. My smile was gone. "Sure," I said flatly, not even trying to mask my disappointment. I must have misread everything.

That quickly, I had forgotten about my headache, but now it was back and with a vengeance. I briefly considered giving him a bogus number. *Do people still do that?* I returned his phone. "I'm sure you'll be fine, Micah." Already over the conversation, I began walking in the direction of the toilet paper. I really needed to get the hell out of here.

"And if it's alright with you, I would love to get to know you better," he said to my back. I turned towards him, greeted again by his warm smile. "I'll be honest, Destiney. You are beautiful, and I'm intrigued." he slid his cell phone back into the pocket of his slacks.

I smiled bashfully. "Thank you, Micah. I would love to talk to you again," I stated, slowly releasing the breath I didn't realize I was holding.

"Sounds like a plan." He let out another light chuckle. "Well, let me get back. I'm sure my niece is eagerly awaiting my return."

"Yes, I'm sure she is. Talk to you later, Micah."

"I'm looking forward to it, beautiful Destiney."

five

MICAH

"Destiney."

I couldn't help but repeat her name as I drove from the drugstore.

This detour wasn't planned, but I was convinced I wouldn't have met her otherwise, and I was grateful for divine timing. And eager to see her again.

Relieved to finally be headed home. I turned on my windshield wipers as the light sprinkle picked up. My office was in Midtown Sacramento, and rush hour traffic in this weather meant I was about thirty-five minutes from my destination.

Malachi and Ella were headed out of town to celebrate their fifteenth wedding anniversary. I'm sure they were excited to escape all this rain. Since I'd still be at work, they used their spare key to let in my niece and nephew. I planned to head straight home after work; I was excited to start the week. About an hour before leaving the office, my niece Gabrielle asked if I could pick up emergency supplies for her. Even though I never had to fulfill this kind of request, it seemed simple enough, and I expected it to be quick.

Turned out I'd been standing in that aisle for several minutes. Unscathed, I resisted the urge to call her. I didn't want to embarrass my dear niece by asking sensitive questions. Apart from that, I was determined to manage mission impossible on my own.

Contemplating what to buy and beset with several options, I spotted her, and I was immediately smitten. She neared me, absentminded and unassuming, carrying cold medicine. She was everywhere but here, as if she had blinders on. I quickly scanned her petite but curvy frame.

She was so beautiful, instantly taking my breath away.

Usually, I'm the type to pursue something I want expeditiously; however, 1 found myself hesitating out of respect.

I was positive she was married.

Then, it was as if the good Lord above gave me a sign. Almost in slow motion, she used her left hand to brush stray locs out of her face, exposing a bare ring finger. She continued walking with no sign of slowing down, and I knew I had to make a move and quick. Having narrowed my options to two remaining packages, I boldly asked her: *"Wings or no wings?"*. Best four words I've spoken in a while. As expected, she was taken aback by my question, but as soon as I explained, her big, brilliant eyes had a spark in them.

I was charmed by everything I saw and everything I heard.

Her smile was wide and infectious. Despite an occasional sniffle, her voice was melodic, light, and airy. I encounter beautiful women regularly, yet it was clear she was so much more. I regarded her chocolate skin, big, vibrant eyes, the tiny gold stud in her nose, and the locs hanging down at her waist. Her ethereal vibe was my jam. I always appreciated a natural queen.

The crazy thing about it is that I got the impression she was unaware of her striking beauty.

Anyway, I was already pressed to see her again.

I made it home and headed inside, grateful to finally be out of the rain and eager to greet my two loves. I barely made it in the door before my niece Gabrielle squealed, skipping toward me.

"Uncle Micah!" She threw her arms around my waist, and I returned a bear hug. "I'm so glad we'll be here for the week!" Her voice muffled against my chest.

"Me too, Gabby girl."

"Thank you!" She grabbed the bag from me. As she looked inside, her eyes grew wide. "Great choice."

I smiled, responding casually, "You know uncle got you."

She quickly disappeared up the stairs to the guest room she stayed in whenever they spent time with me. I placed my work bag in the foyer, then headed toward the living room to find my nephew playing the game on my big screen.

"Hey, man." We did the handshake we'd done since he was just a toddler.

"Hey unc. How's it going?" My nephew Gabriel was fourteen, smart as a whip, super mature, and cool as a cucumber. Although he resembled my sister-in-law Ella in the face, he inherited his six-foot height from my older brother. He and my brother were so much alike personality-wise that sometimes it was scary. My father, brother, and Gabe, as we call him, are all over six feet tall.

"Pretty good man." I sat down across from him on the oversized sectional. "New game?" I watched him play for a minute.

"Yeah, just picked it up. Trying to analyze what I'm looking at to understand the graphics and framework better," he returned, not taking his eyes off the screen. Gabe was brilliant, and he was such a game nerd and a whiz kid. He'd learned to code by fifth grade and was in the process of developing his own app and video game. He played multiple games, but not for fun as most kids did; he was learning the craft by method of reverse engineering. His intel was amazing, and I was excited to see what he would become.

I headed to the kitchen and looked in the fridge to try and figure out what I would prepare for dinner. After contemplating, I decided to order in tonight.

Still consumed with thoughts of Destiney, I didn't want to waste any more time. Picking up my phone, I texted her.

Hello Destiney. Thank you again for allowing me to stay connected with you beautiful

I grabbed bottled water from the fridge. After taking a drink, I called over my shoulder, "Hey, you two, how does pizza and wings sound?"

"Works for me," Gabe replied.

"Yes, please!" I heard Gabby yell from upstairs.

I leaned against the kitchen island, opening the pizza app to place an order. After completing the transaction, my phone vibrated in my hand. Seeing it was her, my heart swelled.

Beauty: You're very welcome. Is your niece all situated? I smiled at her thoughtfulness.

She's fine. Wasn't her first rodeo. I'll keep a stash here for next time

Dots appeared just as I sent it.

Beauty: You're such a great uncle

I thought back to that cold medicine.

How are you feeling?

Beauty: Just a little under the weather. I plan to rest this weekend. Thanks for asking

My response was immediate, and I instantly wanted to take care of her.

I'm happy to bring you soup or anything else you need, please don't hesitate to let me know

Beauty: I can manage. Thank you Micah

I laughed at myself after reading her response. Damn this was crazy. I'd known her for less than two hours, and here I was, coming up with excuses to see her and do things for her.

All I knew was I wanted more of Destiney, and I couldn't wait to see her again.

six

DESTINEY

I woke up late Sunday afternoon to the sun brightly peeking through my drapes. This cold had kicked my ass, and I'd slept for hours. Friday night through most of Saturday, only waking up a few times to pee.

Getting out of bed, I headed down the hall to the living room and drew all the blinds, eager to let the sun in. It rained five days straight, and this much rain was not typical in Sacramento, especially in May.

Stretching for a moment, I basked in the natural sunlight flooding through the oversized bay window. This was one of my favorite places in the house. Daijah and I have lived in the condo for the past two years, and the three bedrooms and two bathrooms have afforded plenty of space for us.

Lately, though, I had the place all to myself. Daijah spent most of her free time at her fiancé's home across town in Natomas. Julian was a great guy, so I didn't mind. Daijah was happy, and they were deeply in love. I was overjoyed for them.

Back in the kitchen, I filled my kettle with fresh water and turned on the stove for a cup of tea. I wasn't back to feeling like myself yet, but I was glad to feel better. I expected to be back one hundred percent within the next day or two.

I started my playlist, noticing an unread text message Daijah had sent me early this morning.

Sibling Bestie: Good morning sunshine. How are you feeling?

So much better today thanks

Sibling Bestie: There you are! I was about to send a search party!

I giggled at her antics. Daijah was so full of personality and zeal, and there was never a dull moment with her.

Sibling Bestie: I'll be home later to get clothes. Let me know if you want a bahn mi. Grabbing some on the way.

I'd love one, thank you!!!

Sibling Bestie: The usual with extra veggies?

You know it Thank you!

My mouth watered. I liked her thinking—no doubt a bahn mi would hit the spot right about now.

I slept so much the past thirty-six hours; I hardly ate anything. I'm not usually a huge fan of sandwiches, but Banh Mi's are hard to resist. Banh mi is a Vietnamese sandwich. They're made on a fresh baguette with pâté or mayonnaise and a delicious combination of pickled carrot and daikon radish. It also has fresh cucumber, jalapeño, and cilantro. The protein varies; traditionally, it would have Vietnamese ham, steamed pork roll, or other meats. Daijah loves to get charbroiled chicken on hers.

The Bahn Mi's around here are the best in town. In South Sacramento, where we live, there are dozens of Vietnamese restaurants on a 4-mile-long strip called Little Saigon. Sacramento, where we were born and raised, is one of the most diverse cities in the country. The food scene is second to none, with so many diverse cultures and cuisines to indulge in.

I had my very favorite playlist going: R&B slow jams from the 90s. As I prepared my cup of tea, my thoughts returned to Micah.

My thoughts of him have been nonstop since I first met him.

I contemplated calling Micah, but I hesitated. I didn't want to disturb family time with his niece and nephew. Pulling up our text thread, I read his messages over again. I smiled, considering how thoughtful he was, offering me his help if I needed it.

I sent him a text.

Hey you, happy Sunday. Can you talk?

The three dots appeared almost instantly, and my heart pattered a little faster.

Micah: Hey, Beautiful. Playing basketball with my nephew. Can I call you a little later?

That's fine

I smiled heading back to my bedroom to finish my tea. I was absolutely looking forward to Micah's phone call.

I took the final sip of tea and decided to wash all the linen from my bed. Clean sheets and a hot shower would do my body good.

My time in the shower had me thinking.

It occurred to me that for the past few days... I'd been feeling things.

Being honest with myself was important; to that end, I needed to acknowledge that.

It's difficult to articulate, but... it was like emotions formerly lying dormant were beginning to awaken.

We'd only been texting so far. Micah had been checking on me around the clock. I always had a message or two from him when I woke up. He offered to bring me soup. He wished me a speedy recovery. Then, he reminded me more than once that his proposition to help me out was still on the table. I wasn't as responsive since I wasn't feeling my best, but I would reply whenever I woke up to pee. Micah seemed okay with that.

And...it was *wild* that I liked him before we even had a verbal conversation.

Yes.

I like him.

I couldn't say if that were a good or bad thing.

Honestly.

Being unsure was the worst part about this.

Whether I was okay with this or not.

How I would proceed. If I proceeded at all.

The idea of Micah was absolutely good. But potentially becoming… something.

That, I wasn't sure about.

I closed my eyes as the hot water cascaded over me. I pictured Micah's warm brown eyes. They were sincere and inviting, and there was a depth and comfort there. He was very handsome—a grown man handsome. That got me thinking, too. It's been quite some time since I've been so eager to get to know someone.

And I wanted to know everything about him. I had so many questions.

I quickly finished up in the shower. I was excited to hear his voice again and didn't want to miss his call. This would officially be our first real conversation.

I moisturized my skin and dressed in leggings and an oversized graphic T-shirt. I had slept so much the past few days that I wouldn't lie down again until bedtime if I could help it. After moving my linen from the washer to the dryer, I decided to head to my in-home office.

I was the only one who worked from home, so I converted the third and smallest bedroom into an office space. It was simple but had everything I needed: a corner desk and office chair from IKEA, where I kept my laptop computer and monitors. I did a bit of digital artwork that I wanted to expand on, so I worked on that here in the office when I had the capacity.

Adjacent to that, I had an art desk with shelves for my pens, pencils, paints, sketchbooks, and canvases. The furthest wall had a floor-to-ceiling bookshelf full of my ever-growing collection, some titles I have cherished since childhood. Though I was a full-time artist and illustrator, I was also a voracious reader. For as early as I can remember, if I wasn't drawing, I would be reading; and if I wasn't reading, I was drawing.

I powered up my MacBook Air and checked my email since I'd been off the radar for the past few days. I sent a few replies and pulled out one of my sketchbooks.

My interest in art started when I was a little girl and has now become a fiery passion. I vividly recall only wanting a new set of crayons and a new coloring book for a birthday or Christmas. Reading and drawing are both my favorite pastimes. Depending on the mood I was in, they were equally therapeutic. I could never decide between them; they both created an escape whenever I needed one.

I'd inherited the art gene and my love of reading from my father. He always encouraged Daijah and me to read from the very beginning.

When Dad discovered I had an artistic gift, he encouraged me to draw daily and challenge myself. I took his advice to heart, capturing everything on paper. I'd draw for hours, filling up more sketchbooks than I could count over the years. My father was a tremendous support, investing in me, paying for art classes and summer workshops, and stressing the importance of honing my craft as a creative. And I kept drawing and creating, always carrying a sketchbook with me.

Most artists do. You truly never know when inspiration will strike. A sketchbook is an instant canvas to capture inspiration on the fly. Any creative person would agree that ideas can go as quickly as they appear. I've found that having a sketchbook handy ensures I can get the blueprint down and explore it later on. That's a regular occurrence for me.

Daijah has always encouraged me to share my art with the public, but I am super shy—inherently so. I don't post any of my work on my social media platforms, and I don't have much presence on social media, period. However, I share my gift with the world by being a muralist. Since I started, I haven't stopped contributing in some capacity to more than two hundred murals in the past eight years.

If someone told me that volunteering for a mural those years ago would bring me here, I wouldn't have believed it. One of the project sponsors liked my art so much that I was offered a yearlong contract, *on the spot*, doing window lettering for a few major retailers in the area. That was so cool, and I learned so much from that experience. I'll always be grateful because things exploded for me after that.

Humming along to Mary J. Blige, I scanned my assortment of more than three dozen illustration pens. I finally decided on my go-to Pigment Liner. It was my favorite pen to work with. I flipped to the next available page in my sketchbook, and in no time, I was well into the groove of my creative genius.

Several songs later, I faintly heard my cell phone ringing. I looked around, realizing I had left it in the kitchen when I returned for another cup of tea. I retrieved my phone from the kitchen, extremely enthralled to see Micah's name on my screen.

My grin was back. "Hello."

"Hey Destiney. Is this a good time?"

seven

MICAH

"This is a great time," Destiney said. Unbeknownst to her, she was damn near seducing me with the lullaby of her soft voice. I turned to my back and propped my arm behind my head, instantly feeling calm. I was fresh out of the shower since returning from the park, so glad the rain had stopped, and the courts weren't too wet for Gabe and me to shoot around for a while. He was a great basketball player and full of energy, of course. Gabe whooped my ass out there. But if I'm honest, my game was off, consumed with thoughts of Destiney. My face lit up when I got her text, and I was eager to return to the house and call her.

"So, how's the cold?"

"A lot better. I expect to return to work tomorrow."

"Glad to hear that. For your information, my offer still stands if you need me to bring you anything," I reminded her.

She chuckled lightly. "Are your niece and nephew still over?"

"Yeah, my brother Malachi and his wife will be back tomorrow afternoon. I'll take them to school on my way to work in the morning."

"Do they stay over often?"

"Oh yeah, this is their second home. And I love those two with my whole heart." I said that with my chest. They were so special to me.

"They're blessed to have you." Our conversation flowed. "So, are you the older brother?"

"Baby brother. I'm taller, though."

"Are you really?"

"Yeah, since about junior high. Man, he used to hate it too." We both cackled. "But I only have him by an inch or so. And we're only eleven months apart. Damn near twins and extremely close."

"That's beautiful."

"What about you?" I quizzed. "Any siblings?"

"One younger sister, we're a year and a half apart. And she's taller than me." We laughed again.

"Serious?"

"Oh yeah. It happened around the same time for us, too. The summer before I was to start eighth grade, and she was to start seventh grade, she sprouted several inches," she continued. "I'm short, but she's really tall."

"Wow."

"We're close too. She's my best friend."

"Love that."

"Me too."

"How old are you, Destiney?"

"You're not supposed to ask a woman her age." I could hear the sarcasm in her voice.

"You're too young for that rule to apply to you."

She laughed, "I'm joking with you. I just turned twenty-seven. You?"

"Oh, you're just a baby. I'm thirty-four."

"I'm a grown ass woman."

I gasped, my theatrics on display, "No way, you curse?"

"All the damn time."

We both cackled again. "You watch that pretty mouth of yours," I teased.

There was a comfortable silence.

"So why me?" Destiney asked after a beat.

"Why you what?"

"Why was I the lucky customer picked to answer your question?"

I was transparent with no hesitation, "Your vibe. Your energy."

It was true.

Destiney had such a feminine aura—it was clearly one of her superpowers. I was only in her presence briefly, but it was comforting and soft. "I watched you for a second before I spoke to you. You're so beautiful and intriguing to watch, might I add. So why not you?" I stated rhetorically.

"Thank you." I could hear her smiling, and I pictured it mentally. She had a beautiful smile.

"I have to say that I'm so glad you did ask me. I may not have stopped otherwise. I tend to have blinders on when I'm out and about. I've often been told that I need to be better about that. More observant of my surroundings."

"I would agree, especially when you're out alone. A beautiful woman is a moving target."

"You've used that word a lot these past few days."

"What, beautiful?" I asked entirely in jest. I already knew.

"Mmm-hmm."

"Since meeting you, your beautiful face is all I've managed to think about. Now I'm wondering how I'm supposed to get any work done tomorrow." I was serious.

"I'm sure you'll manage, Micah."

Well damn.

I loved the way my name rolled off her tongue.

I loved her voice. It was the most beautiful melody in my ear. Demure and soft. But not in a ditzy, damsel-in-distress kind of way.

Not only was she beautiful, but she also had something else going on.

It was a fact Destiney was channeled into her femininity and that shit was super sexy.

Subconsciously, I felt my primal instincts awaken, and I wanted to handle her as delicately as possible. That may be why I insisted on offering to take care of her.

At least, that's what I was telling myself.

"So."

"What's up?"

"What happened with your last relationship? You are single, right?" I was joking with that last question. Destiney was too classy of a woman to entertain me beyond pleasantries if she already had a man. I could tell that much off rip. I knew she was single; hell, I was glad she was single. But I was curious why *any man* would let her get away.

Her soft chuckle cruised through the line, "I am very single."

I chuckled too. "Good to know."

"You are too, I take it?"

"Single as a pringle."

"Wow." She laughed heartily this time. When she calmed down, she answered, "To answer your question though… my last official relationship was in high school. I was just a teenager. So… not much to speak on relative to that."

My head drew back; my eyes grew wide. "You said high school?"

Shit. That would mean a decade ago.

"Yeah. I mean, I've dated a few guys since then, but… nothing serious ever really panned out."

"Hmm."

"I sound like a weirdo to you now?"

"No, no, no. Not at all, sweetheart. I enjoyed getting to know you. Everything about you: please know you can speak freely with me. Always."

"I appreciate that."

"Indeed." I certainly wasn't judging her. My last relationship wasn't recent, either. Not even a little bit.

"What about you?" She volleyed.

"My last serious relationship was in college. Like you, I've dated a little since then. But."

"Nothing to write home about?"

"Nope."

"Dating can be a lot." She sighed lightly. "Not to sound like *that girl*, but... it seems daunting. Repetitive. Bleak. Damn near depressing sometimes."

"Oh, I hear you!" I couldn't help my light chuckle. "And though I don't date often, I try not to focus on that part. Instead, I see it as an opportunity to get to know someone new. I've also learned a lot about myself dating. Learning from my mistakes. My philosophy is not time wasted, but a learning experience. You know what I mean? Life is full of lessons, and they come in many forms. Even crap ass hell dates."

Destiney laughed, "I'm compelled to agree." After a beat, "Typically, college relationships are a bit more serious. What happened with you two?"

I sighed lightly, considering how much I wanted to share. Then, I quickly decided to put it all out in the open. In my mind, it was the best way to establish what I deemed as a new friendship between us.

I could only hope, sincerely, that Destiney didn't run for the hills after my confession.

"We met our sophomore year. Down at Cal Poly, San Luis Obispo."

"Nice."

"Yeah. We found out we were both from Sac, which was cool. Anyway, we were inseparable. And things were serious. We were engaged by the end of junior year."

"Engaged?" She replied, surprised, "What happened?"

This time, I released a heavy sigh. "It seemed like the right thing to do. At the time. Getting engaged. Like a natural progression. My brother was married, and I felt pressure, which I've since realized was all a figment of my imagination. I did care about her. I loved her. Very much. But… we saw things differently. Things that mattered a lot to me didn't mean as much to her." I shook my head. "My mind was a mess. My heart was conflicted. I wanted… I needed to be sure. She deserved certainty. So, a few months before the day we were to be married, I asked for a break. Just to pray and get my head in the right place. You know."

"Yeah."

"I called it all off in the end."

"Wow."

Wow is right.

This shit still got to me. Even now, nearly twelve years later. "I hurt her. But I've made peace with my decision. The momentary disappointment was worth avoiding the severe heartbreak I knew would come later had I gone through with it. I cared enough about her to let her go." I sighed heavily again, but I was relieved. It felt good to share this with Destiney. I hadn't spoken of this out loud in years.

Something else that occasionally crossed my mind: lightning doesn't strike in the same place twice. It's not as simple as *just finding another one.*

I wondered if I'd fumbled my one.

I certainly didn't toss her aside, thinking that I'd replace her with a better model.

I wondered sometimes if I tried hard enough. There's compromise, and then there are deal breakers. I thought maybe I'd given up on us too soon. And I wondered, if I had sought out counseling to address my inner issues or something, could I have salvaged our relationship?

Destiney pulled me from my thoughts, "Well, thank you for sharing this. I get the feeling it's somewhat of a sensitive topic for you."

"I guess so. Yeah." She had no idea the emotions that had come flooding back just sharing that with her. But I was glad she knew this part of me. Taking a page from her book, I queried, "What are you thinking? I sound like a weirdo to you now?"

Her lively chuckle was back again. "No. No. No. No. Not at all." She sounded sincere. I was convinced.

And.

She was so adorable. A contented "Mmm" is what I gave her. My fret having already melted away.

"I respect you, Micah. Even more so now. Your vulnerability. Your honesty. Your transparency. She isn't here to speak for herself, but your kindness and consideration, despite how things ended with the two of you, speaks to your character."

Well.

Can't say I expected that. But I was good with it; we could definitely do something here. Granted, she didn't disappear on me after this. For some reason, I didn't get the feeling she would.

We chatted for a while longer. When the time came, I hated hanging up with her, but I had to get some dinner on the table for Gabe and Gabby girl. Destiney had to get ready to head out to work tomorrow. It seemed she didn't want our conversation to end either.

The plan was to chat again tomorrow evening.

And... *I already couldn't wait.*

eight

MICAH

A few days later, I was at my parents' house, putting eyes on them.

The rain and wind we had days ago left the backyard fence slightly leaning. After surveying it, Daddy and I figured adding some reinforcements back there would be a good idea. This prompted a trip to the home improvement store. I'd already made a mental note that Mal and I would replace the entire fence later this spring.

"Let's head over and get some post-ups. Take a ride with your old man."

"I'll be right out behind you, Daddy."

Between Malachi and me, one of us was checking in at home base every couple of days. They still lived in our childhood home. Mal and I lovingly called it the blue house. My mom's favorite color is robin's-egg blue, and that's the color it's painted. With a crisp white trim. For as long as I can remember. We've given the house a fresh coat a few times over the years.

When I made it out the front door, I found my father in the driver's seat of his pickup truck, the engine purring, waiting for me.

"I can drive us, Daddy."

"I got it. Come on here."

I didn't argue, just proceeded around to the passenger's side. Mal and I drove them as often as possible. When they allowed us to, that is. Though Mommy didn't seem to mind,

Daddy was holding on tight. I fell back without retort each time he resisted. Daddy was fiercely independent, and I understood.

We made our way to the local home improvement store, driving with the windows down; the fresh air felt good on my face. I loved to see the sun out and all those heavy clouds and rain finally gone, at least for the time being. We cruised toward our destination, and Daddy had talk radio on.

As far back as my memory serves, we were always tuned into talk radio in Daddy's truck. He loved music but not in the car. We listened to music for hours at home, but it was always talk radio in his truck. That was his thing. I didn't mind it though. He mentioned once that had he seized the opportunity to finish college, he would have pursued broadcast journalism and made his mark in sports talk radio somewhere. He certainly had the voice for it. The texture of his voice had only grown richer with age. I'd inherited my deep timbre directly from him.

Daddy and I listened intently to the three gentlemen talking about the latest in the world of sports as we enjoyed the ride. This was how things were with my old man. He was seriously the easiest person to be around. He wasn't a man of many words. But anytime he decided to bestow his wisdom, it was always welcomed.

"I can't believe Mal and Ella are at year number fifteen. That's *bananas!*" I broke our silence after a good while.

Daddy nodded, and I saw the trace of a smile. "Seems like no time at all, doesn't it? He said they had a great time in Cabo."

"I bet they did. Missed all this rain, that's for sure."

"No doubt." After a few beats, "What did you three Musketeers get into?" Referring to Gabe, Gabby, and me.

I chuckled, "It was a low-key few days, relaxing around the house. But we enjoyed each other's company. Gabby was mostly on the computer, working on something for school. Gabe had a new game we tried out, and that was cool. The rain stopped long enough for Gabe and me to play a little ball, too."

"Oh yeah?"

"Yeah. You know he whooped my butt out there! He's getting good!"

Daddy released a lively chuckle. "Oh, did he? That's my boy. Bet that shut you up!" He continued laughing heartily, and I joined him, shaking my head. Everyone knew full well I could get a little competitive out there.

"Man! I didn't think he'd get away from me, but he showed out!" It seemed a tad premature to tell Daddy I was actually distracted the entire time. The beautiful woman I encountered with the angelic voice had since captivated my every thought and was living rent-free in my head.

Destiney was a beautiful distraction, and I didn't mind it one bit.

Riding shotgun alongside my father on this beautiful sunny afternoon was nothing but nostalgia. If it weren't for my hesitation, I would have told Daddy all about our exchange and subsequent conversations. Sparing no details. As an inquisitive child, I always loved talking to my old man while we took a ride somewhere in his truck. It was, by far, one of my favorite childhood memories. There were so many pivotal conversations in this setting over the years.

I took another route instead.

"Daddy?"

"Yup?"

"I wonder sometimes if I'll ever find my wife. The older I get, the more I find myself wondering. Do you think marriage is in the cards for me?"

Daddy was quiet, as usual. He tapped his thumbs along the steering wheel and took his time musing over my question. Whenever we came to him with a loaded question like this, he didn't rush about it. Every word he spoke was given thought and intention, which I appreciated immensely. I do my very best to demonstrate the same.

"Have you prayed about it?" He finally spoke.

Not sure why, but my head reared back slightly.

I certainly wasn't surprised. I was a man of faith after all. Prayer was an integral part of my life and my upbringing. I gave his question some thought. In true Daddy fashion he cut the radio off as we continued cruising down the highway giving me space to consider what he'd asked. Mal and I used to get so frustrated when he answered our question with a question. We couldn't appreciate it then, but there was so much value in that. In hindsight I realized he was fostering critical thinking. Often, we had the answer all along, we just needed to consider things from another perspective. As I prepared to answer him, I knew I had to be honest.

I hadn't.

"You know Daddy... I can't say I have prayed that prayer specifically."

Daddy nodded and took a few more moments, always exhibiting a gentle approach in his encouragement. "When you get on your knees tonight, call this out. Make your request known. And ask for a sign. Then, you put in the work." I nodded as I listened intently. So glad for this time together and his wisdom. Always there to help, guide and inspire and I loved that so much about Daddy. He continued, "You can dream, wish and hope. But you must put action behind it. Faith without work is dead. Not only must you believe for it, but you work to secure it. Just as you would with anything else you desire to achieve." He quickly glanced at me, and I met his eyes.

My same eyes twenty-five years older and wiser. "A man who finds a wife finds a good thing." Your good thing is out there son. You pray about it, and then you see about finding her."

I knew it was soon. *Really soon* to feel so strongly.

But I felt like I had found something good in her.

Yes, she was gorgeous and adorable and sweet. And her vibe was fire. But I felt something else. Far beyond the surface.

I couldn't wait to get to know her.

I really couldn't wait to see her again.

Praying silently right then and there I asked God to reveal to me if she was the one.

I hoped she'd be the one.

I wanted so badly for her to be the one.

nine

DESTINEY

"Hey beautiful."

"Hey you," I said casually, trying to play it cool, but I smiled from ear to ear seeing Micah's name on my screen. We'd been talking for a couple weeks now, and it was still happening. And the way he made me feel, it likely wouldn't stop happening.

"I catch you at a bad time?"

"Not at all, this is the perfect time." I sat up straight on the couch, placing my iPad beside me. I was reading the past hour, getting utterly lost in a love story.

And the sex.

Especially the sex.

The indie urban and contemporary romance authors I followed did not play around when it came to this, and I was here for all of it. I suppose it was partly because it was the closest I'd ever come to experiencing the real thing. But I was making do.

All I had to do was dive into a book by one of my favorite indie authors and I was set. The erotic novella I was currently reading was *hot! Hot! Hot!* I could focus on very little else once I started it. I'm a fast reader and I typically devour title after title. Steamy novellas are my very favorite. My daily streak on record was more than five hundred days. Yup. Almost two years straight. My schedule could get hectic sometimes, but I always find time to read every day. Even if it's just a page or two. I took another sip of my tea. I just made it, so it was still hot, and I slurped a bit louder than I meant to.

"What you got over there?" My embarrassment melted instantly by Micah's playful tone.

"Cup of tea. It's how I relax at the end of the day."

"Definitely a great way to relax. What kind of tea?"

"Chai."

"Chai is a great choice."

"Totally agree. It's my favorite." Chai was always tricky for me. Too much sugar was too sweet to enjoy; too much cinnamon made it spicy. Tonight, I accomplished the perfect ratio, and this cup was *everything*.

"Indeed. You prefer tea over coffee?"

"One hundred percent!" I replied eagerly. "I don't mind iced coffee on occasion, but tea is my go-to. I can drink tea any time of day. Any day of the week. What about you?"

"Expresso for me. Only now and then."

"I'm always wired when I have an expresso. If you can even imagine. I'm already on ten most days anyway." We both laughed. "So how was your day?" I asked him.

"Productive overall, but busy. Glad to have you in my ear, helping me relax."

Oh shit.

Micah's voice was already beginning to unravel me. Moments before his call I read an explosive sex scene… now his deep voice was in my ear.

Doing things.

"Glad it was productive," I managed, bypassing the rest.

"Yes, it was. How was your day?"

"Productive as well. I met with some highschoolers this afternoon and they want to paint a mural in their campus theatre. We're brainstorming some ideas."

"Oh yeah?"

"Yeah. These kids are talented with dope concepts. I'm excited to get started."

"Nice. You work with kids most of the time?"

"Depends on the project. Community work will bring in all walks of life. I've worked with kids of all ages. Preschoolers up to high school and college. I've worked with seasoned citizens. Everything in between."

"What's your favorite age group?"

"I enjoy working with them all as long as I get to create something in the process."

"Indeed." That made me smile. I was learning Micah and noticed he said "indeed" a lot. I also noticed how much he enjoyed getting to know me. Things that didn't seem significant about me mattered to him. It was sweet and I felt seen.

And special.

My tea seemed slightly cooler, so I took a few hearty swallows. Warming my throat as it traveled down.

"So. Did I cross your mind at all today?"

I froze. As if Micah could see me. I also damn near choked.

"You alright over there?"

"Ye…" I coughed several times, "Yes, I'm fine thank you."

Once Micah knew I was good he continued, "I'll have you know that I thought about you all day long, wondering if you were thinking of me too. I must admit, I'm constantly thinking of you, Destiney baby."

Baby?

Oh.

Oh. This was a new one. I liked it.

Also, note to self: Micah was a straight shooter. That's certainly a good thing.

But I wasn't ready. And my ass needed to buckle up.

"Really?"

"Yes. Why does that surprise you?" He countered.

I pondered for a moment. "I don't know. You're a busy man. And I guess I didn't think I was that interesting."

Micah thought that was so funny. "You've had me intrigued from the moment I saw you. There are so many things I want to know."

Well.

"What would you like to know? I'm an open book," I said, "You've given me a safe space; I'm comfortable sharing anything you ask me." I was partially honest. It was true. I was comfortable and I wanted to share with him. But I was fiercely shy too. Clearly, I had a crush on him which made me feel… silly? Hell, I don't know. That feeling girls feel when a guy they like is paying attention to them.

Whatever that is. That's exactly how I felt.

"I'm happy to hear I'm doing something right," Micah said.

"Now you sound a little surprised."

He chuckled again. "Come on now, don't leave me hanging. You never answered my question."

I paused for a beat. Then, "Let me put it this way; I'm so glad to hear your voice. I've missed you," I effortlessly shared.

"Hmm." That sounded damn good in my ear, but I pretended not to notice. "Now, to answer your question. I wonder what goes on in that pretty head of yours." He continued, "I said I was intrigued a minute ago. And I am. But that word doesn't truly interpret conceptually what I feel when it comes to you."

My eyes grew wide, and my lips parted.

Shit.

Micah carried on, *"Enchanted?* That too. But… *captivated?* That's it. *Captivated.* You are so beautiful. And… you have a vivid imagination, colorful language, you're so expressive. Passionate. Well spoken. Words aren't big enough for your ideas. Your mind is fascinating." He was silent for a beat, but it was a heavy pause, "Were you the type to daydream as a young girl?"

Somehow, after all that I found my voice, "I was. Always daydreaming."

How'd he even know?

"Mmm." Micah seemed pleased with that. "Destiney, I happen to think you are extremely interesting," he said matter of fact.

"Thank you. You intrigue me too. Deep conversations are clearly your specialty. I enjoy our talks. You should also know you have the calmest, most soothing voice I've ever heard. It's crazy where my mind wanders when you're talking to me." I didn't mean to say that last part out loud. Now I was curious if the arousal I felt could be detected in my voice.

"Is that right?"

Well shit.

Micah didn't wait for a response, "Your voice is also calming. Light. So sweet in my ear. You're likely great at reading bedtime stories," he paused, "And pillow talk."

I giggled nervously. "Never tested that theory."

Micah chuckled. "I also imagine how you might sound when you're being pleased and when something feels good to you."

I definitely felt my pussy awaken. I held my breath, taken aback but turned on by his bluntness. I slowly released the breath I was holding. Then, "Now I'm curious about the same." Surprised by my revelation.

We had a few beats of comfortable silence. And I desperately needed to change the subject.

And my panties.

"So, Micah?" I seized the opportunity before he said something else because I had no idea how I could possibly handle whatever came next.

"Yes?"

"What do you most look forward to?"

"I look forward to many things. Traveling, making memories, having a family of my own. A wife. Children. These are all so cliche, but the fact is, I have everything else."

"That isn't cliché at all. I look forward to some of those same things," I replied, gulping down the last bit of my tea. I sat back on the couch resting more comfortably. "At some point we realize what matters most and what will sustain us when all the temporary things are long gone."

"Agreed. I came to that realization a long time ago."

Micah was a beautiful man saying all the right things. I felt so comfortable.

"Now, this is completely off the record. But I'm a pleaser, and I look forward to pleasing you. In all the ways."

My breath hitched in my throat. My face grew warm, and I knew I was blushing. Thankfully he couldn't see me. "Do you really?" I somehow managed, my demure feelings surfacing. I wasn't sure of what else to say.

"All the time."

I took a moment to gather myself. I had a feeling there was more to come on this. But how could he say that so casually? My mind was going a million miles a minute.

"And... whenever you're ready... I look forward to kissing you."

Shit.

I was not expecting that. But I loved that he told me. And he was such a gentleman about it.

Surprising myself I said, "I look forward to kissing you too."

***

So, I've been giving Daijah the latest. A play by play in real time.

And so far, she loved everything she heard about Micah. One afternoon some days ago, she came home in the mood to tease me. I was in the office working on a commissioned design and she leaned into the office doorway.

"Hey Des."

"Hey Day."

"Catching feelings, are we?" Daijah jested.

I spun around in my chair, finding the silliest grin on her face. I knew she was giving me a hard time because she knew I'd built a wall complete with a fucking barbed wire fence around me.

"That's random." I suppressed my smile as best as I could. When Daijah returned a knowing expression, I shrugged my shoulders. "Maybe?"

"Ain't no maybe! I love this for you sissy. Don't fight it. Go with it. You're already there anyway."

My brows dipped. Not that I disagreed. That was my exact sentiment.

"You are all smiles lately. You're always smiling and bubbly anyway, but you are beaming so bright these days," she nodded with that silly grin again. "You are sprung sissy."

"Aww man. I guess I am."

"Are you afraid to be?"

"Maybe a little bit. But I trust Micah. He is such a good guy Day."

That shit was crazy because it was exactly as she predicted when I first told her about Micah. And it was very soon after meeting him, but I couldn't contain myself.

"So, I met someone."

"Okay." Daijah was deadpan with that one, returning an empty stare, waiting for the punchline. I always got attention from men, but it was never worth mentioning as I didn't often entertain them beyond a respectable hello.

"I gave him my number."

Her eyebrows went high on her head.

"And we've been talking for the past two weeks. Texting, talking. We text and talk all day long."

"Oh damn," she said, suddenly interested. "You like this one."

"I really do."

"Tell me about him."

"He's thirty-four. Tall, handsome. Incredibly sweet."

"Sounds like he's already made quite the impression on you."

"He absolutely has."

"I'm excited for you."

I smiled wide. "I'm excited too. I've already told him so much about you sibling bestie."

It was her turn to smile. "Aww. I hope I live up to the hype."

"Of course you will," after a beat, "So, what do you have planned rest of the night?"

"Wash some clothes. Julian's picking me up around nine."

I looked at my watch. "You're always leaving me," I whined with a dramatic sad face to match.

Daijah chuckled. "Don't say it like that. In a minute you won't even be worried about what I'm doing. You'll be up under your man every chance you get. I think you forgot how much you like that shit. You're such an affectionate person. You like being close to the people you're fond of. Especially someone special to you. What's his name?

"*Micah.*"

"*Oh damn! Look at the way you said it!*" *Her eyes were wide. Her smile too.* "*You're getting the feels already. That's a good thing. I'm so happy for you sissy!*"

That was weeks ago, and I've already accepted that as a fact.

If I'm not careful I am going to fall in love.

That much I knew for sure.

What have I gotten myself into?

ten

DESTINEY

I was bleeding again.

I was constantly bleeding.

It was as unpredictable as it was painful.

Unbearably painful. Not only that, but I would bleed for several days. Ten days or more were typical. And the pain is so intense that some days I can't get out of bed.

Like this morning. The churning and clamping of my damn uterus woke me up.

And a sanguineous presence akin to a fucking crime scene.

For years, I thought it was just a normal part of everything.

My normal.

I assumed I just had heavy, painful cycles.

I am fiercely shy and get embarrassed easily, so I tend to keep personal and private matters to myself. Mostly out of desperation, I opened up to Daijah, sharing these details, and she told me I needed to see an OB/GYN.

Like, yesterday.

I was twenty-three years old when I finally saw a doctor about it, and that's when I was diagnosed with uterine fibroids. That was four years ago, and back then, it wasn't terribly hard to manage. Uncomfortable, sure. I was living with it as best as I could. Managing. But it's gotten progressively worse—especially these past few months.

Lately, it's been horrendous.

The debilitating cramps.

The bleeding between periods.

These days the bleeding lasts much longer, and it's been so heavy I've had accidents while in public. The blood has ruined my clothing. My current wardrobe consists of cheap black leggings. Black leggings that I have no problem throwing away if necessary.

I've had to set multiple alarms throughout the night, so that I don't ruin my bedding.

I learned that the hard way.

The "monthly curse" has taken a whole new meaning for me. Except it wasn't even monthly. It was all the time, weeks at a time and heavy. All the time. As of late, I spend more time bleeding than not. It's like three weeks on and one week off and it's hardly predictable.

I've bled so much, and my iron is so low, I am now considered anemic. I also had to have a couple blood transfusions. Worst of all, during this time I am often exhausted. My energy can be scarce sometimes. Or just plain nonexistent. And I hate that.

I miss myself.

The old me.

Anyway, since things have progressively worsened my doctor is suggesting surgery. As much as I don't want to get surgery, I'm so desperate I'm leaning closer to making this decision with each passing day.

And… it was the irony of it all for me. When I told Daijah I had to laugh about it. Wasn't shit funny but maybe I laughed to keep from crying.

God really had a sense of humor.

Me meeting Micah *of all places* in the tampon aisle.

An aisle I spent more time in than I cared to admit.

I tried them all. I settled on a combination of reusable pads, period panties, and a diva cup on the days that had mercy on me and the flow was light enough. I used so many disposable pads that I felt convicted. I *had* to reduce my carbon footprint and *not* clog up the landfill.

Also, I'm saying this parenthetically; I remember thinking that I could imagine my father being in the same situation Micah was in at some point. Needing guidance on what to get for Daijah and me.

So, there you have it.

That is the reason I shy away from men. I knew relationships would eventually lead to a desire for closeness. Not just on his part either. We would desire closeness. And intimacy. And eventually, sex.

Sex wasn't something I could offer anyone right now.

Not anytime soon. I honestly don't know if it's something I could *ever* offer.

My female department did not appear promising. There were a few unknown variables, and I couldn't guarantee much of anything.

And that shit was depressing.

Anyway, it's been ages since I'd been in a committed relationship, but I have dated a few guys.

And I've always dated men a little older than me. I didn't intentionally seek them out, but it always worked out that way somehow. We just got each other. I've been told many times that I have an old soul. And… if im objective, men my age bore me.

I need psychological and emotional stimulation.

Multidimensional. Provoking. Engrossing stimulation.

Without it, my ass was checking all the way out.

Micah had all the above on lock. Micah is by far the sweetest guy ever. He was also seven years older than me. Go figure.

I supposed I would date again, but I know I'm selective as hell. I've had a couple "almost, but not quite".

I could also admit that I could take things a little more seriously.

That's the first thing.

I was too old for this self-sabotage thing. If that's what you even called it.

For example, there was a guy named Zeke that I hung out with now and then. He really had a thing for me. Like he really, really liked me. Once he told me that I was his *dream girl*. That was incredibly sweet.

And I liked him too. Honestly, I did.

At the time I was twenty-five and he was thirty-one. We hung out several times; sometimes out somewhere, other times at his house. We were never intimate, but we kissed plenty of times.

I remembered him being a gentleman and always sweet to me when we hung out. He always wanted to see me, and it wasn't like I was super busy, I just never really made it a priority.

One Saturday I went to his apartment unannounced, and he was so glad to see me, he hugged me and invited me in immediately. When I stepped inside, I saw that he had one of his boys over and they were watching the game. Zeke was thrilled to introduce us. Since he wasn't expecting me and already had company, I offered to come back another time, but he insisted I stay because the game was almost over.

So, I went to watch tv in his bedroom and at some point, I fell asleep. I must have been sleeping for a while because he'd covered me with a blanket. When I went back to the living room, he hugged me again and took me to the kitchen. He had ordered takeout from a Thai place.

Thai is one of my favorites. Like, top three.

I only mentioned that one time, but he remembered that detail. It was crazy too because as he warmed the food, he told me he was hungry as hell but was waiting for me to wake up so we could eat together. My ass wouldn't have been able to wait as good as that food smelled.

Zeke and I were never official, and had I taken things more seriously we would have headed in that direction. He wanted to be. I evaded that. I don't have any excuses, but I didn't really give things with Zeke my best. I was never mean to him but what I did was mean and inconsiderate. I feel bad as hell thinking back on it. If I ever missed his call, I never made an effort to call him back right away. I avoided making concrete plans with him whenever he asked to see me.

I remember the last time he called me; whatever the reason, I didn't answer so he left me a voicemail. I had completely forgotten about it and didn't check my voicemail till a few days later.

"Hey Destiney, it's Zeke… how you doing? Been thinking bout you… miss you… been wanting to lay eyes on you. I'm trying to give you space because it seems that's what you need… but I don't know because you won't really tell me what you need. Anyway… I guess that's just how it is right?"

He sounded frustrated. And I couldn't blame him. I remember feeling horrible, but I never even called him back. He was a great guy, and he deserved love and happiness. I hope he found it. I know he would make someone very happy.

I didn't know how else to maneuver the dating pool. That was a personal problem of mine. I could admit that. I'm a complicated person. And I really needed to stay out of it. Which

I generally did. And I guess I wasn't missing out on much. Apparently, the dating pool was full of piss.

I had Neeka in my ear telling me all about it.

Neeka was a serial dater and was tenacious as hell. Her ass was determined to find her husband. I told her she shouldn't have to look so hard, but what did I know? My ass was single too.

My feelings were all over the damn place and I was extremely guarded. I hadn't always been, but over time, something switched somewhere.

And something else crazy was that I had a way of leading someone to believe I would entertain them beyond a conversation, but they'd end up disappointed. I didn't do that shit on purpose. Honest to God. I was just being myself. I'm an intellectual. Apparently, men like that because it always happens that way. It came as no surprise. I am attractive to intelligent men. And I'm extremely attracted to them.

I'm a sapiosexual through and through. Conversations are my specialty and my weakness. Especially deep conversations.

I can converse with anyone about almost anything even if I wasn't doing much of the talking. I'm easily intrigued by many different things. I love to coexist with people opposite me, I'll inquire to the point where I'll eventually ask them twenty-one questions. Those questions would beget more, and before we knew it, we would be waist deep. I especially love to nerd out when we uncover commonalities.

But… those amazing conversations do not lead to any lasting relationships.

Mainly because I don't allow them to. I've done enough introspection to admit that.

Daijah has tried to set me up a few times, but things never quite panned out.

I wasn't taking it seriously enough.

Some months ago, Daijah begged me to double date with her, Julian, and Julian's coworker. He and Julian were good friends, and I'd met him once or twice in passing but didn't think anything more of him. Frankly I wasn't paying him any attention. I acquiesced since he was a nice guy and seemed pleasant enough to be around.

The four of us went to a bowling alley and he and I talked a lot. He had a great conversation, and I genuinely enjoyed his company. When the night ended, and he asked for my number I had to let him down. He brushed it off but had inquired about me again a few times. He also seemed always conveniently to be around for something or another. Twice, I'd gone to pick up Daijah from Julian's house, and she asked me to come in and there he was sitting on the couch in the living room.

Later, Daijah revealed that he'd asked if she could get me to come out on the double date and he'd had his eye on me for a while. By then I figured as much.

Eventually we did have that conversation, and I told him it was nothing personal.

And it wasn't. I was being honest. I just wasn't really interested in pursuing anything right now. To be real, I may have considered it if I was in a different headspace.

And not bleeding all over the damn place.

When he asked about being friends, I had to shut that shit down too. I know how I am. I could never just be friends with a guy. Like ever. Tried that. I don't do opposite sex friendships. They aren't good for me.

Feelings always ended up being involved.

Either the guy would end up liking me, or I'd end up having a crush on him.

It honestly wouldn't take much for me to grow sweet on him. If we were friends, we'd be talking a lot, sharing life moments and being there for one another. I'd end up being vulnerable and before I knew it my ass would have caught some damn feelings.

Anyway, I told him, hypothetically, I'd only be friends with him if we were going to explore a relationship. When he asked for a ballpark timeline, I encouraged him to move on.

I'm not even sure what his relationship status is now. I don't think he's married but who knows.

And that's why things were so crazy when it came to Micah.

Micah was the first man in a while to truly intrigue me. And intrigued I was.

We spoke daily. For hours. And our conversations were *fire*. We'd even graduated to FaceTime which I loved. I looked forward to our talks each night. And my feelings were growing.

By now, I was so into him. My little crush had taken off full steam ahead.

I was always giddy every time my phone chimed. Hoping it was him texting me. And when it was, my face lit up. Bright as a Christmas tree.

I was absolutely sprung. From our first conversation.

Micah was kind. Intelligent. Charming. And handsome of course but his quiet confidence and awareness of himself just did it for me. He moved with a quiet swag I was into. His wisdom and maturity absolutely had something to do with my attraction. I couldn't even say what it was exactly. We just seemed to have something. A spark. Magnetism. I didn't know… I felt deep in my gut that it would lead to something amazing. I really liked the way he handled me. And talked to me. I loved it. And I couldn't help but imagine being his. And how beautiful it would be.

I'd never given relationships much thought. I didn't even think it was in the cards for me.

But Micah had me thinking about all of that. A life together. Love. Marriage. Babies.

I saw the way Daijah had effortlessly fallen for Julian, and I loved that so much for her. It really was a beautiful thing.

I guess… I never thought I'd get a turn.

As much as I tried to keep those thoughts under control, my feelings were already invested. There wasn't anything I could do to stop them either. But I was hesitant. Hesitant to give it a try. Reluctant to let things go and stop fighting it. I worried that if I did, he would want something more with me.

Something I wanted too, but something I couldn't give him.

That scared me because I didn't want to lose Micah.

In the meantime, I was trying to slow things down.

But that was becoming difficult.

eleven

MICAH

"So. What was your first job?"

"Chuck E Cheese."

"Aww for real? You had to sing that birthday song?" I guffawed.

"Shit. A million times."

Destiney and I had been on the phone for the past three hours. We took a break to shower, and I had just called her back on FaceTime. We were both lying in bed. I was on my back, one hand behind my head, my other hand holding the phone. Destiney was lying on her belly resting on her arms, her phone propped nearby. Her beautiful face filling my screen.

Since meeting Destiney those weeks ago, most of our evenings ended the same way. She was the last voice I heard night after night after hours of conversing. I had to admit it was my very favorite part of the day. We talked about so many things and the more I got to know her the more my fondness grew for her.

It was so easy opening up to her. I had nothing to hide but just the same it felt good to feel safe and vulnerable. Our conversations always flowed so smoothly. Flowing like waves, we maneuvered from one topic to the next. I noticed we reminisced about our teenage years a lot. Tonight was no different and we'd segued into talking about our first jobs.

"Good grief!" Destiney roared with me. "Gabe and Gabby had a many birthday parties there. That place is too germ infested for me. Seems like all of them kids have a runny nose and sticky ass fingers."

"Now that's a fact. What was your first job?"

"Ice cream scooper."

"That's adorable. Baskin Robins?" Destiney squealed filling the screen with her bright smile.

"Yep."

"You try all thirty-one flavors?" She asked playfully.

"Just about. Funny thing about it, I'm not a huge fan of ice cream anymore. Even all these years later. I've had one too many free scoops."

"Oh man! *I love ice cream,*" she gushed.

I lightly tittered, telling her, "I used to love ice cream too. In this case the perks can be a bad thing."

Each conversation was an opportunity for me to learn more about Destiney and I loved everything I learned. I always took mental notes, storing things for later. I found out she loved green, any shade, but her favorite was jade. She and her younger sister were incredibly close. She called her *Sibling Bestie,* and I loved that.

Destiney was also a Daddy's girl, and she spoke of her father all the time. That made my heart so happy. She never spoke of her mother, and I took the hint not to bring her up. I figured when she wanted to talk about her she would. I was curious though.

Recently, as in just a few days ago, I learned she's a vegetarian which fascinated me. She had my interest piqued there since I didn't personally know many black vegetarians.

But she wasn't overt at all.

She didn't force her views onto me about it. I learned of this detail simply because we were talking on Facetime over our lunch break, and we talked about what we were each having. We did this a few days a week and I noticed the trend that she never had any meat and that's when she casually informed me.

And another thing, Destiney loved all things, art. She was so creative. So talented. And she spoke with such excitement about the things that she felt passionate about. She shared a few pictures of some of the work she had done on murals. It was amazing. Sensational. Her passion for art showed itself in her work and I was beyond impressed with her level of talent. The best part was that she was so humble about it.

Destiney possessed a confidence in herself and was so comfortable in her skin. In a classy way.

Theres a sweet spot for the right level of confidence. A level that isn't too much. And Destiney had the perfect amount of self-assurance. I've found that only a select group of women can pull it off.

She liked to mention she was super shy on occasion, and I picked up on that too. It was adorable honestly. But her confidence was a constant presence. In the best way.

And she was sweet. So sweet. My gosh.

She'd call me sometimes when she was leaving a work site, and I'd hear how she spoke with people. Peers. Counterparts. Colleagues. Associates. Seniors. Children. Superiors. She spoke the same way with all of them. Kindly. Respectfully. Littered with manners, fluff and compliments.

Destiney was a rare breed.

I could dig it. I was into it.

I was into her.

Hella.

"Let me see if I can guess your favorite flavor." I peered at Destiney with low lids with my hand on my chin. As if in deep thought. "Don't tell me."

She grinned, "You won't guess."

"Rocky road?"

"That's Daijah's all-time favorite. But not mine."

"Hmm." I tapped my chin silently.

"What made you guess that?" She asked after a moment.

"You're multi layered a lot like rocky road. An interesting mix."

Smiling she said, "Aww. That's sweet. Want me to tell you now?"

"No, I want another try."

I looked at her and she looked back at me, keeping a straight face. "Mint chocolate chip."

"Oh my gosh that's my least favorite, eww." Destiney laughed after making a gagging sound.

"Least favorite? Why?"

"This is my humble opinion, but Mint flavor belongs in toothpaste or chewing gum not ice cream. There's a school of thought that thinks otherwise but I could never get into mint chocolate chip ice cream."

"I hear you on that. Like the way people can mix savory and sweet. Not my jam either."

"I'll give you one last guess."

"Hmm. Butter pecan?"

"Oh yum, now that's a good one. But not my favorite. It tastes pretty good, but don't you think there's too many nuts?"

"Oh yeah, there's no getting away from those. Like nuts in brownies." I chuckled. "I'm beginning to think you're more complicated than I thought."

"Hey! I'm not complicated. Good ice cream doesn't need nuts. Something already good, doesn't need anything extra. My favorite flavor is vanilla ice cream. Perfectly sweet, not mixed with anything extra."

"Vanilla ice cream huh? Wow. I should have figured."

"Yup. Extra points if it's French vanilla. My grandmother used to make homemade French vanilla ice cream. It's a bit richer because it's made with a custard base. Perfect on top of warm peach cobbler."

"Yum! I can imagine that!" I mused. After a beat, "I know a place near midtown with some of the best ice cream around."

"Really?"

"Yeah, it's called Gunther's. Ever been?"

"Not yet."

"Well, I'd love to take you there. Every ice cream fan must try Gunther's."

"Hmm." Was all she gave me. No longer looking in my eyes, she was now focused on something in the distance.

It wasn't lost on me that she suddenly grew quiet. This was my second time asking her to meet me, and she retreated then, too. As great as our conversations were, I couldn't figure out what I was doing wrong. We'd been talking for about eight weeks now, for hours at a time. I wanted her to be comfortable, but I was eager, I guess.

"You know Micah…" She brought her eyes back to me, pausing, and I waited for her to complete her thought. "Can we take it slow for now?"

"Take it slow?" That question came out before I could stop it, and it was laced with an ounce of sarcasm.

"Yeah, I mean…for right now, I'd love to continue getting to know you better. If that's alright with you."

I sighed lightly. "Is that not what we've been doing? We've been talking for hours night after night. I just want to see you again. I like you, Destiney."

"That's very sweet. I like you too."

"Yeah?"

"Yeah. And I want to see you again too. I'm just not ready yet. But I'll be ready soon."

After a beat, "Tell me when you're ready, and we won't wait a second longer."

"Deal." Her beautiful smile filled the screen again, and I returned one of my own.

Later, after we'd said our goodnights, I was up. Pondering.

I wasn't sure how I would fare taking things slow. But I didn't have an issue trying to figure it out. I could concede that too much too soon could end badly.

We were both intentional about how we wanted to pursue things.

I appreciated courting a woman. I could be patient. Destiney was absolutely worth the pursuit.

I just knew I wanted her. She was beautiful. She was sexy. But I desired to know her so much more. Share space with her. Learn her intricacies.

Destiney captivated my mind, and my thoughts were consumed with her morning, noon, and night. At the same time, I didn't mind doing things differently.

I'd prayed about this, and I wanted this to be it for me.

I wanted her to be it for me. I'd do everything in my power to ensure I didn't fumble this one.

Destiney was precious to me. All of her. Mind, body, soul. Her heart. I was going to handle her accordingly.

And her heart took priority. If she wanted- needed us to take things slow, we would take things slow. It was imperative that I took the time to show her who I was. I wasn't one of those other dudes who only wanted one thing from her. If that meant slow-walking this thing, I was fine with that. I felt good about us and where we were. Most of all, I was never intimidated by a challenge.

I also knew that once we got to the point where we were seeing each other, I would have a whole new world to explore with her. That shit had me excited.

Taking it slow.

I thought about it.

That meant we had an opportunity to get to know each other intimately before any intimacy whatsoever. I'd never touched her. Never kissed her. Aside from the day we met in that drugstore, I never shared any space with her. And yet, I was so far gone for Destiney.

Yet and still… I was perfectly fine with being so gone for her.

twelve

MICAH

"Okay. So, this may seem like a random question…" I told Destiney, then I cracked up. I couldn't see Destiney, but I heard her laugh along with me. Many conversations started this way between us. By now, we've talked about so many things. But we still had many more things to learn about each other.

I reveled in all of this. I enjoyed the process of learning about each other. My fondness for Destiney growing by the day.

Anyway, we were eating dinner together tonight. Kind of.

We both had dinner in front of us. And we were on FaceTime. This was something we did a few days a week.

"No such thing, baby," Destiney volleyed from somewhere nearby. I chuckled at that. I guess she was right. "Hang on just one quick second."

"Take your time." Her phone had been propped up at her kitchen table. And I had my phone propped up in front of me at mine. My plate untouched.

I was waiting for her to start. We always waited for each other.

"You settled?" I asked her once she came back into view.

"Yup. Thank you, baby. Just had to get my water."

"Of course. It's my turn, right?"

"Yes."

I nodded, then prayed over our meals.

We ate in silence at first.

"Beans must be delicious," I teased playfully. She looked up, and I laughed, "Or you were starving. You're so quiet."

She laughed too. "Both! And these beans are perfect. Thank you very much. My best ones yet."

"Nice." Destiney made red beans and rice. We were on the phone yesterday while she picked through them to soak overnight. And she was pretty excited to have them for dinner tonight.

"How's your salmon?" She asked me.

I made honey-glazed salmon and broccoli. "Great. Thank you love."

After a beat, "So what was this random question?" She reminded me.

I nodded. "Right." I forgot for a second. "Can you eat with chopsticks?"

"Yeah? Can you?"

"Yeah. I only learned recently though. So, I'm not that good."

Yes, I was the guy asking for a fork at sushi restaurants.

Destiney gasped dramatically. "No freaking way. *Have we discovered something Mr. Wonderful isn't good at?*"

I cracked up and said, "Oh, stop it. There are lots of things I'm not good at."

"Not really." She pointedly nodded. "You're perfect at everything." She took a drink of water. "Except for eating with chopsticks, apparently."

I shook my head.

"I'm kidding, baby. You'll get better; keep practicing." She took a few more bites. "So, you like sushi? I take it?"

"Yeah! Love it. You too?"

"Mmhmm. There's always lots of vegetarian options at sushi places."

Naturally, my first instinct was to invite her to get sushi. I knew of some places downtown where we could get the best sushi. And I'd love to take her.

But I knew better than to ask. Suggest. Or imply.

She'd likely shoot me down.

Just the same, it was great to learn that detail. I'd been tucking these things away. I figured that at some point, in the *very near future*, I could put the info to use.

I hoped so anyway. I wanted to see her. Be close to her.

And last we talked about it, almost two weeks ago, I agreed I would wait for her.

And I was waiting. Patiently. With much anticipation for the very moment, she would tell me she was ready for me.

I've been ready for her.

Looking at her beautiful face on my screen, she seemed so close… yet so far away.

"Good to know." We segued effortlessly once I thought about something else, we hadn't talked about. "So, you a TV fan? Movie fan?"

"I prefer to read or sketch. So, I don't have time for much TV. But when I do, I love a great documentary. Someday, I'm going to make one."

"Oh yeah? Love a great documentary." I was captivated. "What about?" When I thought I had her all figured out, she'd surprise me with something more. She was so multifaceted and intriguing. I loved it when we discovered commonalities too.

"Not sure yet. I'm interested in so many things. I love journalism and great storytelling."

"Same here. There are some great documentaries out there. What are some of your favorites?"

Her eyes lit up. "There's a few. One is called *Whilemina's War*; it's about a small town in South Carolina where the

AIDS/HIV epidemic has ravaged the black female population. I watched it years ago, and it was life-changing. So many of the women die of complications related to AIDS and HIV because there are so few programs and funding for them for several miles. I've seen it millions of times.

There's another one called *Carmen and Geoffrey* about a husband and wife who were trailblazers as black dancers in the '30s and '40s, but their careers spanned decades. I love the arts in general, but especially the performing arts. Their story was captivating because they broke down so many barriers for many of the black and brown dancers known today. Misty Copeland wouldn't be where she is without Carmen de Lavallade and Geoffrey Holder."

"Wow. I'd love to see them both."

"I own them both…" Destiney began. And I'll admit, I held my breath. I lightly exhaled when she offered, "Maybe we can watch them sometime."

"I look forward to watching," I replied, not missing a beat.

She looked up at me and smiled. Real big. Her smile was beautiful. "Thank you," she said.

I furrowed my brows. "Thank you?"

"Yes. For caring. You care so much about everything that is me. You're so interested and intentional." I smiled too. "No one's really done that before. Only my dad. He still dotes over Daijah and me." She looked down. "No other man has done the things that you do, Micah." She shook her head. "I'd find myself caring for someone… and sharing my heart with them, and then it turned out to be one-sided."

"Hey, lift that chin, baby." If Destiney were with me right now, I would have gently lifted it myself. When her eyes settled on mine, I said, "Listen, I'm intrigued by *everything* that is you. And fortunately for me, those yo-yos fucked up."

She giggled, which quickly became a cackle, "Well, it's nice to know my feelings are being reciprocated. And I'm intrigued with you, too, Micah. Everything about you."

I was pleased with that. And though her suggestion was subtle, it seemed we were getting closer to meeting. And I was very anxious to see her again. To share space with her again. It didn't matter what we did; I just wanted to be with her.

***

I'd been hanging out in the VIP area for the past hour and a half enjoying the band, and this band was hot! Smoke was a five-piece band that did impressive covers of some of the greatest R&B hits from the 90s. Malachi and I went to high school with Solomon, the saxophone player. He was badass at the sax, too. And my best friend, next to Malachi. The other fellas in the band were good guys, and we'd have a chance to shoot the breeze every now and then.

A few patrons were on the small dance floor and dozens more at the two bars on either side. This lounge was a great setting for a night out. Going to the club was never my thing, but I didn't mind a lounge on occasion. I hadn't been out in a while and was enjoying myself. I loved the grown folk's vibe of a lounge. The lights were dim, the music was great, and drinks were flowing.

HomeGrownSol was a black-owned bar and lounge in midtown Sacramento and was a pillar in the black community, specifically in the art space. I read an article covering the tenth anniversary of the grand opening that this was the brainchild of two college sweethearts; *"She was a starving artist and passionate chef from humble beginnings, he was a business minded philanthropist from old money. They both wanted to open a space to somehow pay it forward"*.

Anytime I could support them, I would. HomeGrownSol hosted many benefit concerts over the years and offered their space as a venue, often free for a good cause. They generously opened their doors to up-and-coming artists of many genres to play their music and had indie art shows and weekly open mic poetry nights. It was a great place to spend time and meet great people. But my favorite thing about this place was the food. The chef and co-owner of HomeGrownSol could cook her ass off. The vibrant flavors she could capture were incredibly delicious. Her specialty was Black Southern cuisine with Creole, Caribbean, and African influences. Her passion for great food was evident in all her dishes.

Everything on the menu was fire, but the red snapper and spaghetti plate was my favorite. They also had your typical bar food, so there was something for everyone. And speaking of the food, that was the only reason I'd agreed to come out when Ray asked to meet here. I was overdue for my red snapper and spaghetti fix.

Raymond stumbled back into our VIP section and sat down with a curvy brown skinned chick attached to him. Her dress was too tight and way too short, and it was clear ole girl had one too many to drink. She leaned forward to tell Raymond something in his ear and her titties looked as if they were about to fall out of the top of her dress. I looked the other way, taking a swig from my second glass of brandy and coke.

"You hurry back!" Raymond yelled over the music, slapping her ass. She yelped and almost tripped as she stepped down to exit the VIP area. I shook my head and lightly chuckled.

"What?" Raymond looked over at me, oblivious.

"We getting too old for all that."

"I ain't never too old to entertain a beautiful woman!" He flagged down a cocktail waitress and ordered another round of whatever he was drinking.

"I see that," I returned simply, returning my glass to my lips.

"Man, you better get you some of this. Look at these options. Thick, slim, tall, petite, caramel, chocolate, high yella!" Raymond expanded his arms looking around the lounge, "You can take your pick of the litter in this muthafucka!"

"I'm good," I returned. The truth is, I was mentally somewhere else. A pretty girl came a dime a dozen, and at this point, I desired much more than a pretty face. I wasn't impressed by the infinite options of beautiful women surrounding me. I glanced around the lounge. Tonight, there were many. If I had to guess, the women easily outnumbered the men by three to one. In my peripheral, I could see Raymond glaring at me.

"Man, what's going on with you? You ain't moved since we got here."

Raymond's father is my father's older brother, making Raymond my first cousin. My uncle drove long hauls for a living and was gone quite a bit, so Ray spent a lot of time with us when we were kids. At one point, he lived with us. I didn't know much about Ray's mother besides that my uncle never married her. I think I only met her once, as far as I can recall. I think she was an alcoholic, and Ray didn't see much of her as a child. I believe they have somewhat of a relationship now, but I'm not sure to what degree.

Anyway, Ray is a year older than Malachi, which makes him two years older than me. Mal and I were both close to him as kids. And Ray is hilarious. Always keeping things light. But his ass is wild. Ray chases the ladies like it's going out of style.

He may not ever settle down. As we've matured, Mal and I love him from a distance more and more often.

"You seeing someone?" He quizzed, pulling me from my thoughts. Last he heard, I was single as a Pringle. I hadn't brought a woman around in a number of years.

"Yeah. Kinda sorta." I couldn't refrain from smiling as thoughts of Destiney flooded my mind.

He returned a quizzical expression. "Why am I just now hearing about this?" In Ray's defense, we were super close once upon a time. I would share everything with Raymond and my brother Malachi. I haven't shared much with Ray lately; instead, I go to my brother for everything.

I shrugged my shoulders dismissively in an attempt to downplay it. I didn't need Ray in my business. "There's not much to tell right now. We're not actually hanging out or anything like that but talking a lot and getting to know each other." I took another drink, "Taking it slow."

"She in the pen or some shit?"

Here we go. I grimaced. "Naw!"

"She in another country?"

"Land Park."

"*Land Park!* You bein' catfished my nigga?"

"No Ray. I'm not being catfished," I said defensively.

"How you know that if you've never seen her?"

"I have seen her. On the day we met, we've been focusing on getting to know each other since then. Minus all the physical shit getting in the way."

Ray pondered for a moment. "Exclusively?"

"Yeah. Why?"

"All this pussy at your disposal and you're holding out for someone you can't even see."

"You already know that ain't even my style, cousin."

I'd already told Malachi about Destiney. How amazing she was. How much I enjoyed getting to know her. How much I liked her. From the beginning, Mal wanted the best for us both. And he'd been asking me how things were going. I kept him in the loop, and he knew we were taking things slow. Of course, I couldn't help but share how much my feelings have grown.

"These feelings are just… they're unlike anything I've ever felt. Her beauty is what captivated me, but our conversation, our connection… I like her a lot."

"Sounds like it." Mal chuckled, *"I love it, man. Get your girl. Then, once you get her, never stop chasing her."*

That was the plan. I wanted her, and I was going to get her. And I planned always to remind her how special she was.

"She probably getting it in with some other nigga," Ray said, bringing me back to the present. I peered over as he smirked, accepting his drinks the cocktail waitress returned with.

"Doubt that." I tossed back the last of my drink and handed the waitress my empty glass. I gave her cash to cover my food and drinks and a tip. The band had just finished their set, and the DJ announced he would be up next. I took that as my cue to take my ass home. Rising to my feet, I extended my hand, "I'm headed out, Ray."

"What man?" He glanced at his cell to check the time. "It's still early! You ain't in your feelings because of what I said, are you? I was just talking my shit. You know how I am sometimes."

What Raymond had to say didn't bother me in the least. What I decided to do didn't need to make sense to anyone else. And what's understood doesn't need to be explained.

Furthermore, I didn't give a damn. I would stand behind my decision ten toes down.

"You good cousin, for real. I'm just ready to get out of here." Ray stood to his feet, and we shared a quick embrace. "You really should be right behind me," I chuckled. His lady friend returned to the VIP section and sat beside him. "Be good aight?"

"Oh, I'm just getting started, Micah." He handed her the drink he ordered as he put his arm around her waist, settling back into the couch and getting comfortable. "I'll holla at you."

"Bet." I turned to head out of the lounge, stepping down into the main section. The DJ started spinning, and the congregants on the dance floor grew. I weaved in and out of the clusters of people, using my manners and keeping my line of vision straight ahead. I was near the exit when I felt a light tug on the hem of my shirt. I turned to my right noticing a tall, slim, cutie smiling. She looked familiar, so I turned completely around to get a better look, but her face didn't register. I was trying to get out of here, but I had already stopped and being the gentleman I am, I obliged her.

She leaned into my ear, "Hey handsome, how about a dance?"

"Can't. I'm headed out," I gingerly told her.

"Aww." She placed her hand on my forearm. "Just one dance? I noticed you sitting behind that velvet rope past two hours. I hate I waited for nothing."

Maintaining my gentle tone, I told her, "I'm about ready to go. Not really in the mood for dancing."

Stepping closer and facing me, she placed each of her hands on my shoulders. "I'll come with you," she said with low lids and a sultry voice.

Well, that was forward. I considered it a turn-off being pursued by women, and ole girl was not my type. Not even a little bit. She was cute, but I chased what I wanted when I was on the market. Her persistence meant there were few excuses I could use to get through to her.

"I have someone waiting for me," I said simply. I was partially honest. "Excuse me." I stepped aside and made my way to the exit, leaving her no time to retort.

I texted Destiney as soon as I was back in my car. She likely wouldn't respond tonight, but I didn't care. I just wanted her to know she was on my mind. Destiney stayed on my mind. It didn't matter where I was or what I was doing.

Shifting into drive, I headed back toward my house, ready to call it a night. I couldn't hang like I used to, and my ass was tired.

thirteen

MICAH

It would have been easy to take ole girl from the lounge home with me.

But I was focused on a greater task.

Practicing abstinence was nothing new for me. I was a slow swimmer to begin with, and I didn't start having sex till college. I was damn near twenty-one when I had my first blow job. I had foresight even before I'd physically gotten to that point. I just knew that I needed to protect my heart. I knew how much was at stake in opening myself up to those things. I knew how emotional I was and how easily I got attached.

Ray would always tease me about still having my V-card.

And for every discouraging word, Mal would always encourage me. I appreciated that immensely. People were out here fucking on each other like it was going out of style.

"Don't worry about what everyone else is doing, baby brother. Ain't nothing wrong with holding out. I promise you, sex ain't going nowhere. Fucking before you're ready, ain't gone do nothing but complicate shit."

It was no secret that Ray had a completely different philosophy. He'd fuck anything and everything willing. One time Daddy told Ray, *"His dick would fall off if he weren't more careful about where he was putting it."*

I remember Mal cracking up at that. I joined in with the laughter but didn't see what was so funny. I do now though.

When I got home, I hopped in the shower, and now I was lying in bed in the dark, staring at the ceiling. I had caught a second wind and couldn't fall asleep just yet, so I'd been thinking.

And for some reason, my thoughts drifted to my ex-fiancé. Ayesha.

There was a time I thought of her constantly. Of course, when we were together and in love, but even after we were no longer together, I thought of her.

After everything with Ayesha was officially over, I was confused with exactly what I would do with myself. I did dumb shit that would hunt me later. For example, I hadn't been in a serious committed relationship, yet I fucked a few times without good reason. I knew better but I did the shit anyway. As a result, it was screwing with my mental. Big time.

I couldn't just lay with a woman if I didn't care about her. I must care about her in some capacity to be intimate with her. That's just the way I am.

I was out at a lounge once with Ray. And Erica, a woman from work, was with a few girlfriends. We'd never spoken at work, but I'd seen her in passing. She's hard to miss. Erica is extremely attractive, and she knows it. A few men at the lounge tried to dance with her and talk to her, but she made it clear she wanted me. She kept approaching me throughout the night and was extremely flirtatious. We did end up talking and Erica was so sexually suggestive, I was convinced she would have let me fuck her right out in the open in front of everyone. I was so turned off that it was over before it even started. Yet, for some dumb ass reason, I left with Erica anyway, ending up at her place.

Erica begged to give me head. I let her.

Then begged me to give her the dick. Against my better judgment, I relented.

That was my first and only one night stand. And as I drove away from her house, I was more than pissed at myself. I was irritated and on edge. I knew I should have stayed my ass away from Erica. When I couldn't shake the repulsive thought of what I had done, I went to Malachi.

I still remember that day. I called him on my Bluetooth speaker as I drove away from her place.

"Baby brother." He greeted me pleasantly and I immediately hated that I even called him with this shit.

"Brother," was all I could manage.

"Come on and see me man." His tone reassuring. "I'm at the house."

All I had to say was one word. Mal knew me frontwards and backwards.

I was so thankful for him and our relationship. Malachi, always the voice of reason was the person I needed to get my ass out of that funk. Next to our father, Malachi was the only one I trusted of this magnitude.

We were eleven months apart and were raised like twins. We were so close.

As close as we were, my parents made a point of always celebrating our unique strengths and accomplishments. We did many of the same things in the early years, yet I never felt I was in competition with Malachi. Since my parents celebrated us as individuals, we were confident in ourselves. We liked different things but enjoyed the things we had in common.

When I was a senior in high school, Malachi went away to Morehouse College. That was tough because we were separated for the first time in our lives. I remember him coming home during Christmas break and telling me how much fun he was having. By then, I'd already committed to Cal Poly in San Luis Obispo on a full athletic scholarship. I had a few offers, but I always knew that was where I wanted to go. When I asked

Malachi about the ladies in Atlanta, I couldn't believe what he told me.

"Baby brother, there are beautiful chocolate women everywhere! You almost get used to it," He chuckled.

"Ain't no way man!" I exclaimed.

"I swear!"

When Mommy and Daddy moved him in, I was doing a summer internship, but I may have gotten a sample. But I found out just what the hell Mal was talking about when I visited for my spring break. I really missed my brother, and he was so proud to introduce me to his roommates and new friends. I only stayed 4 days and hated that I couldn't stay longer. But damn! A black teenager from Northern California saw all the good things about the South. The Spelman women he showed me were beautiful and my ass didn't want to come back.

But Malachi wasn't fazed by those ladies. He was laser-focused on handling business and even pledged Greek. And anyway, Ella already had Malachi on lock by then. He only had eyes for her. Quite frankly, in Malachi's world, no other women existed.

I remember when he first met Ella. We went to the same high school. Malachi was a junior, and Ella and I were sophomores. Ella and I had AP Biology together, and one afternoon, he saw us both coming out of class. We weren't walking out together, just exiting at the same time. One second, I saw him standing across the hall; a second later, he ended up right next to me.

"Baby brother!"

"Hey Malachi," I answered with eyebrows high on my head, wondering what the hell he was so pressed about.

*"Who is **that?!**" He pointed at a group of girls nearby talking.*

"Which one? It's like six of them over there."

"Which one you think?"I chuckled, already knowing, "Ella is the one in the green dress."

"Wow." That was all he said, but he was saying a hell of a lot more than that. I knew my brother, just like he knew me. I briefly regarded him; I had never heard him speak that way about any girl. Malachi wasn't a playboy by any means; he only dealt with one girl at a time. That was something my father drilled into us. But Malachi never seemed invested; it was more so passing the time, I guess. I could tell off rip, this one would be a little different. As it would turn out, he was smitten with Ella from the start.

"You know her?" He asked, pulling me from my thoughts.

"Kinda," I shrugged. "We have AP Bio together. She's smart as hell. We worked on a group project before. She's nice too," I offered. It mattered a whole lot whether the girl was kind. To me, anyway. If it wasn't one thing I couldn't stand, it was a mean ass girl. And don't be cute and mean. Your ass is damaged goods as far as I'm concerned. Ain't nothing remotely attractive about that shit.

Malachi looked me in the eye. "Brother. If you're already interested in her, I'll back off."

My mother always told us never to let any girl come between us. "There are too many women out here for that kind of foolishness", she would say. We never expressed interest in the same girl. Plus, I was a slow swimmer when it came to the ladies. There could be a girl interested in me, throwing hints all day, and I wouldn't know if one hit me right in the head. Malachi and Ray would always tease me about it.

Admittedly, Ella was out-of-this-world beautiful. In a class all her own.

But I hadn't even seen her in that way before.

I hadn't even thought about her like that until now. If I were honest, I wouldn't have minded getting to know her, but I didn't take the opportunity. That was my bad.

"You go ahead. I'm not," I returned confidently.

"You sure?"

"Yes, I'm positive."

They were inseparable very quickly after that. Once we graduated high school, Ella joined Malachi in Georgia. Headed to Clark-Atlanta on the first thing, smoking.

As they say, the rest is history.

When I talked to Malachi following my lack of judgment with Erica, he had to remind me of something.

"That's not you, baby brother. You've never been the casual sex type."

Mal was right, and I'd say that with my chest.

At that point, I was thirty-two years old, and I could count on one hand how many women I'd slept with. Counting my ex-fiancé Ayesha, I had been intimate with four women total.

I made the decision then: the one finger remaining was for my wife. Considering that, I decided to be abstinent.

I'd been abstaining for two years now, preparing my heart and my mind for my wife. I knew I needed to stop with the foolishness and clear out all the shit in the way.

Staying ready is better than having to get ready.

***

I met Ayesha during our sophomore year at Cal Poly. The crazy thing was, I'd been hearing about her since freshman year and had no idea. I still remember my roommate Tyson coming in one night after being out with his girlfriend Laila. He told me Laila also had a roommate from Sacramento, and maybe we should meet each other.

He said it casually, and I brushed it off. On a few occasions, he'd mentioned going to hang out with Laila, and if I wanted to roll, he could ask her to bring her friend. It didn't register that he was talking about the same person all that time. He never told me her name, nor did I ask, so I couldn't have known.

To that end, I guess I was indifferent about meeting someone. That's likely why I wasn't too pressed about it. My spring semester was intense; I was playing baseball and didn't have much free time between practices and my very rigorous course load. I wasn't sexually active either so women in general were an afterthought. Somehow Tyson made time for all of that. Anyway, whenever Tyson mentioned Laila's friend, I'd brush it off.

But then, I finally did meet Laila's friend.

And everything changed.

I remember that night.

Vividly.

Ty and I were chilling in our dorm. We'd been working and training hard for the past several weeks. Nonstop. And for the first time since the pre-season started, we didn't have practice that day or a game the next.

"You tryin to hit M.U.?" I asked Ty. I was eager to get out.

"Yeah! I'm down."

The Memorial Union was a hangout spot just off campus frequented by students. It was your typical college bar scene: cheap appetizers, loud music, pool tables, darts. Once Ty and I arrived, we linked up with a few more friends and shot the shit for a while. We'd probably been there for close to two hours, and Ty walked away from our table at some point. When he returned Laila was with him whom I'd met on several occasions. Laila was cute and super sweet, and I liked her for Ty. After I stood to greet her with a friendly side hug, I sat back down and went back to absently scrolling on my phone.

"Quit being rude man!" Ty snapped.

I looked up in confusion. "I said 'hey'. What are you talking about?"

Ty shook his head. Laila giggled, "Micah there's someone I'd like you to meet if that's alright."

I looked back at Laila. Right beside her stood a young woman I hadn't noticed before. I could see why Ty thought I was being rude. The bar had gotten so loud and so crowded, and clusters of people were moving around our table. I stood immediately but I was speechless. Whoever she was had me stuck. I held her eyes for just a second, but she quickly looked down. I continued staring at her and noticed her fidgeting under my gaze. I don't even know how long I stood there but I was in awe.

I could not believe how pretty she was.

"Ahem!" Ty said obnoxiously breaking me from of the trance I was in.

Laila giggled again, "Micah this is my friend Ayesha. Ayesha this is Micah."

I took her hand in mine, "Very nice to meet you, Ayesha."

"Likewise." She gave me just a second of eye contact and as she removed her hand, she looked away again. She was shy but that wasn't an issue. I could work with that.

"You and Ayesha probably have a lot to talk about, you're both from Sacramento," Laila offered.

My head snapped in Ty's direction. He smirked at me already knowing and I was floored. This was her.

Anyway, Laila was right. Ayesha and I fell into a comfortable conversation, our segues were effortless, moving from one topic to the next. It was the most effortless conversation I'd had. So easy that hours passed. At some point Ty and Laila headed out, but Ayesha and I stayed at M.U., conversing more and enjoying each other's company.

Close to midnight, I walked her back to her dorm, and we made plans to meet the very next morning.

"Tyson, why didn't you tell me! I would have been met Ayesha!" I playfully punched him in the shoulder. I sat on my bed and began removing my shoes.

Ty shook his head, "Man, that's on you. Ain't like I didn't tell you!"

"Yeah, but you ain't said all that! She's so pretty. And her vibe is insane! We talked for three hours about so many things."

Ty nodded. "Ayesha is cool. Yo ass lucky she was still available."

I couldn't disagree there. I playfully cut my eyes at Ty, "Did you know Laila was bringing Ayesha to M.U. tonight?"

"I may or may not have had an idea."

"Of course, you did!" I threw the t-shirt I had just taken off at him.

"Man get this shit off me!" Ty threw it back just as forcefully. "You should be thanking me."

"I'm just playing. Hell yeah. Good looking man."

Ayesha and I met the next morning at a coffee shop on campus and fell right back in. Talking about everything under the sun. I learned so much about her. She asked the same about me. We discovered that Ayesha and I attended rival high schools. Her dad is a pastor, and my dad is a deacon and since we both grew up in the church we bonded over those things.

It turned out Laila had been trying to talk Ayesha into meeting me too, but she was consumed with school herself. Ayesha was going for her BSN and minoring in Child Development. She loved children and wanted to be a Pediatric Nurse Practitioner. She had such a passion for children and nursing. She mentioned the graduate programs being quite competitive, but she was undeterred, determined to graduate with high honors. I was impressed.

We managed to spend all our free time together. As often as we could, considering. In so doing, we quickly fell for each other.

It was easy to do.

I'd never been in love before, and Ayesha was just my speed. Everything happened organically. She wasn't in a hurry to move faster than we needed to. I never felt pressure from her, nor did I pressure her about anything.

Another one of the many things we bonded over was the choice to wait. We were both virgins, choosing to abstain. It was such a relief learning we were on the same type of time. The craziest thing about college were the women offering me the pussy. Women I hardly knew. Shit was wild. It was the same for Ayesha. She was pretty as hell, and a lot of guys took their chances shooting their shot, only wanting one thing from her. But she was a good girl, and they eventually moved along.

Anyway, Ayesha and I were together more than a year before we went all the way. And very much in love before we even considered taking things there.

I called Malachi one day to talk about it. I told my brother everything and I trusted him with everything. He was in his senior year down at Morehouse and by then he and Ella were already married.

"We're thinking about it. We've been talking about it. A little more lately. Guess I'm just not sure."

"Okay. Why is it that you're unsure?"

"I don't know. I can't really put my finger on it. It's a big step. And I'm hesitant because there's no going back after that. Know what I mean?"

"Yep. No doubt it is. Listen, I know you love Ayesha, but things change when you start having sex. Not necessarily for the better all the time. Dynamics will shift. There's no harm in waiting a

little longer. Seriously, baby brother. Think about it more. Keep talking about it. There's no need to rush into sex."

I took Mal's advice, and we waited. When we decided we knew we were ready to make love, I called him then too.

"The most important thing is that she's comfortable. She'll be nervous, she'll be in her head, but help her relax. Tell her you're nervous too. And you will be. Remind her how much you care about her. How much you love her. Take everything slow. That's the key. Hold her and kiss her for a long time. Focus on that. Let everything else happen organically."

"Yeah."

"But I get the feeling you were already thinking this stuff."

"Oh yeah?"

"Yeah. I mean, I've taught you everything you know."

"Man, shut up." We both cackled.

So, I met Ayesha at her dorm, and we headed back, hand in hand. I figured our first time would be at her place because she'd feel most comfortable there. Surprisingly, Ayesha wanted to be at my place. I told Ty about the plans Ayesha and I had, and he agreed to stay away from our dorm, planning to chill with Laila.

I tried to chill out, but my mind was all over the place, especially about what was to come.

This was it.

We made it back, and I checked in with her immediately. "Ayesha." I found her beautiful eyes on mine. "Are you alright?"

She nodded.

"Please use words with me, baby."

"Yes. I'm fine."

Mal called it.

I was extremely nervous. I knew Ayesha, and she was nervous, too. I could tell—likely a little scared even.

I turned on soft music for us, and we kissed on my bed.

And kissed. And kissed.

It was our favorite thing to do, and up until now, it was all we ever did. This was our first time being completely alone like this. Ever. The moment was surreal. Despite our plans to consummate our love, the innocence of it all made everything that much sweeter.

After kissing for a while, we talked a lot—more than anything else—partly to talk through the jitters and nerves.

But also, I wanted to make sure Ayesha was good. I wanted her to relax. I knew that would help when the time came.

So, we talked through everything, and I checked in with her ad nauseam, asking what I could do for her, how she was feeling, what she was thinking, and what she needed from me. Ayesha did the same for me, too. Conversely, I shared what I was thinking, how I was feeling, what I wanted to do before I did it, and what I was doing while I did it.

"Are you comfortable?" I asked her.

"I am. Yes."

"You need anything?"

"No baby. Thank you."

"Do you like what I'm doing?" I asked. I was level-setting. I began with one finger, and now I had two inside of her. My hands were large, and my fingers were thick, so I was careful. Slow. Deliberate. Gently, I worked my two fingers in and out of her.

"Yes, baby." Ayesha spread her legs wider.

After a beat, I told her, "I like it too. Mmm." Her opening was so tight around my fingers. Slick with her essence. "You're getting wetter. Does this feel good to you, baby?"

"Yes." I heard traces of a moan. "Are you… enjoying what I'm doing?" She politely asked. I looked down at my hard dick in her hand. Ayesha was jerking me. Ever so softly. It felt amazing. This was our first time venturing this far, and I was enjoying the feeling. I was relishing the view, too, so much so that crystal clear precum was showing itself.

"Definitely. You're making me feel good, too, baby. So good." It became increasingly difficult to concentrate. But I persevered. Keenly aware of my movements, ensuring she was feeling pleasure and nothing else. "You see what you're holding… that won't feel like my fingers."

"I know."

Resisting the urge to get lost in the moment, I focused on her. Looking for any signs of distress. Nonverbal cues. Anything. I considered her pretty face intently. Ayesha's eyes were closed now, and I let her rock, but I kept mine open. Currently trained on her soft, delicate fingers wrapped around my dick, giving him all the love and attention. She had a nice rhythm—a mid-tempo cadence, yielding flaring veins. The sight alone was sending me.

We'd been indulging for the past thirty minutes at least, and neither of us had brought each other to orgasm—the epitome of callowness. Yet…there was something so beautiful about not knowing what we were doing that we were learning together. Experiencing everything for the first time. Together.

"So… are you sure?" Still stroking her with my fingers. Still gently moving in and out of her. "You can change your mind. Even right now, you can. I don't mind. I respect you so much, and I love you so much. I can wait for you, baby." This was the most precious thing Ayesha had, and she chose to share it with me.

I was so pleased she chose me. And I was contented my first time was with her too.

"I know. I love you, too. And I want to. I'm sure."

I held her eyes. Searching. Thinking. I wanted her. But there was no hurry. I revered her virginity just as much as I revered mine. "What's on your mind?" I volleyed after a beat.

She sighed. "The pain."

Yeah.

There it was.

I hated the fact that this would hurt her. I wished it were me instead.

"I know baby. I know. Hold on to me. Squeeze me. Scratch me. Do whatever you need to do."

When things with Ayesha ended, I felt that I'd fallen short because she gave herself to me, and I didn't end up wifing her. That shit messed me up because I knew how much it meant to her.

It also meant a lot to me, and I grieved that loss for us both.

It was one reason I went back and forth about ending everything. That fucked with me for years.

The guilt of it all. I went to Mal about that, too.

"Ayesha gave me her virginity. Something so sacred. And…" I shook my head. *"I walked away from her."*

"For what it's worth, you gave her your virginity too, baby brother. The fact that this still bothers you means your heart is in the right place. It was then, and it is now," Mal said. *"You aren't a bad person. Don't look at yourself that way."*

I appreciated Mal's words, and I received and believed them too.

fourteen

DESTINEY

It was a productive Saturday.

I had an appointment with Daijah early this morning to get my locs retwisted. Daijah has been caring for my hair forever—since we were kids. In our teens, she'd do hair for our cousins and friends. She has the Midas touch for real. Doing hair as a side hustle, she stayed booked and busy.

Eventually, Daijah got her cosmetology license, and a few years ago, she walked away from her corporate job and went into business full time. She does all hair types but specializes in natural haircare—locs in particular—and she's one of just a few certified Sisterlocs consultants in the region. I always get stopped on the street about my hair, and I send all inquiring minds her way. Her shop is doing really well, and I am so proud of her.

After my appointment, I went to the grocery store, washed my car, and even vacuumed the inside this time. I never really felt like doing that, so it was a big deal. When I sent Daijah a picture of that giant vacuum at the carwash, she replied with a million laughing emojis.

India and I met at our favorite coffee spot this afternoon and chatted for a good while.

I love cute coffee shops. And I love catching up with India anytime I can. I adore her spirit, and she was a beautiful soul inside and out. I couldn't have been more blessed to have met her. We were literally twin souls. I was often misunderstood, but I never had to explain myself to India. We just get each other because we're so similar. She gives so much of herself, just like I do. I don't know anyone else like me. And then I meet her and I'm like, are you fucking serious? It's like me again.

And India is solid. She's super protective of me and always has my back. I am just as protective of her, and I'll always have hers. Most importantly, I was so glad to be able to get her out of the house so she could breathe. India has a lot going on at home, and sometimes I worry she'll crumble beneath it all. India was my girl. I'd always be there for her.

After chilling with Indie, I went to the grocery store. Once I got home, I finally got caught up on my laundry.

Throughout the day, I'd been texting Micah. As we always do.

This morning, I woke up to a message from him. And it was so sweet.

Micah: My cousin thought I was crazy, being a wallflower at the lounge. But all I could think of the entire night was you baby

When I read that, a silly grin swept my entire face as I quickly typed a reply.

He replied right away, and I grinned even bigger.

You were thinking of me?

Micah: I am always thinking of you. And good morning beautiful

I'm always thinking of you too baby

He'd gone out with his cousin last night and wanted me to know he had been thinking of me. I felt so special. Micah called me beautiful as if it was my name. I was still getting used to it. That was incredibly sweet. Everything he did was thoughtful and sweet.

Micah had so much reverence for me.

As a woman. As a person. It was something I'd never seen.

Not like this.

I was jealous of any woman that had his attention before me. Crazy, too, because I didn't have a jealous bone in my body.

What's for me is for me, and what's not mine isn't my concern.

I don't covet a damn thing that belongs to someone else.

And the truth was I didn't leave room for anyone to get close to me. I filled my free time with commitments and projects, and I preferred things that way. Then, I wouldn't have to face the fact that I was lonely. That I didn't have anyone. No one was missing me or looking for me. But now that I had Micah- well, I didn't have him, but I knew him. And getting to know Micah as I have these past several weeks made me want him for myself. I was breaking all kinds of my "rules".

Where I didn't befriend men, Micah was absolutely a friend. A close friend.

Where I wasn't checking for a relationship, I wanted one. With Micah.

I called him, and we spoke briefly when I came in from the grocery store. He had gone to play basketball, and later, he planned to head over to his parents' house to spend some time. I loved how close he was to his parents. He visited them at least once a week, and they spoke every few days. Family was important to him, and that meant so much to me.

As productive as my day was, I thought of Micah at every moment. As usual. He called me right before I got in the shower, so I told him I'd call him back once I got out.

And there was something else.

I wanted to see him. Badly. So bad I could hardly stand it. I'd gotten out of the shower a while ago. Did my moisturizing routine. Now I was lying on my bed, wishing Micah was here. I felt an overwhelming gravitation toward him that I couldn't even explain. I had only been in his company once, but through our conversations, I was getting attached, and it was becoming increasingly challenging to continue staying away. I felt silly because I wasn't exactly sure how to tell him. He asked to take me out twice, and I'd declined. That was all it took because he hadn't asked me again since. I couldn't blame him, and knowing Micah and his thoughtfulness, he was waiting for me to initiate this next step.

He was more than patient.

I didn't know a man who was more patient.

I was the one who asked to take things slow. I know full well the ball was in my court. And I didn't want to take things slow. I wanted to see Micah. And I wanted to be with Micah.

And I'd come to the realization that it was about time I made a move.

My feelings for him were beginning to become overwhelming. At this point, I was ready to let it all go and let things unfold as they may. That felt right, natural, and like the best thing to do.

I held my phone in my hand, contemplating. I knew I could always be honest with him. I reasoned that, at minimum, I would no longer be suffering in silence.

That was good enough for me.

I exhaled a frustrated breath and opened our text thread. I quickly typed a message and hit send before I changed my mind. I had just placed my phone down when I heard it chime. I knew it was Micah, but now that my feelings had been revealed, I was almost too shy to read his message. I was also much too eager not to read it.

I really want to see you

Micah: You can see me anytime Beautiful

I lay on my back, considering my response. Bearing all, I responded more bluntly this time.

I really want to kiss you

His reply was immediate.

Micah: When?

Oh shit.

I held my breath, contemplating and unsure of what to say next. I couldn't go back on it now.

Not that I wanted to.

My phone chimed.

Micah: Drop your location and I'll come kiss you goodnight

I glanced at the time; it was close to eleven. I didn't want him out this late just to kiss me. I'd feel horrible if something were to happen. I saw dots appear. I started to type some flimsy excuse of a response just as I saw an incoming call from Micah. Likely because I was taking too long to reply. I sat straight up in bed, considering my excuses, and answered just before it rolled to voicemail.

"Hey."

"Hey. You okay?"

I wanted to be near him… and his smooth baritone in my ear at this hour was a dangerous combination.

And…I felt my pussy beginning to purr.

"Yeah. I'm okay."

"You sure? For a second, I thought I'd get your voicemail. And you still haven't sent me your location."

"Micah, it's getting late. You really shouldn't be out this time of night," I said pleadingly.

"I want a goodnight kiss, sweetheart. Or were you joshing me?"

I contemplated for a few beats.

"Destiney baby."

"Yes?"

"I would love to kiss you right now."

Shit.

"We can't kiss yet."

"Why can't we kiss yet?"

"If we kiss, you just may fuck around and fall in love with me," I returned using an ounce of sarcasm.

He roared with laughter. "Is that right? You that kind of kisser?" I could hear the smile in his voice.

Smiling, too, I replied, "I'm certain you want to make an informed decision, Mr. Walker."

Another beat of silence.

"What if I want to fall in love with you, Ms. Evans?"

Pulling up our text thread, I dropped a pin, my smile still wide as I considered my words.

Throwing all caution to the wind, I dared, "Come kiss me then."

Micah paused for a moment. "Seventeen minutes. Or will you fall asleep on me?"

"Tell me when you're outside."

"Bet."

fifteen

MICAH

It was a leisure Saturday.

For once in a long time, I slept in. I woke up around nine this morning, which is sleeping in for me. Most of my mornings begin before six.

Since I wasn't on the schedule for any games, and nothing else was planned, I made a hearty breakfast and then took a walk. It was brisk out, but the sky was clear, and the sun was shining. I lived in a subdivision full of multicultural and multigenerational families. I wasn't engaged with my neighbors beyond pleasantries, but everyone seemed friendly.

My neighbors on one side were a Hispanic family with four small children. We moved in five years ago, around the same time. At that time, they were on baby number two. There's also an older woman living there, who I assume is the children's grandmother. I see her every now and again whenever she walks the children to the playground.

The neighbors on my other side were a middle-aged white couple with an empty nest. I knew they had at least one daughter who came around occasionally, mainly during the holidays and the summertime. I figure she's in college or something.

I made my way toward the running trail that weaved through the park. It didn't take long since I lived just two blocks away. Many people were walking the trail. Some walked briskly, while others took a stroll like mine.

Many people were out walking their dogs. I love dogs. I've considered getting one on many occasions. A bit of company in my spacious home would be nice. They're great companions, truly man's best friend. I've been back and forth on that since I travel semi-frequently for work, and I would have to figure out a dog sitter often. We'll see.

I continued my stroll through the tunnel of trees. I could hear the gravel under my feet as I enjoyed the view of the man-made lake the trail looped around. A woman running with her Lab passed me. I couldn't help but smile.

We had a golden Labrador Retriever growing up. I would get one of those if I decided to get a dog. Mal and I loved her. We named her Tweety, after the cartoon character. Looney Toons was one of our favorite Saturday morning cartoons. Ray would always tease us for giving our girl puppy a boy's name. I think Ray was jealous because we had a dog, and he couldn't get one. We argued back and forth about Tweety Bird's gender all the time. I always thought Tweety was a girl. Ray swore Tweety was a boy. I still don't know the answer to that.

But anyway, Tweety was a great family dog. She was house-trained and affectionate. She learned a few tricks, and we took her with us when we rode our bikes or went to the park. She grew up right along with us, and Mal and I cried like babies when she finally died at thirteen years old. Mommy and Daddy cried, too.

I took my time walking and made it home after about an hour.

Once back at home, I hung around the house for a while. I went into my home office to check my email. Mal and Gabe stopped by briefly, and I told Mal I planned to see the parents later. He'd gone by two days ago. Between Mal and I, one of us was at the house every few days, and both of us spoke with them regularly. My parents weren't the type to text, so we had to pick up the phone and call them if we ever wanted to talk. I was okay with that when it came to those two. I preferred hearing their voices anyway.

After Mal left, I installed a few floating shelves in my bedroom. I put that project off for a while but was glad I finally did it. I had a small collection of books, and my bedroom was the perfect place for them. I talked to my boy Solomon, and we decided to meet up and play ball. Afterward, I went home to shower, and then I headed over to the blue house to see Mommy and Daddy.

When I entered the front door, my dad was walking toward the hallway, carrying a light bulb. He handed it to me.

"Hey Son."

"Hey Daddy."

We hugged one another after I locked the door behind me.

"I need the light in the hallway restroom changed. You mind taking care of that for your old man?"

"I don't mind at all, Daddy. Let me kiss Mommy before I do that." He patted me on the back and headed to his recliner. As usual, I found Mommy sitting on the couch with a book in her lap. She was always in the middle of a book for as long as I can remember. My mother was an avid reader and belonged to the same book club for something like twenty-five years. I leaned down and kissed her cheek, hugging her warmly.

"Hey Micah Bear! How's my baby boy?"

"I'm good, Mommy. How are you?"

"It's been a great day so far, even better now that I have eyes on you."

Once I fixed the lightbulb, Dad and I enjoyed some 7-Up cake with vanilla ice cream. Mom was an excellent cook and a phenomenal baker. She made most of her desserts from scratch using family recipes. She had been teaching Gabby how to bake a few of them, and she was getting pretty good at it.

Dad and I went to the backyard to put his ladder back in the shed. I was in his shed all the time, and one look around told me all I needed to know. He hadn't used the ladder in a while, and I could see he moved a few things around to get to it.

"Let Mal or me handle this next time. You shouldn't be doing too much heaving lifting, Daddy." Daddy drove garbage trucks for a living, and the work did a number on his back after all those years.

He chuckled, "My bride didn't tell me that light was out until a few minutes before you got here. You know I never use that restroom."

I chuckled, too. "I'll take my grievance up with her then." Malachi and I both told them to leave these things for us to take care of. They didn't need to do anything; we could handle it for them, but they still wanted independence. And Daddy could be stubborn.

I understood.

They were in their early sixties and still very healthy and active. God willing, that would be me one day. Mal and I offered to move them into our homes whenever they were ready, and whichever they chose would be okay with either of us. I had a feeling they would likely choose my house because I had a bedroom on the first floor. Malachi's home was larger, but they wouldn't want to deal with those stairs. Eventually, Mal would get tired of those stairs, too. Hell, I was already tired of the stairs in my house.

Mal and I paid off the rest of their mortgage two years ago, and Daddy was able to retire. Now that they have more free time, we encourage them to go away now and then and see some places. But they don't seem interested. Mommy isn't a fan of airplanes, and Daddy wouldn't sleep well in a hotel past a night or two.

I spent a couple hours with my parents then headed home to get my ass in the gym. Mom's cake was so good I had two slices and needed to work that shit off. Of course, before I left, Mommy found a reason to mention my love life…or lack thereof.

"You wouldn't gobble up these sweets so fast if you had a wife baking for you, Micah Bear."

Daddy laughed loudly as I smirked.

"What if she doesn't bake?"

"Then I would teach her, of course."

"Touché Mommy. Touché."

I desperately wanted to tell Mommy and Daddy about Destiney. I was eager as hell to tell them about her. I could hardly contain myself. I liked her so much.

She was so special to me.

But I was conflicted.

Though I felt confident in the connection between Destiney and me, we weren't seeing each other physically. If Destiney was worth mentioning, that meant we were serious. If we were serious, I knew Mommy would want to meet her. I wanted them to meet, and I looked forward to the day I could bring Destiney to meet them. But I didn't even have a ballpark estimate of when that would happen.

I was trying to see Destiney my damn self.

I thought of Destiney all day long—I always did. We text each other throughout the day. Earlier, I spoke to her while I was at the court with Solomon. Now, I was home and settled in, waiting for her to call me once she got out of the shower.

Imagine my surprise when she texted saying she wanted to see me.

I stood from my bed and made a beeline to my dresser, quickly throwing a pair of Nike sweats over my basketball shorts. I headed down the stairs two at a time, my thoughts in overdrive. I felt a mix of emotions. Of course, I was excited and wanted to see her too.

But I almost didn't think the day would come.

I laughed out loud in spite of myself.

Grabbing my keys, I secured the alarm and put on my Nike slides. I sent Destiney my ETA, reversed, and waited for my garage door to close. Just before pulling out of the cul-de-sac, I read her reply.

Drive safe. See you soon

I felt giddy as a teenage boy with a crush. It had been several weeks since we shared the same space, so that was one reason to be excited. I'd also imagined what our first kiss would be like, how her lips would feel on mine.

I mentally replayed the last portion of our conversation. Destiney was probably facetious, but I was as serious as a heart attack. I was convinced I could fall in love with her after a kiss. I was already in very strong like, and I had only seen her once.

Destiney had grown to become a close friend and confidant. We talked and texted all day long. For hours. About everything and nothing. I loved the way her mind worked. She sent me pictures of things she found interesting or links to an article she wanted to tell me about. My favorite part was the end of a long day when we could have an uninterrupted conversation. Destiney was always the last voice I heard each night. She was so open and honest. Funny and intelligent. I shared everything with her, never feeling judged. I welcomed her into the deepest depths of my soul and shared things I'd never shared with anyone. Mal and I were close as close could be, but this was a little different.

More than that, her beautiful face consumed my thoughts day and night.

Destiney was unbelievable. She was incredibly comfortable in her skin, unconcerned with the opinions of others, yet so kind and compassionate whenever she spoke to someone. Everyone who encountered her felt seen and valued, especially me.

It was close to eleven, and few cars were on the road. I was on a mission to get to her, making it from my home in Elk Grove to Destiney's home in Land Park within fifteen minutes. I pulled onto a quiet residential block and killed my engine. No sooner than when I alerted her that I was here, I heard her front door open.

I smiled from ear to ear. My anticipation was building by the second. I immediately got out of the car to meet her. She descended the few steps toward me, her waist-length locs swaying with each step. She had the sweetest smile adorning her beautiful face and I damn near lost my mind fixated on everything before me. She wore black biker shorts and a grey tank top. I'd forgotten how much taller I am. I likely stood about a foot taller. She couldn't have been any more than 5'3'.

"You are so beautiful Destiney," I found myself saying as soon as I reached her. Her face was bare and held a natural glow. Fuck. She had no business looking this good.

"Thank you." She smiled shyly.

Unable to contain myself, I embraced her, and she fell into my arms naturally, resting her head against my rapidly beating heart.

I felt like I was in the damn Twilight Zone. We'd grown so emotionally close that it seemed like a lifetime had elapsed. It was as if one day was a week's time.

"And thanks for coming to see me, but you really shouldn't have." Her voice was slightly muffled as she spoke into my chest. She hugged me around my waist just as firmly as I held her.

"I'll come see you anytime, sweetheart." I needed Destiney to understand that I meant that. I rested my chin on top of her head, and she settled into my embrace. She belonged in my arms. I never wanted to let her go. She belonged to me.

I had missed her, and I told her so.

"If I'm honest, I missed you too, Micah. Something vicious."

I continued to hold her close, savoring the moment. Closing my eyes, I inhaled her fragrance deeply, committing her notes to memory. She smelled like a lovely mixture of citrus and coconut. She was intoxicating. All five of my senses were stimulated by her pheromones, and I could feel my dick coming to life. Damn. I didn't want her to feel the brick in my pants and think I came here for all the wrong reasons.

Wanting another look at my baby, I took a slight step back, resting my hands at the small of her back, mindful not to venture off too far. Her head was down, so I gently lifted her chin with my finger. She looked up, but her orbs evaded mine.

"Hey, look at me." Speaking gently with a fragment of firmness, "Are you good?"

She smiled at me. Her eyes were now trained on my quizzical expression.

"It's nothing personal. I promise," Her sweet voice just above a whisper. Destiney pushed a few of her stray locs over her shoulder. Observing my puzzled visage, she said, "I get embarrassed easily. Especially when I'm around someone I'm crushing on," She revealed, through a confident smile.

I chuckled lightly, captivated by her sincerity yet again.

She was the cutest thing I'd ever seen.

I released my hold and took her hands into mine, threading our fingers. I felt a spark and wondered if she felt it, too.

"No need to be embarrassed sweetheart. I have a crush on you, too. And you know what? I am absolutely crazy about you," I avowed. "And I promise you don't have to miss me so much." I rubbed the soft skin of her hands with the pads of my thumbs. "But you already knew that."

Destiney smiled again. Really big this time, showing all her pearly whites.

Her smile was breathtaking. Goodness. She was so fucking pretty.

Since sharing that detail moments ago, she'd given me her beautiful eyes. And I gave her mine.

I felt pretty damn good, as we stood there, holding each other's hands and each other's gazes. I don't know what she was thinking about, but I was losing myself in her. Her eyes held depth. And curiosity. And vulnerability. And I was drowning. Falling…

"So glad it's mutual," she released a breath followed by a low chortle.

"It is positively mutual, Destiney baby."

We shared a comfortable silence. Eyes on eyes.

Her hands were still in mine, and it felt so good to be in her space. She brought me a calmness I couldn't explain. I hadn't even realized when my erratic breathing had returned to normal. A passerby would see two people holding hands, but there was much transpiring. As a grown ass man, I never gave hand holding much thought, but this shit right now was hitting different.

I noted our interlocked fingers and how her tiny hands looked intertwined with mine. My hands were massive in comparison. As she caressed my digits with hers, I regarded her attention to our mingled fingers. There was an art to this, and Destiney had it down to a science. Her tenderness and affection were on full display right now. Another attribute that truly set her apart.

I could dig it.

I continued stroking her hands, lost in deep introspection.

My mind was everywhere, but somehow, at the same time, it was right here with her.

Trying to figure this out. This intense chemistry. It was Kismet. Synchronous.

The energy was so thick I could feel it around us.

None of it made any sense. Yet it all made perfect sense.

Feeling so strongly for her, after never being near her. Caring for her as deeply as I did, solely on the essence of who she is. I felt this… this gravitation.

And this calmness. It was as if I was exactly where I was supposed to be.

With her.

There weren't any words, but the insurmountable peace I felt with her led me to one conclusion.

Recalling our conversations since day one, my confidence in her, and the peace and serenity she afforded me.

The assurance, devotion, and protection I desired to bestow her generously… I felt this confirmation in my spirit. And I knew right here at that very moment that Destiney was it for me.

Destiney is my wife.

And I had plans to make good on that very soon.

But right now, I really wanted to kiss her.

I gave her hands a gentle squeeze, considering my next move. I didn't want to be intrusive or assume she still felt the same. After contemplating for a moment, I said, "I'd love a kiss before I go. Would that be alright with you, beautiful?"

Gazing into my eyes, and without pause, she said, "I'm good with that."

I didn't waste any time leaning into her, gently pecking her soft, full lips. Slowly, I pecked her lips again, and again and again, lingering longer each time. Destiney hungrily kissed me back. When our lips remained connected, she parted, giving me access. And damn… I loved her taste. Our tongues danced together as we naturally fell into a rhythm we seemed to know by heart.

It was so easy with her.

Destiney was a phenomenal kisser. Gentle but eager.

Her tongue had a mind of its own. Brave and confident, she explored unfamiliar territory. I made my own moves as she welcomed me into the sweetness of her mouth. I couldn't help but wrap my arms around her waist, deepening the kiss. I felt relief when Destiney returned the gesture, wrapping her arms around my neck. I was pleased she felt comfortable doing so.

Light smacking sounds emitted from us, and I held her even tighter, getting lost in a trance. Her block was so quiet, and we were so consumed that a dog howling somewhere in the distance is what broke us from our reverie.

I don't even know how long we kissed, but I enjoyed every second of it.

Kissing her was unlike anything I'd ever experienced.

I loved kissing her.

I could have kissed her all night.

Destiney released her arms from around my neck, bringing them to rest on my shoulders. I lessened my grip around her waist, settling in the small of her back.

"Wow." was all I could say after such an explosive moment.

"Ditto," she said shyly.

"Well. That takes care of that." I rubbed her chin with my thumb. "Have a good night, beautiful." I took a few steps backward and leaned against my car. Never taking my eyes off Destiney as she headed toward her front door.

She was almost to her door when I heard a languid giggle. She turned on her heels. "I should mention… now that we've kissed. I just may get attached to you."

"I'm good with that." I tossed back.

Destiney really had no idea.

sixteen

MICAH

It had been seventy-two hours since I put eyes on her.

Since I had her in my arms.

Since I kissed her lips.

I could think of little else since seeing Destiney and sharing that kiss.

Her beautiful face consumed my thoughts. Remnants of her taste hypnotized me.

That night repeatedly played on a loop in my head.

Being close to her again was surreal. And she was so beautiful—my goodness, more beautiful than I remembered.

I wanted to kiss her all over. Hell yeah, my dick was hard, but I wasn't even thinking about sex. Not right then, I wasn't. I'm super affectionate and express my love and adoration through physical touch, and I like to receive the same. I was cool if she wasn't ready for an affectionate overload. I was willing to rock with her till she got there. Though I got the impression she'd come around pretty soon. Her heart and soul were open and available, giving me a sensual vibe.

None of that took me by surprise. She's an artist, and artists are passionate people.

When I'd made it back home, I floated up the stairs and ended up sprawled out on my bed, my head in the fucking clouds. I don't even remember driving home or pulling into my garage. I went to plug in my phone and noticed a text from her asking me to let her know once I had made it safely. I messaged her back telling her I had, and she replied instantly with her usual goodnight text.

Meanwhile, my dick was hard as fuck in my sweats. I hadn't masturbated in months. I came dangerously close that night. Destiney was such a great kisser. She tasted incredible. I got the feeling she tasted just as delicious between her lower set of lips and that had my shit rock hard.

I eventually fell asleep, enraptured with thoughts of her. Those same thoughts plagued my mind when I woke early the next morning.

I woke up at 5:30 this morning, pushed through my workout, and then took a quick shower. While I cleansed myself, my thoughts returned to her soft hands and the gentle way she caressed mine.

Destiney was showing me something. I never thought a gesture as simple as hand-holding could be so sensual. With Destiney, it was. Her tiny hands were swallowed by mine, but they commanded attention. They were soft and dainty and made their presence known.

I wondered what else her hands could do.

Despite my distraction, I managed to stay on schedule, and after a light breakfast, I was out the door on time.

As I rode the elevator to the third floor, I considered just how productive I would be today. If the prior days were any indication, prospects were meager. I could still feel her soft lips on mine and the groove of her sweet tongue. I couldn't wait to make love to her finally.

Just the same, I could wait.

I looked forward to it but didn't want to rush anything about this. We were going at the right pace, and things were right where they were supposed to be. I was not going to mess up a good thing just to get my damn rocks off. Patience was a virtue, and I planned to exhibit the patience of Job.

I strolled toward my corner office. The floor I worked on was generally quiet later in the week as most of the department worked a hybrid schedule, only coming into the office on Mondays and Tuesdays. After connecting it to my monitors, I sat in my office chair and brought my MacBook to life. Laurie, my assistant, was working from home today and had already sent over her morning email with a few updates. Once I'd been brought to speed, I responded to her email, thanking her for the debrief and wished her a great Thursday.

I opened my calendar and sighed in relief, pleased that no meetings were scheduled until the afternoon.

I decided to look at a project charter for a merger we were considering. I'd already reviewed it several times, but thorough due diligence was critical since we were still in the project planning stages. The numbers looked promising, but I couldn't be definitively sure of any anticipated risks without taking a deeper dive. As System Vice President, I needed to ensure we made the best decision on what to include in our deal terms.

I opened a report, deciding I needed to review an outline of the project scope, resources, and dependencies.

"Knock, knock."

"Come on in." I returned, never looking up from the spreadsheet I was reviewing.

"Where are your glasses, boss?"

I looked up to find Ellington standing before me with his laptop bag slung over his shoulder.

I returned an inquisitive expression.

"You gone look like an old man prematurely scrunching up your face and squinting like that." He laughed. "Put your eyes on and take some of that strain off!"

I returned a boisterous laugh, reaching over and fishing my glasses from my briefcase.

"How's that?" I placed them on my face, peering back at Ellington.

"Much better." He chuckled. "You keep squinting like that, and those wrinkles will set in and never go away."

"You're right, E." I smiled, adjusting them on my face.

"What brings you in? You're normally working from home on Thursdays."

"Baby's teething, and I need peace and quiet. I'll get back and relieve Jayla once I get a few things done here."

"Gotcha. I'll be heading out to lunch after my afternoon call. You're welcome to join me. Or let me know if I can bring you back anything."

"Thanks, but no thanks." He patted his shoulder bag and replied, "She still managed to pack her dear husband lunch with a cranky baby and very little sleep."

"You're a lucky man, Ellington." I returned gingerly.

"You know me better than that. Luck doesn't have anything to do with it." He pointed up toward the sky. Like me, Ellington was a man of faith.

"I hear you, man."

"Well. I'll be at my desk; let me know if you need anything, boss." He said, retreating out of my office.

"Appreciate you, E," I called behind him.

"Yes, sir!"

I continued my analysis and moved on to a Pro Forma I needed to review. Expenses and revenues were critical for future projections, and a Pro Forma was the best way to determine what to expect. These could be cumbersome, but I planned to knock out a significant portion before my afternoon conference call.

"Hey, Micah! Good morning." I quietly sighed, attempting to mask the annoyance I felt at the sudden presence of this individual. "Well, good late morning! It's nearly eleven." She was extra chipper. Annoyingly so. I looked up as Erica padded into my office, uninvited, swaying her hips exuberantly. "I've got Noah's Bagels in the breakroom for everyone. I can grab one for you."

"No thank you." I'd since returned my attention to my computer.

"You sure? There are quite a few everything bagels. I know those are your favorite." She sang that last part, provoking my subtle eye roll. If she saw it, she didn't react.

I looked up at Erica to find her already looking at me expectantly. Erica needed to find something else to do. She was an attractive woman, but this wasn't happening. Mixing business with pleasure was not a good idea. Even under different circumstances, I wouldn't have dated her.

I curse the very day I went home with her that night at the lounge.

I knew better. That was two years ago, and Erica was still trying to make something happen. A constant thorn in my side. Furthermore, she was chasing the men all over the building. She thought I didn't know about it, but everyone knew it.

She even tried it with Ellington and that shit pissed me off. Her ass knew Ellington was married. Erica saw a good thing and wanted to mess it up. Simply because it wasn't hers. Ellington was a good man. Professional. Hardworking. Kept to himself, and he loved his wife and his baby. Erica peeped that and was up for the challenge.

I loathed women like her.

No. Damn. Good.

One day, Ellington confided in me that she spent too much time at his desk. In a particular instance, Erica came to speak with him and had her cleavage out.

Just plain disrespectful.

Ellington came to see me immediately and told me he couldn't continue working with her. She made him uncomfortable, and it was beginning to create an interference. We relied on the Administrative Coordinators when we had to meet with other department heads—namely, C-suite executives. Erica worked magic, securing meetings with people with the most challenging calendars you've ever seen.

Many of the people we worked with were in high demand and critical to the progression of the project timeline. She was vital to our department, and I understand why Ellington hesitated telling me. Knowing Ellington, he just wanted to keep the peace. I immediately made the executive decision to trade administrative coordinators with my colleague. Their coordinator was a recent college grad named Jackson. He worked well with our team and was just as efficient as Erica, and I was glad to have him.

I expected we would see less of Erica with this change. Maybe we'd even stop seeing her altogether. The other department sat on the other side of the building. Literally, complete with their own bathrooms and elevators... yet somehow, Erica still managed to find her way over here.

I didn't want to take anyone's job, nor was I above it. If I heard one more complaint, I would dismiss Erica, no questions asked. As System Vice President, I had the latitude to do so.

"I'm positive, Erica. Now, if you'll please state your business, otherwise I need to get back to work here."

Erica stood in front of my desk, making a show of straightening out her black dress. I'll admit she looked great. She was tall. Had long, toned legs. Always wearing high heels, she walked impeccably in.

"I did want to ask you. Would you like to have lunch with me this afternoon? Or sometime next week, maybe? We don't have to go far. I'm fine with the café downstairs."

I sighed. In addition to our one-time sexcapade we did have lunch together here at the café on the first floor. It was just the once, and I realized pretty quickly Erica wasn't the type of woman I wanted to continue to build with. I'd even told her so.

Sighing, I said, "Erica. We've had this conversation. More than once." And we had.

She wasn't getting it.

"I just don't get it!" She snapped. "What's wrong with me Micah? Huh? I know I'm pretty. I'm smart. I parade myself around in front of you, and you don't even notice me!"

"Erica. I never said there was anything wrong with you."

"Then what is it?" She was a little calmer now."

"We aren't compatible," I told her for the umpteenth time.

"So, I'm only good for one thing, huh?"

I sighed again. "The way we met each other was unconventional for me. And things happened in an unconventional order. That's not the norm for me, either. I assure you it wouldn't have gone that far if I had formally met you first."

Erica reared her head back as if she'd been slapped. Her face immediately settled into a scowl. Brows connected. She was offended by that. All I did was answer her question.

Furthermore, what I'd told her for the past two years didn't seem to land.

I should have been blunt to begin with.

Erica slowly crossed her arms, peering at me through cut eyes. "Just who do you think you are?" She seethed.

I said nothing. But my antennas were up. She sounded eerily calm.

"For your information, you aren't all that, Micah! I'm an incredibly good catch. Plenty of men want me! And whoever I choose would be lucky to have me! You're crazy for letting me go!"

"I guess so," I said, shrugging my shoulders.

Erica huffed loudly, stomping out of my office.

I sighed again, rubbing my temples. Just that quick, I had a tension headache. I hoped this meant she'd leave me alone for a while.

I sat for a moment, unable to return to the spreadsheets open on my desktop.

I glanced at my wristwatch. It had hardly been about three hours since I arrived at the office.

I sighed another exasperated breath.

I was no good right now, and I was much too distracted. My head was about to explode between Erica's shenanigans and my yearning for the woman I truly wanted.

Thinking for another moment, I exhaled at the revelation. It was simple. Her voice alone was not enough for me anymore.

I wanted more.

I needed more, and sharing space with her regularly was the only remedy. I could only hope she felt the same way.

On impulse, I picked up my phone and called the one woman that had me besotted.

She answered on the second ring.

"Hey, you. Good morning."

I closed my eyes, moved by her soft voice, sounding sweet as a lullaby.

Not wasting any time, I said, "Destiney baby, I want to see you again." I continued, unable to stop myself. "I thought I would just go back to everything as usual, but honestly, I've been enamored with thoughts of you since seeing you. Being in your company. Your beauty. Your scent… your kiss. Especially that kiss. You are all I've been able to think about."

She released a breath I didn't know she was holding and chuckled lightly.

"Me too."

"Yeah?"

"Yeah."

Damn.

We were silent for a few beats.

"Can I be honest with you?" Destiney volleyed.

"You can always be honest with me, love."

"Well… I have longed for you too."

"Have you?"

"Oh yes. Especially the way you kiss me… it's been at the forefront of my mind."

Goodness.

"Why didn't you tell me?"

"A little shy. Embarrassed. Silly, I know, but I'm glad it's out in the open now."

"Can I take you out, baby?" I asked boldly. "If you are comfortable… seeing me again."

"I'd love to see you again."

"Is tomorrow night, okay?

"It's perfect."

"I'll pick you up at seven if that's alright."

"What should I wear?"

"Something comfortable."

"I look forward to it."

"Likewise."

It was no surprise that the rest of my day flew by.

seventeen

DESTINEY

Just got here. Once I've parked, I'll head inside

Instead of letting Micah pick me up for our date, I convinced him I could meet him instead.

Maybe I knew then that I would do this to him.

Micah sent me the address to where we were meeting and texted me once he left home, headed that way. Now that he had arrived, he texted me, letting me know. As each text came through, I shamefully hung my head as if he were standing right in front of me.

I had every opportunity to tell him I wasn't coming… but my pathetic ass didn't have the decency to take it.

About five minutes after his last text, my phone rang in my hand. I saw that Micah was calling me, and I let his call roll to voicemail.

After seeing Micah the other night, I was so consumed; it was ridiculous. I thought I was before, but this was another level entirely.

Like Tamia, I was so into Micah. My feelings for him grew with each passing moment. I liked him so much, and talking to him was so easy.

Effortless.

Being near him seemed even easier. This was wild because I felt like… almost as if… I was falling. I wouldn't know for sure, I suppose. I've never fallen before. Never been there before.

But this feeling was so strong.

And something else. I don't know what it is, but there's something about conversations when it's dark.

Late-night convos are grown, sexy, unfiltered, and unpredictable.

Feelings are bound to be caught.

Any existing feelings are guaranteed to grow deeper.

Assured to develop into something stronger.

Conversing with that special someone… you had the feels for… when the sun went down… and the hour was far spent…was…dangerous. But in the best way.

I was feeling the hell out of Micah. The majority of our deeper conversations happened at night. Nighttime was my favorite time.

And once we kissed, that was it.

I am consumed even more so now. I was partly joking with him when I casually mentioned getting attached after kissing him. But that's precisely how I felt.

All bets were off. You could stick a fork in me. White flag frantically blowing in the wind.

Micah was everything. He smelled good. He looked great. 6'3 and 230 pounds of solid muscle. He clearly took care of himself. When he held me in his brawny arms, I felt safe with him. Protected.

I'd imagine someone of his stature would appear imposing to some people.

But Micah was a gentle giant. A big cuddly teddy bear. And I felt right at home in his arms. Something I wanted to feel all the time.

And when he kissed me, my mind was blown.

First, no one has ever kissed me the way he kissed me.

He captured my lips, cautiously. Gently. And his kisses were so delicate. Tender. Unhurried. I noticed that it was his m.o., taking his sweet time with me. Making it a point to ask me first.

But when Micah kissed me, it seemed he was savoring the moment as if he didn't know when he'd get the chance again. His lips were full and soft.

And his tongue. Oh. My. Gosh…

He took my breath away.

Simply put, it was amazing. Panty wetting.

Micah brought a serenity I hadn't even realized I needed, and I wanted to be wherever he was. I didn't want him to leave. I was seconds away from inviting him inside.

Literally.

I wasn't thinking about jumping his bones.

Okay, maybe I did. Very briefly.

But honestly, I pictured a grown ass comfortable atmosphere. Maybe some wine with some chill music, conversing the way we do. I enjoy an occasional glass of wine. Those elements paired with a good conversation… I imagine that being a risqué combination once you start feeling warm inside. And I wanted that with him.

And Micah has been abundantly clear about his feelings for me. Unmistakably.

That's probably the one thing I appreciate the most. Last night, I was all in my head. Feeling shy. Typical for me. I was so shy that I couldn't even make eye contact. I was comfortable. Very comfortable. But since I liked him so much, I felt bashful. And Micah helped me relax. Effortlessly. Not only with his words, which are unmatched, but his actions. It is absolutely apparent how he feels about me.

And it's nice to know how he feels without needing to ask. I'm not the type to need constant reassurance.

Well, maybe I am. Sometimes.

But, anyway, being reminded how much he likes me. How beautiful he finds me... ineffable. Considering I feel the same way especially. There was a time or two... or three, where I liked a guy much more than he liked me. And I was taken advantage of.

I've even had a few one-way platonic friendships. That shit was really wack.

Wack as fuck. Didn't feel good.

But this was definitely an equal exchange—mutual gratification.

Yeah. Micah was everything.

When Micah asked to take me out, I said yes without hesitation. I wanted to spend time with him. Go on dates like normal couples do. But... once I thought about it, I knew I likely wouldn't go through with it.

I'd been bleeding—a lot.

Last night, I went to sleep dreaming of Micah and woke up to underwear full of blood and soaked sheets. Things with my "issue of blood" were going from bad to worse.

Nonetheless, I felt terrible for flaking. I wanted to see him, but I was in my head. Bad. If I'd met up with him, I'd probably be too damn self-conscious and overly anxious even to enjoy our time together. He would notice, and it would ruin an otherwise lovely evening.

Now I felt immature and pitiful, lying across my bed and wishing I was out with Micah.

He called me again, and I watched the phone vibrate in my hands.

I sighed, fed up with myself. He was more than patient, and I was wasting his time with my teenage shenanigans. What the hell was my problem?

My phone chimed with a text from him.

Micah: I'll head home since you're not coming. Please at least let me know you're okay

I could have cried.

I'm sorry

It was the least I could offer him; besides, I didn't know what else to say.

He replied immediately.

Micah: I'm glad you're okay sweetheart

I didn't deserve him.

And if I didn't get my shit together and quickly, I knew I'd lose him before I even had him.

eighteen

MICAH

I entered my home through my garage, not even bothering to cut on the lights. I grabbed bottled water from the fridge and sat at my kitchen island in the quiet darkness while I drank it.

I was so eager to see Destiney again finally; disappointed was an understatement.

Shit. I was more than eager. I was juiced.

Disappointment didn't seem fitting either. Gutted was more like it.

Destiney didn't give me much to go on, so I wasn't sure how to feel as it related to her. I thought I'd made her feel comfortable. I was confused as to why she agreed to meet me if she wasn't ready. I didn't pressure her. If she had said not yet, I would have been totally fine with that instead of her flaking.

If I'm honest, I was a bit frustrated with her mixed signals at this point.

Destiney hadn't been in a relationship for a long time. Had never been in one in her adult years. I was cognizant of that. During our conversations, Destiney was opening up so much. We both were. And I could see that her heart and feelings were extremely fragile, which was why I was gentle in the way I handled her.

This was the third time I'd asked to see her. I figured after we kissed, we were past that.

I guess I thought wrong.

Maybe she only agreed to meet because I'd brought it up.

Maybe I'd have to wait for her to initiate when this happened.

Maybe I needed to fall back even more so and let her lead.

I just hoped it would be sooner rather than later.

My phone illuminated the room, and I exhaled an exasperated breath, seeing that it was Destiney calling me. I certainly wasn't angry with her, but I wasn't exactly in the best headspace to take her call. I didn't want to snip at her.

While I waited for her at the restaurant, I called her twice and texted her several times, which all went unanswered. Until she told me she was sorry.

I'm not even exactly sure what it is she was sorry for.

Opting to text her instead, I typed a message and headed upstairs to get changed.

I took a shower, changed, then hung out downstairs to watch TV.

The one television I have in my home is in my living room. I haven't had a TV in my bedroom for several years. I had one in my bedroom years ago and hardly watched it. In my opinion, which I know is unpopular, my bedroom was for four things: resting, reading, conversing, and love making.

Malachi always clowned me about that, naturally. His ass had televisions all over his home. His main screen was eighty inches, I think. The shit was huge, but it fit their expansive living area. I wasn't much of a TV person anyway. I didn't even purchase a TV right away. When I finally decided to get one, it was for Gabe and Gabby to have something to watch.

I flipped a few channels and ended up on sports highlights. But I wasn't watching.

My mind went back to Destiney.

It never left her, if I'm honest. I glanced at the clock realizing we'd usually be wrapped in a deep ass conversation by now. It dawned on me that this was the first night in several weeks we hadn't had one. I texted her, asking if she was still up. She responded with affirmative, so I called her.

She answered on the first ring.

"Hello." She spoke softly in my ear.

"Hey." My tone held an element of firmness. "How was your day?" I asked, briefly, disregarding the elephant in the room.

Destiney was silent for too many beats, so I said, "Destiney. What are we doing?" She needed to let me know something. Maybe I was losing my patience.

If she didn't know, she was about to find out. When she was still silent, I continued, "I want you. I want to see you. And I've made that clear to you. But these mixed messages. I just…are we finished, or are we done?" That last line slipped out before I could stop it. More silence filled the line, and I honestly wanted to hang up.

She finally said, "I'm so freaking frustrated Micah."

"What has you so frustrated?" I asked evenly.

"I was too shy to meet you today." She revealed.

"Shy?" I pressed. Chuckling but wasn't shit funny. "I need more than that, Destiney."

She sighed. "I was too shy to meet you today…because… I suffer from severe uterine fibroids, and I'm bleeding. I'm too embarrassed to go out because if I don't go to the bathroom every half hour, I could bleed through my clothes. It makes me uncomfortable and gives me the worst anxiety. I literally have to cancel plans and stay at home because the bleeding is so excessive."

Wow. There it was.

"How long have you been dealing with this?" My voice was tender now, laced with concern.

"Few years now. Since about my early twenties."

I didn't have sisters, but I have a mother, and one day, I got a crash course related to monthlies. I have an impeccable memory- that can be a blessing and a curse. Depending.

Anyway, I vividly recall my introduction to this occurrence when I entered my parents' bathroom searching for my mother. I had to be about six years old. Maybe seven. Ordinarily, when their bedroom door is open, we can come in. When the door was closed, we had to knock first, in case Mommy wasn't dressed.

I walked into their bedroom and proceeded to their ensuite restroom because I heard her in there. I entered the bathroom as Mommy had just stood from the toilet and pulled her pants up. I entered without bothering to announce myself, and in so doing, I caught a glimpse of a toilet bowl filled with crimson. My pure and innocent eyes had never seen so much blood before, and I was terrified.

Within a matter of seconds, I was hysterically crying my little eyes out, convinced my mother must have been dying. Malachi came running when he heard the commotion. He was none the wiser but was just as hysterical once he saw me in that state. After my mother comforted us, she took the opportunity to explain.

"Don't cry. Mommy is fine." She gently pulled us into her arms. "It's called menstruation, which happens to a woman every month. I promise everything is okay."

In my teen years, I had girlfriends who would mention the cramps, bloating, and discomfort.

I hadn't heard of uterine fibroids, but based on what Destiney shared with me, I could imagine things must have been much more severe than a monthly cycle. My heart immediately softened for her.

"Is it painful, sweetheart?"

"Wasn't so bad at first. But these past three months have been really brutal."

"Hmm. Is there anything I can do?"

She lightly chuckled. "You're so sweet, Micah, but no. It's just something I have to deal with."

"Thank you for sharing something so personal with me. You really could have come to me love."

"I know, Micah…" Destiney exhaled heavily. "I should have told you sooner. I'm so sorry for flaking on you today. It's just embarrassing. This issue has affected my life in all areas."

"We'll get through it together. And I'm always here, we can talk about it. About anything. Please come to me even if it's uncomfortable. All of you is safe with me."

"Alright."

I wanted to hold Destiney in my arms. Though I couldn't sympathize with her, I did empathize with her situation.

"I need to see you." I proclaimed boldly.

"I want to see you too."

"Can I come to you?"

"I would love that, Micah."

"Have you eaten?"

"No, I haven't."

"Give me an hour, and I'll be right there. I'll bring dinner with me."

nineteen

MICAH

"I absolutely love your lips, Destiney baby."

"I love yours too."

I really did love her lips. They were so soft, her mouth was so sweet, and her tongue was wicked. My baby could kiss. I captured her lips again, gently sucking her bottom one. We'd both been sucking lips amidst messy tongue swirling.

We were in Destiney's living room, lying on her couch, kissing each other into oblivion. I was on my back, and she was settled between my legs. When I arrived, she kissed me at the door, leaving me desiring more of her kisses.

I stopped on my way to grab us sandwiches from Jersey Mikes, and we ate in the living room while we watched Juice on BET. Now, the TV was watching us.

After we ate, we settled on the couch, and Destiney surprised me by cuddling up so close to me that she eventually ended up in my lap. Everything was good in my hood. That's when I asked her for another kiss.

Apparently, we were on the same type of time.

This brick in my pants was bulging against the zipper in my jeans, and Destiney had been grinding against it. We were basically dry humping. She was sending me places the way she snaked her body on top of mine. I knew she could feel how hard I was beneath her.

My dick was hard as steel. But she couldn't truly know how much I wanted her at this moment. I wanted her so badly.

The fact that I was in her home with her lying in my arms, my lips on hers would do for now.

The fact that I was in her personal space was hugely significant. But just the same, I couldn't help but desire to get closer to her.

As close as I could.

I was vigilant and cautious with each move I made. This was chess, not checkers.

When I came by to kiss her goodnight, we kissed passionately. It was a perfect first kiss.

But nothing like this. These kisses tonight were wet and sloppy. Nasty. The kind of kissing that would typically get something started. It had been years since I made out like this, and I was here for all of it.

"I need a break baby." Destiney broke our kiss, bringing me out of my thoughts. She laughed a little, wiping her mouth, then mine. I could agree. We had been kissing for quite a long time. So long we probably should come up for air.

"Whatever you want, love." I placed a peck on the top of her head as she laid on my chest.

"Whatever I want?"

"Whatever you want," I reassured.

"I can't have what I want right now."

"Try me."

She was still on my chest, silent as I rubbed circles in her back.

Finally, she said, "When I'm bleeding, I don't... I don't feel confident. I don't feel sexy. It's holding me back. I feel dirty and gross. Even right now, would you believe me if I told you I'm feeling incredibly self-cautious?"

"Hmm." I continued to rub her back softly, trying to formulate my next statement. I knew this was extremely personal, and I appreciated her vulnerability. Our phone conversations were all over, and we talked about so many things, including intimate topics. She had already shared with me that she hadn't been intimate for a few years.

She also revealed to me that these feelings were awakening for her again. So, I knew what she was referring to. I'd told her it was the same for me, too.

"First, please don't say that again. You are not dirty or gross. You are not. Women bleed. I know this situation is not ideal, but I promise we will figure this out and get you better, sweetheart." I was serious. I meant that shit. The very last thing I wanted was for her to feel this way.

Destiney was silent, and I continued musing over my thoughts. Despite her situation, I had an insatiable desire for her. Her situation didn't deter me. I wanted her better, of course, but establishing my position and making it clear that she was the woman I wanted was my goal.

"Destiney baby?"

"Yes."

"Do you know that I find you incredibly sexy?" I hadn't shared this specific detail with her before, but there was no time like the present.

She lifted her head from my chest. Her beautiful eyes held my gaze. "Really?"

"Indeed. You are super sexy. Beautiful yes. But sexy as hell. If nothing else, I need you to be so very confident in that."

"Wow. Thank you, Micah." She leaned forward, kissing me sweetly. "Never been called sexy before."

"Get used to hearing it, sexy."

She lightly tittered. "You're so sweet, Micah." Her head returned to my chest. Then, "Transparency moment. I find you sexy too."

She was so cute. "Is that so?" I asked, chuckling lightly.

"Very much so."

"Appreciate you." I resumed rubbing small circles on her back. I had an idea and carefully considered how I would approach bringing it to her. "Since we're having transparency moments, can I tell you something else?"

"Of course you can."

"Hmm. Give me a moment to get this together."

"Okay."

I was a straight shooter, but I didn't want to cause her to cower by making her uncomfortable. "Alright. So, I want to get closer to you, baby. Intimately."

She looked up at me again. Eyes wide. "Closer how?"

"You may think I'm referring to sex. But I'm not. I know we aren't there yet."

"So, how do you mean?"

"Shower with me." Destiney averted her eyes, but I continued, "It is incredibly intimate washing each other's bodies." She had a look of hesitancy as I continued, "I promise, it will not lead to sex."

After a beat, she gave me her eyes, nodding. "Alright."

"Are you sure?"

"Yes, I'm sure."

"Alright love. Lead the way."

After Destiney cut off the TV and the lights, I grabbed her hand, following her down the hall into her bedroom. I glanced around. Destiney's bedroom fit her personality down to a T.

It was comfy and inviting with eclectic décor. There were various shades of green everywhere, with purple accents. I was greeted by a coconut scent, which I loved. It added to the comforting ambience of her bedroom. Coconut must have been her favorite scent. I noticed a few coconut-scented body butters and candles on her dresser.

Her bed looked like a place where she got the best sleep. It had a fluffy lime green comforter and lots of pillows. I knew she loved to read, which explained the purple and white polka dot reading pillow. I hadn't seen a reading pillow in years.

Destiney beckoned me toward the ensuite, telling me to go ahead of her to get the shower started, and she would join me momentarily. She probably needed a moment to talk herself through her nerves, and I could understand that. There were few things as intimate as couples in the shower.

Once in the bathroom, I closed the door behind me to give her some privacy.

I removed my clothing, folded it neatly, and placed it on the vanity. I turned on the shower and gave it a minute to reach the desired temperature. Destiney probably preferred her water to be a little warmer than I did. Women could take incredibly hot showers and baths. I didn't know how that shit was even possible. After a moment, I heard music coming on, and that's when I noticed the Bluetooth speaker in the far corner of the bathroom. It was a slow jam, which was a great idea. Another moment later, I heard a knock on the door.

"Come on in, sweetheart." I was naked as the day I was born, standing there in her bathroom.

Destiney cracked the door, and I saw eyes peering back at me. "Micah…" she said hesitantly.

"Are you alright?"

"Yes. But I'm a little shy," She revealed.

"No need to be shy, love," I told her gingerly. She remained on the other side of the door, and I remembered the hummingbird nightlight when I entered her bathroom moments earlier. "Would you feel more comfortable if we turned the lights out? This nightlight will be bright enough for us."

"I would."

"Indeed." I turned the lights out, and Destiney entered the bathroom wearing a bathrobe. "Is that better baby?" I asked as I brought her to me, wrapping my arms around her. I wanted her to be comfortable; hopefully, she would be since this was her space.

"Yes. Thank you."

"Of course. Anything you need, you tell me."

"Okay."

I reached into the shower behind me, and the water was perfect. Taking her delicate hands in mine, I kissed both of her palms. Went back and forth. I didn't rush the equal peppering of kisses on each of her hands. Humming, I pressed, "Destiney baby…" now kissing the tops and undersides of her soft fingertips. "I plan to kiss you. A lot. If you're good with that."

"Absolutely fine with that."

"Alright. You ready love?"

"Yes, I am." I took note of the shift in her voice. It held a sultry tone, and I was with it. Slowly untying the belt of her robe, I gently removed it from her body. Kissing her all the while. I took my time kissing her lips, then kissing her neck and bare shoulders. After placing her robe on the hook behind the door, I took her hand in mine, bringing her with me as I entered the shower. She stepped in behind me, and only then did I scan her silhouette. Salivating instantly.

It wasn't long before we were kissing heavily again. I took Destiney into my arms, rubbing her upper and lower back as the water cascaded over us. Her skin was so soft. Damn.

We kissed for a good while.

Flush, skin to skin, no barrier between us, and I could feel the stiff peaks of her nipples. She wasn't the only one who was excited. My dick was hard as hell, pressed between us and there was no hiding it. Destiney's arms were around me, and she moaned softly as I continued to caress her body.

"That feels so nice, Micah," She told me.

"My pleasure baby." That shit had two meanings. All in due time. And I looked forward to it. I kissed her lips. I kissed her forehead, her cheeks. Her neck and her shoulders. Her fingers.

When the time came, I planned to kiss and caress every single inch of her body.

When I arrived earlier, I grabbed her hand and didn't let it go right away.

Holding hands was such a thing with her. Destiney is the best hand holder there ever was. And her hands are so soft. I was a little surprised since she works with her hands so much. As an artist. Creating masterpieces. Painting and sketching for hours a day. I figured maybe that meant her hands wouldn't feel so velvety smooth.

I was beginning to love bringing them to my lips. Kissing her fingers was my new obsession.

Destiney's hands were pretty. Petite, matching her petite stature.

Slender, delicate fingers. Perfectly manicured nails.

Evidently, she maintained a top-notch exfoliating and moisturizing routine.

Breaking our kiss, I surveyed Destiney with low lids. Her doe eyes peering right up into mine. "Sweetheart…"

"Yes." An alluring tone in her voice. Still. I'd caught that inflection moments before, which sent excitement rushing to my groin.

The lighting was dim, but I could see the desire in her eyes. The same desire I had for her. I held her face gently in my hands, my lips just a whisper from hers. "Would it be painful if I touched you? There? If you're comfortable. But I don't want to hurt you if you're tender during this time."

She began, "I…you…" Sensing her trepidation, I lowered my hands, holding her firmly at the waist. Continuing my gentle caress of her skin. I'm sure my question surprised her, and she was likely feeling bashful. But I needed her to understand. She had no reason to be embarrassed with me.

"I'm a grown man. I'm not afraid of a little blood, sweetheart."

Destiney shook her head as she chuckled. "Hardly a little." There wasn't an ounce of mirth.

"The water will wash it all away."

She waited a beat then asked, "You sure you want to do that?"

"I am, Destiney baby."

She took a few beats. Then, "Okay."

"Okay?"

"Yes. Okay."

I placed an arm around her waist, anchoring her close to me, then made a graceful motion of lowering my other hand to the apex of her. I gently cupped her. My massive hand covered her in its entirety. She was smooth. And… fuck. There was an intense heat emanating from her.

Destiney quivered softly as I applied pressure, gently moving my palm from side to side. Arching her back, she leaned into me. Her soft moans music to my ears. She was incredibly responsive as I squeezed and palmed her there. Connecting our lips again, I applied more pressure, pushing the heel of my hand against her. It was clear she liked that, so I did it again.

I liked it too. I was so turned on. Hard as hell. To the point that it was painful.

Rocking her hips slowly, she moaned against my lips.

"Destiney Baby?"

"Yeah?"

"Can I put my finger inside you?" Speaking close to her ear, still applying pressure. I could feel her pearl, showing itself. Got damn... using the heal of my hand I applied pressure there too. Connecting our lips again before she could answer me, I swallowed more of her faint moans.

Destiney broke our kiss, giving me her eyes. "If you want to."

"Do you want me to?"

"Hell. Yes."

I released a faint chuckle as I gently nudged her upper thigh. She understood my silent request and immediately spread more for me. I returned my hand to her center, then, unhurried, carefully pierced her sanctuary with my middle finger. There was some restriction. I decided one finger would be plenty.

I held her even closer to me. "Destiney baby." My strokes were gentle and slow.

"Yes?" She murmured.

"Is this okay? Am I hurting you?"

"You're okay… not hurting me at all."

I was back in her ear, "You sexy girl." I'd never been intimate with a woman while she was bleeding, but things didn't feel any different to me. "Everything feels perfect," I told her. I planted a few kisses on her cheek, then moved up to her forehead, remaining there for a moment.

Destiney moaned, and I felt her subtle nod against me. "It feels perfect to me, too."

Ever so slightly, I increased my pace, grazing my thumb over her swollen pearl. I brought my lips lower again, now tenderly pressed to her neck. I could feel the vibration of her vocal cords as she released a faint moan. She liked that.

Yeah.

We'd eventually get around to washing ourselves.

But first things first.

twenty

DESTINEY

"Byyyyeee Miss Destineeeeeey!"

"See you later, Sasha!"

Sasha was such an adorable seven-year-old little brown cutie pie and super polite. I'd taken such a liking to her right way. All of these kids have my heart, but little Sasha was one of my favorites. Likely because she reminded me a lot of myself as a child; she had a big smile and an even bigger personality. She was imaginative and creative and could draw pretty well for her age. Sasha already had something special. And I told her so.

I knew how impressionable kids were and wanted to always speak life over them. You never knew how that would impact their confidence, especially the ones expressing interest in the arts. There was a school of thought that STEMS were significantly more important. Many adults would discourage kids from artistic expression altogether.

I couldn't disagree more. That shit would grind my gears every time. Yes, STEM fields are vital, but the arts also matter. Tremendously. I would continually cultivate creativity with people of all ages, especially children.

"I'll miss you! See ya next week!" She'd come running back to me, grabbing my legs tightly one last time before she took off again behind the other kids, headed across the quad where all their parents were waiting.

"I'll see you next week, my friend!"

It was close to four o'clock now. Thankfully, the weather was great today. Warm enough to be comfortable. But not too warm. Officially summer. And Sacramento had very high digits in the summer months.

The artists and crew had to arrive at eight thirty a.m. and get everything set up. The kids arrived at 10 a.m. This morning, we had fresh fruit, granola bars, and water for them. Around noon, we had sandwiches and chips for lunch donated by a local deli. We were painting the mural outside a Boys and Girls Club in an underserved area of South Sacramento. We extended an opportunity for the kids in the summer day camp to help with the project. About two dozen kids came out today, from age seven to thirteen.

The mural would be bright, colorful, and lively, showing children of various cultures and ages playing together around a large oak tree. Scattered throughout the mural would be phrases in multiple languages. Spanish, Italian, and Portuguese. Japanese, Korean, Yoruba, Swahili, and many others. The phrases roughly translated to the English word unity. The concept was dope, and I loved the diversity it represented.

The key to a lasting mural was good quality paints, which could be costly, especially for larger murals. We secured generous sponsors who provided everything we needed, including supplies and meals. I was willing to sign on even after learning the artists wouldn't get paid much.

But that's the nature of the beast. Some community projects don't pay as handsomely as the others. I applied for a few grants, and if those came through, I could make up the difference that way. Even if those fell through, I would be fine. I eventually planned to secure another gig on the days I wasn't committed to this project. It was such a great cause; I was just grateful to be a part of it. Especially getting to work with these kids. Making a positive difference in their lives meant a lot to me.

It was a productive day considering. Getting the kids to work for extended periods of time can be a challenge. Understandably. They had such limited attention spans, but they're so proud of their hard work and love helping. Collaborating with kids is always a joy for me.

We have to keep a close eye on them, though. If someone isn't paying attention, one of the younger kids can take a paintbrush and ruin something in just three seconds flat! I've seen it happen.

The mural was along the side of the building, facing the street. Such a great place for it. It would definitely be a neighborhood focal point and look great once it was done. This would be a large project. Twenty-four feet by eighteen feet. Approximately four hundred and thirty-two square feet.

There were seven of us, including India and me. Half guys and half girls. All of us were in our twenties. We all worked really well together and made up a talented group, I dare say. Typically, the number of sessions is based on the size of the mural and the number of muralists. This mural was organized over consecutive weekends, and today was session number two of six sessions scheduled.

Even though we'd been out here most of the day, we couldn't yet call it quitting time. It wasn't unusual for muralists to work after hours when necessary, and today, we would need to stay a little longer to ensure the project was completed on schedule. With just the muralists remaining, we could work with little interruption and really get into our element. I'm sure we'd accomplish a great deal of work now that the kids had gone for the day.

I successfully mustered up the excitement to engage with the kids. And I could put my face on when I was interviewed by the press that came on site. I was trying desperately to hang on to that excitement. I needed it to get through today.

I was still bleeding. Today made day number seventeen. That's almost three fucking weeks of this shit and it didn't seem that things were slowing down. But I wasn't in that much pain. However, I realized that maybe I was convincing myself that I wasn't. I know for a fact that my pain tolerance is higher than the average person's. I was accustomed to these massive cramps. Someone else would likely be curled in a ball somewhere. Although I was tolerating the pain, I didn't have much energy. Anyway, I was a little sluggish but pushing through it.

I hated being away from home for hours like I did today. But I didn't have much of a choice. So, as always, I kept a change of clothes in my car and a sweatshirt in case I needed to tie it around my waist. And made sure to take frequent trips to the ladies' room. If not, I would almost always have a leak.

I learned that the hard way.

"Yo! This portrait is dope, Des!" India said as she walked up behind me. India and I were working on opposite ends. I'd already gone by to see how her section was coming along. It looked amazing.

Everything India did looked amazing. My bestie was incredibly talented.

"Thank you, girlie. I'm getting better at these. In a minute, I'll be as sick as you are with portraits."

"Girl, stop. You're already there! In the meantime, I'm getting a handle on my lettering. You're the lettering queen! I think Brandi had us mixed up when she assigned us."

Brandi was a hippie white chick, a freaking beast with a paintbrush and Artistic Director-Extraordinaire of this project.

Generally, there's a director in charge of the design and execution of the mural. They're tasked with organizing the artists, identifying their strengths, and assigning them accordingly based on their talents.

I was good anywhere, really, but I would have expected to be working on the lines and lettering and India the portraits. Instead, we were flipped, which was fine. But it was still funny.

"Yeah. She probably did." We both cracked up.

Many people got India, and I confused. We worked on multiple projects together, and we'd been mistaken for each other plenty of times. Though I didn't mind. Funny, we didn't resemble one another, but we were always together and had similar personalities. And almost always, we were the only two black chicks. This project was no different.

When we broke for lunch earlier, I called Micah, and we spoke for most of the lunch hour. I sent him a few pictures, and he loved our work so far.

The night he came to my place was the last time I saw him.

That was almost two weeks ago.

I missed him something fierce, and I desperately wanted to see him. Be near him. But I was trying to keep my distance since I was still bleeding so much.

This was the worst. I was beside myself, and I missed him terribly.

But… I just couldn't be near him. Not only was I feeling insecure as hell, but I also knew I couldn't offer him anything physical. All we could really do was kiss, which I loved. I absolutely loved the way he kissed me. The way he kissed me and the way he touched me had me fantasizing.

I should be embarrassed at the amount of fantasizing I'd done these past two weeks.

Anyway, Micah is a grown man. He needed more than kissing. Eventually, it was only a matter of time. And…I wanted to be the woman who satisfied those needs. He certainly deserved it. Micah was so considerate. Thoughtful. Sweet. Gentle.

And Micah made me feel sexy, which is entirely new for me. I feel confident in myself as a woman. I know I'm an attractive woman.

But sexy is different.

Micah just had a way with shit. I can't even put my finger on it, like when we were in the shower. I was so nervous. But my nerves were dispelled immediately.

Micah made sure I was comfortable, checking with me before he did anything.

Everything he did required my permission.

I didn't know if he was being extra conscious because of my situation or if that was just him… ever the gentleman. But my goodness. Even when we kissed, unless I initiated it, Micah was asking first.

He had no idea how much I appreciated that.

My first sexual experience was… not good. I tried to forget about it and compartmentalize it.

And it remains my only sexual experience.

Considering that, it seemed that Micah knew precisely how I needed to be handled without being told.

I loved the way Micah handled me.

And I didn't express it, but I took notice of Micah's prominent erection when we were lying on my couch. Micah's dick was hard as hell. I felt it grazing me multiple times when we were in the shower.

Crazy too, because he didn't even take care of himself. Not in front of me anyway. That shit had to be painful for him.

That entire experience had me in my feelings, not only in the moment but also after the fact.

I concluded that my feelings had grown deeper than before. I attribute this to the careful way Micah handled my situation and me. I can't say exactly what I expected, although I wouldn't dare say I was surprised.

Micah has already proven himself to be compassionate. Sensitive. Hypersensitive to what I'm dealing with. His compassion revealed itself early in our friendship and was a constant presence.

That was just Micah. Compassion came second nature.

But not all my feelings concerning this were warm and fuzzy.

For one, I felt incredibly selfish.

My loudest thought of all, aside from how much I loved everything Micah was doing to me, was that I wanted Micah all to myself. I wanted to be with Micah.

Yet, I couldn't offer Micah anything beyond conversation. And making out.

That wasn't okay.

Something occurred to me a long time ago.

Something I desperately tried to ignore, hoping that by doing so, maybe I could make it go away.

And as hard as I tried to ignore it, I couldn't make it go away.

It was time I faced the music.

The fact of the matter is that I just needed to let Micah go. Leave him alone. Let him be.

That was inevitable. I also felt an immense amount of sadness. I cared about Micah so much. I knew he cared just as much about me. Hurting him was the last thing I'd want to do.

The sudden influx of moisture in my underwear pulled me from my thoughts. It was about that time I went and checked on things.

I put my paint brush down and removed my black rubber gloves. I prefer wearing gloves while working on a mural. I have sensitive skin, and it's easily irritated, so the extra barrier protects me from the harsh chemicals and paint we use. Of course, it keeps the skin clean but also helps prevent accidentally transferring paint or chemicals to other surfaces and accidental smudging. Not all painters wear them. I get a better grip on my brush with gloves than without.

"Indie, I'll be right back, headed to the ladies room." She was back in her zone, working away. She smiled warmly, giving me a knowing expression. I shared my diagnosis and everything I had been dealing with, with India a while back. She was constantly checking in with me, and I didn't feel so alone with this.

Once I was securely in the restroom stall, I saw that my pad was soaked, and I noticed I had passed a few rather large clots. I switched out my pad, and when I wiped myself, I saw another large clot on the toilet paper. I stood up to flush and saw one in the toilet.

Groaning, I buttoned my pants and then washed my hands. I just wanted to go home. It was almost five, and the team would likely work until at least six before packing it up for the night. I felt terrible for bailing early, but I was sure Brandi would understand.

I pulled my backpack over my shoulder and exited the restroom. I needed to find Brandi and let her know I would be leaving.

Taking a few steps, I felt a gush between my legs. I considered going back into the restroom but decided to wait until I got home.

I took another step, and that's when everything went black.

twenty-one

MICAH

"Which hospital?"

"Sutter Medical on Capital."

"Does she know you've called me?"

"No, she doesn't. But she'll get over it. I know she misses you. And she can use some cheering up. The doctor admitted her, and she's scheduled for surgery tomorrow morning. She's not happy about any of this."

"I see. Well, thank you so much for calling me, Daijah. I'll be there as soon as I can. Is there anything I can get you on my way?"

"No thank you, Micah. Julian went to get me something. He should be back any minute. I look forward to introducing the two of you."

"Likewise. I'll see you all soon."

I ended the call, exhaling in exasperation.

Now I knew why Destiney was hiding from me.

She was still bleeding.

When I left her home two Fridays ago, I was confident we'd made progress. We'd gotten so close.

Intimately close.

Shit was surreal.

A fucking fantasy I could have only imagined. A fantasy that somehow came true. A high I was still coming down from.

Seeing Destiney in person was significant in itself. But she let me do more than that. Destiney allowed me into her personal space.

She let me kiss her. And kiss her I did.

Till I got tired.

She agreed to shower together. She let me wash her body. And my goodness, her body was just as beautiful as I imagined. The lights were dim, and my sight was limited, but I could take in everything through my unrestricted touch.

She let me feel her mound. She let me grace her haven with my finger… fuck. That had me painfully hard.

Things went no further than that, but it was all good in my hood. I didn't go to her home to have sex with her. I wanted to show her she didn't have to avoid me. I wanted her to know I still wanted her.

So, when I left her that evening, I felt everything was finally out in the open. From my perspective, I figured she would be comfortable enough to be near me even during that time.

But… since then, it seems we've regressed. In my mind, we'd taken strides forward, only to take several steps back.

We talk daily, as usual. But Destiney continues to have a reason to evade my attempts to see her. Always an excuse. At one point, I considered pulling up on her, then quickly decided against it.

When we spoke this afternoon, Destiney was onsite doing work on a mural. She gushed about all of the cute kids there helping out. She sent me a few pictures, and I was beyond impressed with everything I saw.

But for the life of me, I couldn't comprehend this. She was at a worksite and seemed to be having a great time in her element, doing what she does best.

But she wouldn't let me see her.

If I'm honest, I was pretty frustrated. And I was beginning to take it personally.

Those feelings dissipated immediately when Daijah called me.

Destiney lost so much blood that she passed out at the worksite, and an ambulance was called.

After hanging up with Daijah, I quickly got out the door and hopped in my car to get to my baby.

The sun was beginning to set. It was a beautiful Saturday, and it reached ninety degrees. It's not too warm since Sacramento got a lovely Delta Breeze. Today, ninety didn't feel like ninety. It was close to seven thirty in the evening now. We had about an hour of daylight left. The days were long during summertime in Sacramento.

I merged onto CA-99 Northbound. According to my GPS, I would arrive at the hospital in about fifteen minutes.

As eager as I was to get there and lay eyes on Destiney, I was nervous about walking in on her unexpectedly.

I could only hope she would be glad to see me. If she was worried about surgery tomorrow, I hoped seeing me would lift her spirits.

I made it to the hospital, and once I parked, I entered through Emergency and headed straight for the information desk. They hadn't moved Destiney yet, so they sent me straight back.

As I neared her room number, I spotted Daijah standing in the hallway, speaking to a tall gentleman I assumed was Julian. Daijah and I had only spoken on Facetime, but I recognized her immediately.

Destiney and Daijah favored one another. Daijah is tall, much taller than I expected, possibly 5'9. But Julian towered over her. I'd say he was at least 6'2. He may have had me by an inch if we weren't at eye level.

"Micah!" Daijah whisper, yelling. We were right outside of Destiney's room.

"Hey, Daijah. Thanks again for calling me." I hugged her, then shook Julian's hand. "Nice to meet you, Julian. I'm Micah."

"Same here man. I've heard so much about you."

"Get in there because they'll be back any minute to move her upstairs." Daijah gestured with a nod of her head. "Once she's settled, they'll be starting a blood transfusion. She may not be in the mood for company at that point."

I nodded and headed inside.

When I entered the room, Destiney peered up in surprise. She looked a little tired, but her beauty shined through. Her eyes were red, puffy, and glossy. She had been crying.

I held her gaze, giving her a warm smile. I'm here now, and I plan to help her feel better. As best as I could. I placed the flowers I picked up for her on the windowsill and then made my way to the side of her bed. I leaned over to kiss her forehead.

"Destiney baby," I said, gently taking her hand in mine kissing it. I.V. be damned. I held her hand firmly between both of mine.

"Daijah called you," She stated meekly.

"She did."

Destiney rolled her eyes. "I'm going to get her."

"From there?" I asked rhetorically through a chuckle.

"None of this is funny."

"I agree. I was wondering why you kept avoiding me. Imagine my surprise when I got a call that you were rushed to the E.R. because you'd lost so much blood." I told her evenly.

Destiney looked away from me. "I wasn't avoiding you."

"No? What do you call that?"

"Micah. You wouldn't understand."

"Right now, I don't. But if you open up to me a little more, I may. Or I can at least try. You won't even give me the opportunity." My frustration revealing itself without my permission.

The room was silent, aside from the monitor beeping every few seconds. Finally, she said, "I always feel insecure when I'm bleeding. The smell. The constant wet feeling. The anxiety. It's so unpredictable that I can't even get close to you because I can't guarantee we will ever be intimate."

I saw a tear fall and used my thumb to wipe it from her cheek gently.

"Baby. You're here now. Let's focus on getting you better." I lifted her hand back to my lips, kissing it again. "We'll get through this together."

Destiney shook her head. "You have to move on, Micah."

"What?"

"You're a good man and deserve more than I can ever give you."

"Destiney, what are you talking about?" Dumbfounded, my eyes were glued to hers.

"I'm having surgery tomorrow morning. And after that, I won't be able to have children."

Her eyes welled with tears, and my heart broke for her.

"Destiney baby..."

She pulled her hand from mine and snatched away when I tried to reclaim it. "I'm so sorry, Micah." She broke down, weeping so hysterically she could barely speak.

All I wanted to do was hold her tightly in my arms. I pulled up the chair against the wall closer to her bedside. Then

I took a seat. She wouldn't look at me. But I proceeded anyway, "Sweetheart, why are you sorry? None of this is your fault." I wiped her tears as they continued flowing down her beautiful face.

"I know how much you want to be a father." She managed, "I'm not the woman for you. We should just stop while we're ahead." Still looking straight ahead.

Still refusing to look at me.

What the hell was going on? How did we get here?

"But I love you Destiney. I'm in love with you," I spoke gently, but insistently. Destiney's head snapped in my direction, giving me her eyes for a few seconds, and I saw something there.

Something I could hardly describe in words.

It was something intense. Something ardent.

Fervent.

It was almost as if… maybe… no. Wait... could she possibly...?

Before I could ruminate any further, Destiney averted her gaze. I probably surprised her.

I was surprised myself.

Not with my feelings. But rather my declaration. I didn't plan to share my heart under these circumstances, but the words came out before I could stop them. And this was how I felt. Truly. And I knew it was soon, but there was no doubt in my mind.

I'm in love with Destiney Evans.

"You're the most important person to me now. You baby. We can always figure out the rest," I told her.

Looking past me, focused on something in the distance, she said, "Just go home, Micah."

My eyes grew wide. "Destiney. Please."

"You already told me you wanted children. And I won't be able to give you any. Just leave." She pulled her hand from mine; I'd since reclaimed it and turned away from me. She covered her face with her hands, weeping. The sight of it pulled at my heartstrings.

I didn't want to leave her. I couldn't, not like this.

"Destiney, baby… let me be here for you," I pleaded. I didn't want to be anywhere else.

I didn't want anyone else.

"Get out, Micah!" She said firmly, her voice at least two octaves louder.

Daijah must have heard her because she entered the room wearing a concerned expression. Julian didn't come in behind her, so I assumed he'd gone home.

A few nurses came in a moment later and began preparing to move Destiney upstairs. The room suddenly grew loud and crowded. I stepped back, rubbing my hands over my head, unsure of what else to do.

Daijah silently nodded toward the door, and I followed her out into the hall. Sighing, she said, "Go on home Micah. I think that's best for right now. You won't need to worry. I'll stay with her tonight, and our dad will be back first thing tomorrow."

I rubbed my forehead. "Did you know she was having that surgery?"

Daijah nodded. "Yes. But she needed to be the one to tell you."

"I understand. Will you please text me tomorrow with an update? I just want to know how she's doing. I won't come back if she doesn't want me here."

"Of course I will." She smiled warmly.

"Thanks, Daijah. Please let me know if I can have a meal delivered tomorrow or if you need anything at all."

"I will. Goodnight Micah. Get home safely."

"Thank you, Daijah. Goodnight."

Walking down the hallway and out toward the parking garage, I was beside myself.

I'd just poured my heart out to Destiney. Professing my love for her for the first time.

I didn't expect her to say it back, but breaking things off was the very last thing I had in mind.

She avoided my eyes and didn't want to discuss things first.

We certainly could have at a better time.

I thought we had something.

Was all of this a figment of my imagination?

No. There's no way.

twenty-two

MICAH

I left the hospital with no particular destination in mind, merging onto the CA-99 Southbound freeway.

I didn't feel like going home.

I certainly didn't want to bother Malachi with this. Not right now.

Just before I cranked up, I texted my boy Soloman to see if he wanted to get into something. Play some pool. Get a drink. I realized he may have been occupied. Probably at band rehearsal. Or playing at a gig somewhere.

The freeway was full of vehicles.

People were enjoying the warm evening and were likely headed out to their prospective locations for whatever plans they made for this Saturday night. It was still fairly early. Sunroofs were open. Droptops down.

I just kept driving, eventually passing the Florin Road and then Sheldon Road exits.

I'd cut the music off, so it was dead silent in my car. I needed the quiet because my thoughts were loud as hell. Running rampant in my mind.

I felt like the rug had been pulled from under me.

Destiney hadn't lied.

We talked at length about children. Children in general. We both worked with children.

We often talked about future children.

I was always up front with that. I pretty much told her from the beginning that I dated with the intention of marriage and a family.

I hadn't realized that I belabored the point so much she thought her new reality would cause disarray on my part. Create divergence.

And as much as I wanted marriage and fatherhood, I was almost settled with the idea that maybe it wouldn't happen for me.

Until I met her.

Now, those dreams were dashed. Again.

No. This wasn't the first time.

Marriage and fatherhood were things that seemed just out of my grasp.

This sudden change of circumstances was another situation that seemed to confirm that.

Another situation… concerning a child I almost had, who never got the chance, was something I thought about often. They would be about thirteen now, right between Gabe and Gabby.

My wife to be, at the time. My now ex-fiancé, Ayesha, aborted our baby. That was the beginning of the end for us.

We'd gotten engaged, but she wanted to finish school and get her footing before we got married and started a family, which I could understand.

But the way she went about it all…

She didn't tell me she was pregnant right away. When she finally shared the news with me, she'd already decided she wasn't keeping it.

Yeah. That was the beginning of the end.

***

My phone vibrated with a text from Ayesha.

Can you meet me in front of Kerr? Really need to talk

I was surprised to hear from her because she'd been distant for the past couple of weeks. Although it was a pleasant surprise.

We were kind of in a weird space. We hadn't seen much of each other lately, and the last couple times we'd hung out, I could tell something was off about her. Of course, I asked her about it, but she kept saying she was overwhelmed with her course load.

She doubled up on her science classes in preparation for grad school, and it was taking its toll on her. Her physics class in particular was kicking her ass. Her words, not mine. I'd never taken physics, but I took chemistry, and that shit was almost the death of me so that I could understand.

I offered to take her out to a movie or something, but she said she was too tired. At that point, I didn't know what else to do besides give her space.

Needless to say, I was glad to hear from her.

I gathered my things as I shot her a reply. I wasn't a far walk from Kerr Hall.

Yep, 20 minutes

I wasn't sure what she wanted to talk about, but I was glad to get to see her.

When I arrived, she was sitting on our bench, and the sight made me smile instantly.

This was the bench we would always choose if it wasn't taken. Kerr Hall was a place we met often when we first started hanging out because she had many classes in that building.

We had our first kiss two years ago, right on the front steps.

It was the sweetest kiss.

Literally and figuratively.

I can still remember the cotton candy bubblicious flavor of her tongue. She'd been popping her gum nervously right before I asked if

I could kiss her. My nerves were just as bad, but I was ready to feel her lips on mine finally. She was on the same type of time because she was throwing hints right at me, nerves and all.

Ayesha looked up at me as I approached. She was smiling, but it didn't reach her eyes.

"Hey. You good?"

She shrugged her shoulders. "Depends."

"Depends?" I halted in my tracks. "You want to talk right here?"

"Sure."

I sat beside her on the bench and took her hand into mine. Once I threaded our fingers, I kissed her softly on the lips. "Something's been up with you, baby. Please talk to me."

She regarded me for a moment, and I held her gaze. Her eyes were different today.

Empty. Dark bottomless pits.

Ayesha began talking, and I regarded her pretty face, still searching her eyes. For what, I wasn't sure, but I needed to make sense of all this.

I was so preoccupied that I wasn't registering whatever she was saying. I was so caught up in my thoughts, but I swear I heard her say she was pregnant.

Pregnant? I had to be mistaken.

"What did you just say?" At this point, we'd been love-making for a while, and we were always careful. There were only a couple of times I hadn't strapped up, but I pulled out in time.

Regardless, here we were.

"I said I'm pregnant, Micah." Her tone was vague. I couldn't get a read on where her head was.

"Okay." I nodded. "Do you know how far along we are?"

"Just left the campus clinic. Exactly eight weeks today."

"How long have you known?"

"About two weeks."

Ah. Now I knew why she'd been avoiding me.

"Why are you just now telling me, Ayesha? I would have gone to the clinic with you."

She shrugged.

"You could have told me when you found out. You know that." *She said nothing. I pressed forward anyway. "How are you feeling?"*

She chuckled, but it wasn't in amusement. "Sick. Always nauseous. I can hardly eat anything. Nothing stays down."

"Yeah. I can imagine this first trimester will be tough." I rubbed her lower back. "Hang in there baby. I can get you whatever you need. Please tell me what it is. I want you comfortable." She looked away from me as I asked, "How are you feeling about our baby? Being pregnant." I wasn't sure how I felt, but I'd have to think about that later. Ayesha and our baby are my sole focus right now.

She shook her head. "Shocked. Stressed. Terrified." She finally revealed.

"I'm shocked too," I told her honestly. "But try not to stress. It's not best for you or the baby. This is a little scary, and I can understand you feeling terrified. But we can handle this together."

We sat for another moment in silence as I processed everything. This was a lot and would no doubt change our lives.

"I just don't know how I will explain this to everyone." She said after a moment.

"Who said you had to?"

She grimaced. "Micah. I came out here for college. Not to get pregnant! I'll owe people an explanation!"

"What people? Aside from your parents?" I evenly asked, more so rhetorically.

I already had an idea. The fact that Ayesha was a pastor's daughter inherently made her a spectacle. I understood because the church we grew up in was no different. Mal and I were good friends with our pastors' kids growing up, and I knew the troubles they experienced all too well.

People with nothing better to do were watching and waiting, always running back to tell the pastor and first lady something they saw or heard.

I understood the shit firsthand because it was similar for Mal and me. Daddy was chair of the deacons, and Mommy was an usher and taught the children's Sunday school class—practically our entire lives.

The gossiping women in the church irked my damn nerves. Half the ass whoppins Mal and I got were behind some shit they ran back telling. We were only being kids, but they just wouldn't leave us alone.

I could understand Ayesha's position to a degree, but we were in college now, hundreds of miles from home.

We were also grown.

I didn't give a damn what someone back home thought of what I was doing now.

She was still walking the line. I wished she would free herself from all that pressure.

Especially since she didn't have to yield to that anymore.

"I thought about it, and I can't go through a pregnancy, Micah."

"Everything will be fine, and we'll get through it."

"I can't."

I gave her a quizzical expression. "You can't, or you won't?"

She said nothing.

"Ayesha."

"I need some time… alone. I need to figure all of this out. I just need a few days, Micah."

Alone? The hell. "Why are you running from me?"

"People will talk…"

"Ayesha... people will talk regardless. You're a grown woman." She said nothing.

I realized then exactly what the issue was.

If I'm honest, I realized this a long time ago.

Ayesha cared too much about the opinions of others. Entirely too much.

To further complicate matters, Ayesha didn't have a spontaneous bone in her body.

She had to plan every single thing down to the smallest detail.

Anything that happened had to be planned.

It was as if simply thinking about doing shit on a whim made her uneasy. Even the smallest, most trivial things.

Back during our sophomore year, I heard about a poetry slam at a spot just off campus. I wanted to surprise her with tickets and make a date night out of it. We are both fans of spoken word poetry, so I thought it would be something chill to get into.

Anyway, I texted her, telling her I had a surprise for her. That was my first mistake.

Initially, she asked for hints. When I wouldn't give her any hints, she began begging me to tell her.

She finally wore me down because she wouldn't stop insisting. Once she knew, she casually laughed it off, saying she didn't like surprises, and they gave her anxiety.

No shit.

I never did that again. If I wanted to do anything nice for Ayesha, I needed to tell her well in advance so she could plan for it.

So, things like finishing graduate school, establishing her career, marriage, and having kids had to go in that order, and there was no room for a change of plans. No wavering.

Her compulsive desire to micromanage everything had been a point of contention in our relationship. Honestly, it was the only one, but it was major.

She had no idea, though.

As significant as that was, I kept it to myself, which was another mistake. I knew I couldn't change her; nor did I want to. It was who she was.

Part of me wondered if that shit would change even if I did say something. I'm such an easygoing, laid-back person. I'd tried all for naught to encourage Ayesha to try to let things just be.

Why be so type-A and meticulous about everything?

That seems exhausting.

Her micromanaging, stringent, and compulsive traits made it extremely difficult to exist in the moment because she was always in her head about everything going perfectly. Shit was wild.

Conversely, there were benefits to her extremely detailed planning.

I could concede that my time management and study habits had improved significantly since having Ayesha in my life.

Being a student-athlete was a beast. Quite honestly, it was a balancing act and not for the weak.

Especially at the collegiate level.

I figured my high school habits were going to work in college, and I was sadly mistaken.

I wasn't the most disciplined to begin with, and incorporating the additional responsibilities along with my habitual procrastination was a disaster waiting to happen.

Shit wasn't good.

I didn't have enough time in the day for much of anything. I wasn't sleeping well because my mind was cluttered with all the shit I had to do. I was exhausted at baseball practice. Fatigue significantly impacted my performance and my coaches weren't happy.

Shit, neither was I.

Naturally, things in the classroom were no better. I was always playing catch up on papers and cramming for exams. I knew shit was bad, but I couldn't seem to free myself from the funk I was in.

When midterm grades were pulled one of my coaches called me in and told me I'd be dropped from the sports program if I didn't improve. That shit was a reality check.

A few nights later, I revealed to Ayesha that my scholarship was on the line. Simply put, she helped me. With everything she had going on, she still managed to help me.

Foremost, Ayesha was instrumental in helping me get my time management together. When I finally started prioritizing what I had to do, it left more time for the things I wanted to do.

Ayesha had excellent study habits, and she kindly shared those with me. Consequently, my grade point average improved. I went from a less than stellar student to an excellent student. I wasn't on the dean's list, but I was damn close.

I owed all of that to Ayesha.

"We aren't even married." She pulled me from my thoughts, rising from the bench. Taking a step, she turned back to face me.

I stood too. "Then let's get married."

"Micah. It's not that simple."

"It's not?"

She sighed, "That's impulsive."

"We're engaged. What difference does it make?"

I closed the space between us, taking her hands into mine. "Look, I know you wanted a beautiful wedding, but we can do that later. Be my wife. Then let's handle the rest of this together. I got you. Always."

She shook her head, undoubtedly in disapproval. "That's not how this was supposed to go…we had goals."

"Ayesha." I hung my head trying to gather my thoughts. I wasn't getting through to her. "Sometimes things don't go according to plan. That's life. We can't control everything."

"I can control if I'm a mother."

My eyes grew wide.

There it was. "Meaning you kill our baby?" I huffed in frustration. "You can accomplish your goals and some with me as your husband. I won't keep you from fulfilling your dreams. If anything, I'll do all I can to help you and support you. I'll take care of you. And our baby."

She pried her hands from mine. "I have to think about this."

"Us getting married or the baby?" I pressed.

She paused for a while. Longer than I liked. "The baby."

"What is there to think about? I want our child."

"I don't know if that's what I want right now."

Growing desperate I said, "You can sign them over to me. I'll raise it. You won't even have to be involved."

I saw a look of surprise which faded just as quickly as it emerged, "Carrying this baby is my choice, Micah."

I took a step back. "I'll get with you later Ayesha," I said that in defeat and really that's exactly how I felt.

It dawned on me at that very moment: she'd already decided.

She called me here to inform me of that and probably didn't expect the reaction I'd given her. "I'll see you around. I guess." I quickly walked away with my mind going a million miles a minute. If she had anything to say I didn't hear her. My thoughts were in disarray, much too loud for me to hear anything anyway. Walking away from this conversation was my best move for now. I needed to stop while I was ahead before I said something I'd regret.

It was her choice, but her ass was being irrational.

I couldn't believe this.

She was seriously contemplating killing our baby. To make matters worse, I got the impression she wasn't concerned about considering my feelings in her decision.

This wasn't the Ayesha I fell in love with. The Ayesha I knew adored children and now she was going to kill ours. All for optics. At least that's the impression I was getting.

It was clear we saw this differently and I didn't even know where we stood.

One thing I did know; if she decided to go through with this decision, I couldn't confidently say we would survive this.

And we didn't survive it.

We drifted apart.

We finished up at Cal Poly. Graduated. Came home. And I immediately put some distance between us, asking for a break to figure it all out.

I think I already knew it wouldn't happen.

Marriage.

I prayed. I even fasted.

Bringing myself to officially end things was the difficult part.

So, I consulted with the three people I knew wouldn't steer me wrong.

"You know son, there's no easy way to let her down but there is a respectable way. This is a woman you deeply cared about once upon a time," Daddy said.

I nodded. "I still care for her."

Mommy said, "Please be gentle with her. Do not do this in a text message and not over the phone. Meet her and tell her. You owe her that much."

"No one should marry someone they are not one hundred percent sure about. As much as I hate to say this, it sounds like she isn't the one. For you that is. If you're questioning things you can't work through, you certainly aren't the one for her. She deserves a man who would marry her with no hesitation." That was Mal.

***

After driving aimlessly, I exited Elk Grove Boulevard, arriving at Elk Grove Regional Park.

The park is huge, more than a hundred acres. It's a nice family park, and I've been here many times over the years. Lots of birthday parties. Family barbeques. Little league Baseball games. Music festivals.

A Saturday afternoon in July was a great day to spend at a park like this. There was a big city pool. Mature trees offering lots of shade. I could see people packing up and headed home after what I'm sure was a great day making even greater memories.

There was a miles long walking trail that weaved through the park. It had a lit path at night and quite a few people were walking along the trail. After pulling into a parking space, I shut off my car and I sat for a moment watching people come and go.

A small bridge straight ahead came into view. I sighed.

This was the very place Ayesha, and I met when I'd made the decision to walk away from her.

I guess now I had some idea of how Ayesha must have felt that day.

I arrived promptly at the appointed place and time. Ayesha was already waiting and spotted me as I made my way to her.

She was leaning against the railing of the small bridge that went across the lake.

She smiled brightly. I returned a smile and as I approached her, I knew she could see my smile didn't reach my eyes.

"Hey." I reached in for a hug.

"Hey."

We walked along the lake in silence. I suppose neither of us were sure what to say.

I hated this shit.

We'd been on a break for the past few weeks and today was the day I needed to officially end everything.

I knew this would crush her.

But I was here for one reason only and I didn't want to delay things any further.

I just wasn't sure how to begin.

"How are you?" I asked after a while.

"You kidding?!" Ayesha stopped walking to face me. "Micah, I've been a mess lately. Beside myself. I should be the happiest woman in the world, knowing in a few months I'll be marrying the love of my life. But instead, I've been consumed with... this uncertainty. I thought you loved me." She hung her head in defeat.

I stepped closer and gently lifted her chin. "Ayesha. You're an amazing woman. I fell in love with you for so many reasons. Your kind spirit. Your sweet nature. Your heart for children. Your passion for equitable health. You're smart. You're pretty." The corner of my lips lifted, and she smiled weakly. "I'll always love you. But...I can't marry you."

I saw the warmth leave her eyes.

"Is there someone else Micah?"

"No there isn't."

"Well...do you need more time? We can push back the wedding," her tone was hopeful.

My gaze fell away from hers as I sighed, "I don't need more time. I want to end this. Here."

"So that's it?" She yelped on the verge of tears. "How could you do this to me!" she belted when I didn't answer. She hung her head, covering her eyes as she wept audibly and uncontrollably. I went to wrap her in my arms to console her, and she snatched away from me. "Micah don't touch me!"

"Ayesha, I'm sorry."

"Micah, I can't believe you!" She managed through her tears. She pushed past me, but not before roughly forcing her ring back into my hand. I hadn't even noticed when she took it off.

She walked back toward the parking lot, and I followed her at a distance to ensure she made it to her car alright. I could still hear her crying and by now she was hysterical. I watched as she put her car in reverse and slowly drove away.

I'd never felt as low as I felt in that moment.

I hated myself for the pain I caused her. I looked down at the ring and chucked it into the water. Then, I continued along the path surrounding the lake with my hands in my pockets. I had nowhere else to be, so I took the time alone to process my thoughts.

I knew I'd broken her heart, and it tore me up inside.

But just the same, my heart was broken for another reason entirely.

She'd killed our baby.

This was one detail I hadn't told anyone. But I knew I needed to let her go if I couldn't move past that. She didn't deserve having her decision held over her head. Least of all, entering a marriage where I held that against her.

Ayesha deserved a man who would love her unconditionally.

A man who would move heaven and earth for her.

I prayed sincerely they found each other soon, and she could forget about how much I hurt her.

One random afternoon after a handful of years, Mommy told me she saw Ayesha's mom out shopping, and they spoke briefly.

Ayesha had gotten married and had two daughters. I was genuinely happy to hear she'd been doing so well. But that was the last I heard. I never bothered to keep tabs on her after that.

I felt that it was for the best.

twenty-three

DESTINEY

"Would you like children, Destiney baby? I'd love to create life with you. If that's what you want to do."

"I absolutely would."

"Would you?"

"Yeah."

"Indeed. If it were up to me…I'd love a son first."

"Oh yeah?"

"Yeah. That way, whoever came next will have a big brother looking out for them."

"Hmm. I like that! I never had a brother. Big brothers seem so cool to have."

"For sure! I can confirm it's as cool as it seems."

"Yeah. Then we'll need one more… boy or girl, it wouldn't matter. But our son will need a partner in crime."

"Oh, for sure! I need Mal. I'll always need my brother."

"I hear you. I need Daijah. I don't know what I'd do without her."

***

I woke up early the next morning, feeling exhausted. The events from the night before played on a loop in my head. I was drained. Physically and mentally.

I hardly slept. Since I'd had the blood transfusion and needed to be frequently monitored, the nurses came in several times. To that end, I was also trying to process my new reality, and I'd been crying nonstop.

I noticed Daijah in the chair across from me, knocked out. She probably hadn't slept well either.

I was so angry at her yesterday when Micah walked in, but I knew she was only trying to help cheer me up. I reluctantly admitted to her that I'd been avoiding him. She was furious with me. Saying I was being irrational and ridiculous. Quickly, she realized how much I missed him. She also knew I wouldn't have called him myself. I felt terrible for the way I spoke to her.

I felt even worse for the way I spoke to Micah.

I'll never forget the sadness in his eyes when I demanded he leave. He was trying to be here for me and support me, and I pushed him away.

The shocker was when he spoke those three words.

For the briefest of moments, I felt that maybe, just maybe, everything could be okay.

It would be okay.

With Micah, love seemed to be enough. The way he made me feel left me without a doubt that it would. But... he would only be settling with me.

But he loves me.

I love him too.

It was so soon. But there was no way I could control that.

We'd been acquainted all of about four months. Saw each other three times, counting our initial introduction. Actually, I counted four times, including yesterday.

We weren't even officially *us*. Definitely friends. Close friends. But Micah wasn't officially my man. I wasn't officially his woman. Though in my head, we were. Micah didn't make me feel any less than his. We never had that conversation, and establishing things crossed my mind a couple of times over the course of what we were doing, which was basically talking.

We talked night after night, but it was never mundane. Ever. We did so much more than talk. So many topics were uncovered. No subject was off limits. And we got right to it.

Conversing. Musing. Discussing. Debating. Analyzing. Commentating.

Articulating. Reflecting. Joking. Laughing.

Shooting the breeze.

Learning *from* and *about*.

Teaching *to* and *about*.

Mastering each other's idiosyncrasies.

Getting all caught up in one another.

So caught up that we messed around and fell in love.

Wild.

Guess none of that mattered now anyway.

I would likely never get to tell Micah I love him, too. That made all of this so much worse.

As awful as I felt, I tried convincing myself that this was best. In a matter of hours, I will have a total hysterectomy. I would never be able to give him any children.

Micah made it clear from the beginning that he wanted a wife and children. Meeting Micah made me realize I wanted that too, and children came up often during our talks.

We'd somewhat unofficially decided that two children would be the perfect number.

I couldn't expect Micah to be with me if he wanted children I couldn't give him.

Glancing at my cell phone, I saw it was nearly seven a.m. My father would be here soon since my procedure was scheduled for nine a.m.

I glanced at my phone again, for the umpteenth time. Despite everything I'd said to Micah, I held a glimmer of hope that I would hear from him. I had no new notifications, so I laid back, closing my eyes.

Each morning began with a good morning text, and our conversation would continue throughout the day. I wanted to text him, but I felt awkward and embarrassed after what I said last night. I couldn't simply reach out as if nothing ever happened. After analyzing my behavior, I knew that my emotions had been all over the place, and I'd made the mistake of reacting in the thick of it all.

Now, here I sat, covered with a heavy cloud of remorse and regret. The shit was suffocating.

I wish I hadn't told Micah to leave.

I really wish I hadn't told Micah to move on.

A nurse came in—a different one than last night.

"Good morning, Destiney," she said warmly. "I'm Trisha, your new nurse. Your night nurse is off shift. I'm going to check all your vitals, and then in about an hour, we will get you prepped for your surgery, alright?"

I nodded silently as I felt tears welling up again.

I was only twenty-seven years old. I couldn't believe I would lose the ability to carry children.

I don't even remember passing out.

My mind went to India.

I learned that India came searching for me when I hadn't returned for a while. Once they called an ambulance, India called Daijah. India came to the hospital yesterday when I first arrived, but she couldn't stay long because she needed to get back to her parents.

I sent her a text message.

Good morning, Indie. Thanks again for having my back

As the nurse finished and headed out, I glanced at Daijah. She was still asleep. There was so much commotion as the nurses came in and out pulling their cart through that loud ass door. I was surprised it didn't wake her. Daijah had to be exhausted, but I was eager for her to wake up. I needed to apologize to her. Last night my stubborn ass had an attitude with her even after she told me something selfless and beautiful.

"Des, if you can't have babies, I'll just have babies for the both of us. I'll be your surrogate as soon as you and Micah are ready. And we'll raise our babies close. Just as close as we are."

When she mentioned Micah, I grimaced, though she couldn't see.

Daijah and I had our heated exchange just before her declaration, and by then, I had turned away from her.

Of course, she hadn't a clue that everything with Micah and I had gone-to-shit.

Who knew what the future would hold, but I didn't even thank her for the offer.

It was bad enough; my pathetic ass wouldn't even look at her.

I saw my phone illuminate and grabbed it quickly, hoping it was Micah. It was India.

Indie the Bestie: I love you and I'll always have your back. See you later this afternoon

Leave it to India to bring positivity to a fucked-up situation. I smiled despite the disarray I felt surrounding me.

I returned my phone to the table beside me, quickly dozing off again...

***

"Good morning, Daijah."

"Good morning," she returned flatly and expressionless as she folded her blanket and began straightening up the corner she had slept in.

I woke up about fifteen minutes ago. My nurse had just returned to tell me they'd start my prep. My father called me a moment ago, letting me know he was here and parking and that he'd be up soon.

"Thanks for staying with me. You sleep okay?"

"Sure. And I slept as best as I could sleeping in a chair." She placed the folded blanket in the closet. "I'm headed down for a cup of coffee and need to call Julian. I'll be back."

Daijah made her way across the room and was almost out the door before I said, "Daijah… wait." She halted and slowly turned to face me. "I'm so sorry about last night. I was mean to you, and you didn't deserve that." I let tears fall from my eyes. "You're my best friend. I can't believe I let my emotions lead. I'm so sorry. I've been praying, and if this is God's plan for me, then so be it. It could have been worse. I was thinking, what if I had passed out while I was driving? I could have killed someone."

"Or yourself."

"Yeah."

"But you didn't. You still have your life and so much to look forward to. You won't have to deal with these fibroids anymore, and you'll be back to feeling better soon." Daijah came to my bed and hugged me warmly. "All is forgiven. I love you, Des."

"I love you too Day."

"Let me go call Julian. Have you already talked to Micah?"

"No, I haven't."

She returned a quizzical expression.

"I can't call him after the way I spoke to him yesterday."

She sighed. "Just tell him you're sorry. You've been through so much in the past twenty-four hours. I'm sure he'll understand."

"I can't. Yesterday, I told him to move on... I broke things off with him."

"You did what?!" Daijah gasped in surprise. *"Why?!"*

"When I found out about the surgery, I figured he's better off without me. Micah wants children Day. In case you forgot, I won't be able to have any in just a few hours. My lady parts will be taken from me, and I'll resemble a fucking blown out cave." I laughed despite it all. Maybe to delay the inevitable tears.

"Des, Micah cares about you. Have you talked about it? Do you even know if that's a deal breaker?"

"He's tired of me." I sighed, deciding to evade the question.

"Here's an idea; start with *I'm sorry.*"

I shook my head. "Then what? I still can't give him what he wants. I need to leave him alone. It's better this way." I didn't truly believe that. But I was trying to convince myself it was. I cried softly as Daijah sat on the edge of the bed holding me in her arms.

"Ssshhh. Don't think about it right now. Once we get you home, we can talk this over more."

I continued crying into Daijah's shoulder. I'd cried so much I was surprised I still had tears left.

I got the feeling that Micah and I were *officially* finished.

That had the waterworks going full blast.

twenty-four

MICAH

It was after eleven when I woke up for a second time. I had been up since seven this morning although I didn't sleep much at all last night. Of course, my mind was on Destiney heavy.

I almost texted her out of impulse.

We both normally greeted each other with a good morning text. Most mornings we would have a minute to talk after we got our day going. We would text back and forth all day long and in the evening, we would end our night talking for hours until Destiney was falling asleep on me.

Just one day off that routine threw me off kilter.

Emotionally, I was in shambles.

A mess.

I was heartbroken. Simple as that.

This was the most heartache I've ever felt in my life.

Interestingly, I didn't feel this way when things ended with Ayesha. Not even close.

But I imagine that's how she must have felt. I'll never forget the sound of her cries as she walked back to her car that day at the lake. Especially since it was all because of me.

There was something else, too; I didn't like the fact that I seemingly compared these moments with Destiney to the parallels I had with Ayesha. But somehow, albeit subconsciously, I still found myself doing it. It occurred to me that maybe it was happening because that was my only other serious relationship and therefore my only point of reference.

Either way I didn't like that shit.

These were two very different women. Two completely different relationships, with polar opposite dynamics. And I've changed. I've matured of course, but beyond that, I was in a place where my decisions were made consciously and with foresight. Back in college I can't say I was thinking my present decisions would have an impact on my life five, ten or fifteen years from now.

I threw my legs to the side of the bed, but I didn't get up for a while. Just sat there. Thinking.

I glanced at my phone again. I expected to hear from Daijah shortly. Destiney would probably be out of surgery in the next hour if she wasn't already out. Daijah texted me this morning as promised after they'd taken Destiney back. She said the surgery was expected to last up to three hours. Daijah, Julian, and her father planned to stay there most of the day and her friend India would be staying the night since Daijah stayed last night. I offered to have a meal delivered but she assured me Julian would be taking care of them.

Julian seemed to be a chill dude. I would have loved to converse with him more and I would have under different circumstances. Hopefully we'll cross paths again.

That was solely based on how Destiney chose to move.

When I woke up earlier at seven, I got the feeling Destiney's mind was in shambles, just like mine. I would have loved to comfort her, but she didn't want me. I was hoping she would text me just to open that door, but that was too hopeful. I said a prayer for her and sent her positive thoughts anyway.

Even still, I cared for her so much. She was crazy if she thought I would just move on with a flip of a switch, simply because she asked me to.

I love Destiney.

I knew I did for a while.

Whether she could carry my children or not made no difference to me. I still want her. She's my wife and being forced away from her had me quickly becoming unraveled.

We hadn't experienced each other yet sexually but I already knew she was the woman I wanted. Just in these past few hours I was becoming a shell of myself pinning after her.

I glanced at my cell. Again. Somehow, I missed the notification of a missed call from Daddy. I also had a couple unread messages from Solomon. He was likely responding to my messages from last night. I'll check in with him later.

I called my old man but got his voicemail, so I called Mommy. She was likely the one calling me from his phone anyway. She used dad's phone more than her own. Mommy's cell phone was hardly charged half the time because she used it so infrequently. If I didn't reach her on her cell, I would call the house phone. My parents still had the house phone connected with the same phone number since Mal and I were in middle school.

I called Mommy's cell and surprisingly she answered.
"Micah Bear!"
"Good morning, Mommy. How are you?"
"It's a great morning! How are you son?"
"I'm alright Mommy." I tried my damndest to hide the sorrow in my voice. I likely failed miserably though. She was quiet for a moment which let me know she knew I wasn't being honest. And I was grateful she didn't press. But knowing her, she would bring it up again. "Is Daddy nearby? I missed his call this morning."

"He's down at the church for the men's coffee and bible study." My parents still attended the church we grew up in. Daddy had been a deacon there for many years. Now that he was retired, he had more time to participate in the various men's fellowships. They met for a coffee, prayer and bible study a few times a month and he seemed to enjoy attending.

"Come by today when you can. By the time you get here maybe I'll remember whatever it was we needed." Mommy laughed and I did too.

"I'll likely go to the store before I head that way. Need anything?"

"How about a few lemons? I have a taste for lemon pound cake."

I smiled at that. Mommy knew exactly how to cheer me up.

Her lemon pound cake was delectable. She captured a true lemon flavor that was so delicious. Her secret was to use fresh lemons. The fresh squeezed lemon juice made a lemon glaze that was incredible. She used extract whenever she was in a pinch but not often. Her presentation alone was award winning; that beautiful citrusy perfection looked too good to eat with the lemon zest sprinkled on top. Her lemon pound cake was my very favorite dessert of hers.

"You're the best."

"I do okay." Mommy tossed back laughing.

"See you in about an hour."

"I'll be here, my Micah Bear."

***

"More?" Mommy asked, gesturing toward my now empty bowl sitting in front of me.

I'd just finished my second serving of pot roast, with red potatoes and carrots. It was seasoned perfectly, tender and so delicious. Daddy was still at the church, but we expected him home any minute now. "No thank you. I've had plenty. Plus, I don't want to eat all Daddy's food," I said through a chuckle.

"Oh nonsense! He'll be fine. There's always plenty," Mommy assured me, but I already knew.

My mother was an excellent cook and kept the three men of her life fed past satisfaction. As early as I can remember, there was always a warm meal for us on the table. Always a freshly baked cake or pie to go with it. Our friends wanted to come by just to get a taste of something Mommy cooked. And there was always plenty to go around. None of them were turned away. Ever.

"I can't take another bite Mommy." I was beyond full, and I made it a point not to do that often.

"I'll pack some up for you."

There was no reason for me to argue. Mommy wasn't going to hear any of it.

We both stood from the table at the same time, she made her way to the stove, and I headed to the sink to wash the few dishes in there along with the bowl, spoon and glass I used.

"Hmm! Looks great!" I peered over my shoulder as Mommy removed the pound cake from the oven placing it on the cooling rack. "I'll let this cool off and I'll get started on my glaze in a little while."

"Yum. It smells even better. I need to let this food go down before I can eat anything else." We both laughed.

Mommy moved in beside me at the sink, rinsing the dishes I'd washed, placing them in the dishrack to dry.

"So, who is she? Tell me about her."

My movements instantly stilled, and I slowly looked over at Mommy.

She was already looking at me, smiling expectantly. Eyebrows high. Warmth in her eyes.

My mouth opened slowly but I couldn't find my voice. I pressed my lips together, quickly opening them again. "How did... what are you talking about?"

"*Micah Bear.*" She gave me a knowing expression. "Only a woman would have you behaving this way."

My jar dropped. "What way?"

"I know you. *Someone* has your heart," she said gently. There was still a smile there too.

I was heartbroken at the moment, but I smiled too anyway. I couldn't help it if I tried. That was the effect Destiney had on me.

"When did you plan on telling me about your sweetheart?" This was a legitimate question, and I wanted to tell Mommy about Destiney a long time ago.

I sighed, "Well... that's complicated."

"Complicated how?"

I proceeded to telling Mommy everything. From meeting Destiney back at Walgreens, to our nightly conversations.

How amazing she is.

How beautiful she is.

I confirmed her suspicions, telling her I'm in love with Destiney. And she listened intently.

Then I told her what happened just yesterday.

"Try to imagine where she's coming from. She's been bleeding on and off. Lost so much blood she goes unconscious. Wakes up in a hospital. Gets the news she's having an emergency surgery. A surgery that will leave her unable to bear children. My mind would be in disarray too, I can't even imagine."

I could appreciate all of that. I understood.

Mommy continued, "She may have been saying things she didn't mean in the heat of the moment. Sometimes we hurt the people closest to us just because of proximity. It isn't always personal." I continued to wash, and she continued to rinse. "You know Micah, I don't think she really meant that. To end things. She probably misses you and needs you but doesn't know how to say so. Especially now. She's made a mess of everything and probably doesn't know how to fix it."

"Mommy… I get it. But I'm starting to lose it. It's like we're going in circles. We take a few steps forward only to go backwards. She keeps pushing me away from her and I keep coming back expecting things will be different. As much as I want them to be, maybe she doesn't know how to handle this. She's never been in a committed relationship. She hasn't entertained a man beyond surface level conversation in years... she's also nearly a decade younger than me. What if we can't figure this out?"

"But son, what if you *can*? The two of you care a great deal for each other. That much is obvious. Give her some space. Some time. For now."

I nodded but I said nothing. I finished washing the dishes and now I was leaning back against the counter. Pondering everything Mommy was telling me.

"At some point you'll need to have a conversation. To find out what she needs from you to make this work. And you tell her what *you* need."

"What if we can't give each other what we need?"

"Then you part ways. But at least you discussed it. You don't want to go through the rest of your life wondering 'what if'."

I nodded. *That*, I could agree with.

twenty-five

DESTINEY

"Everything, everything Princess?"

I was visiting my dad at the house Daijah, and I grew up in. My dad and I were sitting in the backyard under a big tree. I found out just a few years ago, it was called a Blue Oak Tree. It was our favorite place to hang around when Daijah and I were little. It was huge. It had an expansive trunk, sturdy branches and lush leaves. Had the best shade. We loved to climb it. Bravely venturing as high as we could go until we were too afraid to go any further. Climbing down again.

My dad built us a playhouse right beside it. Now there was a hammock in its place, perfect to lounge in on a warm day like this one.

I leaned my head on my dad's shoulder as we ate our popsicles. "Yeah. Everything is everything."

"Good, good. How was your appointment?"

I had an appointment this morning. Six weeks post-op and I'd finally been cleared by my doctor. I'd still need to take things easy in general. I planned to go back to work in a few days. No heavy lifting for a while longer. No strenuous activity.

Slowly but surely, I'd ease back into my pre-surgery routine. I was cleared to drive again, which I was very excited about. It wasn't as if I had too many places to be as of late, aside from my appointments. Daijah and India were giving me rides whenever I wanted to go somewhere. I appreciated them for it. Immensely, but there's nothing like your own independence.

Speaking of surgery, instead of a hysterectomy I had an abdominal myomectomy. There were a number of fibroids, some larger than four centimeters, relatively large considering, but they were able to successfully remove them all. Still leaving my lady parts intact. I would continue to get a menstrual cycle and though I had a leery feeling about still getting a period, I could live with that. My doctor would keep an eye on everything as I continued to follow up with her.

All in all, I had a smooth speedy recovery. I already felt so much better. My energy was returning to normal. I wasn't in pain. I felt like a brand new me. The best part of all, I can still have children. It was the best news I'd gotten in a long time.

"It went great! All cleared."

"That's great news princess! Thank God!"

"Yes. Thank God!"

"How's Micah doing?" My dad never formally met Micah, but by now he'd heard a good deal about him. There wasn't anything to report as of late. I think my dad figured we reconnected by now. A significant amount of time had passed. Six weeks to be exact.

"Not sure dad. Haven't talked to him."

My dad nodded. After a beat, "Can your dear old dad tell you something without upsetting you? I'm not choosing sides; I just want to share my thoughts."

That was something dad did a lot. With Daijah and me, he had a gentle approach whenever he wanted to express something he thought contrary to how we felt about the matter. Especially during our teenage years.

"Sure, dad."

"From what I can see, Micah has proven himself worthy of you." I sat up straight, urging him forward. "No one deserves you at your best if they aren't for you at your worst.

You were down pretty bad Princess. But Micah came running as soon as he heard. That man loves you. It's clear."

I nodded in agreement. And understanding. "He does. He told me so. I love him too, dad. Except he doesn't know that I do. Never told him." I shook my head, still dealing with the residuals of my shitty decision.

"What are you waiting on?"

I shrugged my shoulders in lieu of a verbal answer.

"If this man has proven himself worthy and he wants to be there for you, wants to be with you, let him. No reason to fight it."

I nodded, "I don't know if it's that simple."

"One way to find out. Call him."

I sighed, "Just like that?"

"Sure." Dad shook his head. "Must you kids insist on complicating everything?"

We both laughed. I guess he had a point there.

"Just give him a call. Have a conversation. Share your heart. Promise you'll think about it?"

"I promise dad."

"That's my baby girl." He leaned over and kissed my forehead. I giggled at the way his cold lips felt.

"Dad!" I screeched, wiping off the moisture he left on my forehead with the back of my hand.

He cracked up at that. "Thanks for having a popsicle with me, Princess."

I smiled big. "You're welcome."

I headed home shortly after my conversation with my dad. He lived about ten minutes from Daijah and me. Not far at all. Close enough for us to get to him quickly should he need us.

When the lease ends in a few months I've considered moving back home. Daijah would be moving in with Julian and there was no reason for dad and me both to live alone. He was getting older, and we were growing more protective of him.

We were all he had.

My mom passed away almost seventeen years ago, after an aggressive breast cancer ravaged her body. It all seemed to happen so quickly. I was ten years old; Daijah just nine.

I remember them telling us she was sick, and it seemed very quickly after that she was gone. It's still such a raw place for me, emotionally. I try not to think about it. Some days just visiting my childhood home is difficult for me. All these years later. My mother's memory is very present there. Daijah took her death pretty hard. She was incredibly close to our mother.

Anyway, it's one reason I don't speak of my mom as much. I like to think of her as away on a trip somewhere. It's my way of coping. I've gotten ridicule for that, but I don't care. When I speak of her, especially to someone unaware, I have to acknowledge she's no longer here. Physically. And I have to speak of her in past tense. I don't like to do that.

And my dad. He's my hero.

As cliché as it sounds, he really is. I always admired the strength he had, raising Diajah and me while extremely heartbroken. He and my mom were high school sweethearts. Together since they were fourteen. I was so young when it all happened, some of it is a blur. But I remember hearing his cries from our bedroom. Late into the night when he thought we were sleeping. That went on for years.

I can remember the women who tried to come in and play on my dad's heartbreak and vulnerability. They seemed to come out of the woodwork.

From all directions.

The women at our school, or at our church. Single moms of kids on our volleyball team, or girl scout troop. Those women had no chill. Swooped in and tried their hand when he wasn't even emotionally available. Trying to convince my dad of all the reasons why he needed them. Impressing upon him why he needed to move on. Tried to persuade him that marrying them was a good idea and insisting we needed a mom. Especially once we arrived at pubescence.

But my dad wasn't interested. Not even a little bit. No one could get close enough. His sole concern was Daijah and me.

Once I got home, I hung out on my bed. Thinking about everything my dad said. He approved of Micah. Site unseen. I couldn't blame him. Micah was everything. And I missed him so much.

We still hadn't spoken. Or seen each other.

When I learned I could still have children, all I could do was thank God. I was so grateful. Beyond words. I cried. And I felt like this was a sign. Confirmation that maybe Micah and I could still possibly work things out.

My next dilemma was figuring out the best way to approach him. I wanted him back. Desperately. I worried that each passing day I didn't reach out, my chances of reconciliation were dwindling.

And I didn't know how I would go about doing it but I was sure going to try.

I just hoped it wasn't too late.

So, it was the end of August now and summer was coming to an end.

I was over this heat. Been over this heat. Sacramento has very warm summers. So yeah. Over the summer and ready for fall. Fall is my favorite time of year. Fuzzy socks. Apple pie. Pumpkin flavor galore.

I couldn't wait.

I felt my phone vibrating beside me. It was a text from Indie.

Indie the Bestie: Yay!! We're going to hookah tonight. Need to celebrate your good news!!

After my appointment, I updated India, letting her know I was all good to go.

Hell yes!

Indie the Bestie: I know you're clear to drive but I'll pick you up. How's seven?

Perfect

Indie the Bestie: Daijah coming?

If we can get her from up under Julian LOL I'll ask. Probably will. We're so overdue for a girls night

I texted Day in the group chat, checking to see if she wanted to join Indie and me.

Sibling Bestie: I am there!! Plus Roni and Vic

Indie the Bestie: FUNNERS!!!!

I laughed at that, then I started my playlist.

Throwback slow jams were my go-to any day of the week. I got comfortable on my bed letting the smooth grooves of Avant mentally take me away. "Read your mind" was an oldie but goodie.

Micah could read my mind.

Damn. I couldn't help but think back to the intimate moments Micah and I shared. I thought about those a lot. I didn't need any music.

I missed him. So much. I missed our talks. His text messages. His voice in my ear. His laugh.

These six weeks I had been home recovering from my surgery, I felt like I was damn near on house arrest. And since

I couldn't do much aside from reading, and sketching; I was forced to sit with myself. Sit with my feelings. Face my lackluster decisions.

And I wasn't pleased at all with what I had done.

I wondered also if Micah missed me as much as I missed him. Or if he thought of me at all.

After what I did, from the beginning leading up to yelling at him forcing him away from me… I wouldn't be surprised if he told me to kick rocks.

But. I still hoped. Wished. Maybe, there was a chance we could be we. Us.

I wanted that so much. More than anything.

My mind began to wander thinking about things I probably shouldn't. Like, I thought about whether Micah was giving it to someone else now. I felt a tinge of something akin to jealously thinking about that. I tried to move on to something else.

For reasons I do not understand my thoughts ventured to my first sexual experience. Which I tried not to ever think about.

Normally I can keep those thoughts back. But today… I was no good. Thinking about my dad. Thinking about my mom. Thinking about Micah. Wondering if he was still thinking of me, or if he was on to someone else. Someone else more deserving.

My mind was a mess.

I'm so glad India and I would be going to smoke.

I needed to decompress.

But these fucking thoughts were so fucking loud.

I turned to my stomach pulling a pillow over my head. Trying in vain to block them out. It was past time I talked to someone about this. A professional. I should have a long ass time ago.

I wasn't raped, but I was pressured. Regardless it was an encounter I do not like to think about.

Daijah had been hanging out with this guy. Since Daijah and I did everything together, whenever I took Daijah to chill with him, I'd stay and chill too. We went often. A couple days a week at one point.

We always hung out at his apartment and had the place to ourselves. Daijah's guy was an only child with a single mom that worked two jobs. She was never home.

At the time I was seventeen and Daijah was sixteen. Anyway, Daijah's guy had a cousin that was always over whenever we came by to hang out. The more time Daijah and her guy spent together, the more his cousin and I saw of each other. He was seventeen too and he liked me. He asked me to be his girlfriend right away. He was cute I guess, so I considered it. The first time he asked I told him it was too soon. I didn't know him like that. As I got to know him, I wasn't interested in actually being with him. He asked me more than once. Saying shit like, *"I'm just wondering when you gone stop playing and be my girl."*

Obviously, I said no. His personality wasn't my type. But it was chill kicking it with him.

And he was a good kisser. Whenever Daijah and I went over, the cousin and I made out. Which was a mistake. I've had a damn decade to think back on that situation and I really shouldn't have been kissing him.

Once, Daijah and I were over, and the cousin and I had been making out for a while. Eventually we were dry humping. I could feel how hard he was through his jeans. I'd let him touch my boobs a couple times, but that was the extent of it. Before Daijah and I went home, he said something like, *"We won't be kissing forever."* I remember being confused, trying to figure out just what he meant by that. We'd never talked about having sex. Actually, we didn't talk much at all. Not that I would have agreed to that anyway. I was still a virgin. We were only kicking it, and that's all we were doing.

I should have ended everything right there.

But I didn't. And the very next time Daijah and I went there, things happened.

It started like all the others. The four of us hung out in the front for a while. After some time, he stood and put his hand out, silently asking me to follow him. That's when we'd go be alone, also giving Daijah and her guy time alone. I looked at Daijah, and she smiled at me. I smiled back then he led me down the hall to his cousin's bedroom. He lay on the bed and invited me to join him. I did, and we proceeded with our making out. At some point, he started going for the button on my jeans, and I stopped him.

"I just want to finger you."

I thought about it for a second. We'd never done that before, but I didn't see the harm in it. "You gotta wash your hands first."

He jumped off the bed with haste, going to wash them.

Once he returned, he made quick work of unbuttoning and unzipping my jeans, but I kept them on.

He didn't waste any time putting his hand inside and went straight for my center, moving my panties to the side. I was jolted in surprise when he quickly forced his pointer and middle fingers into me.

"Damn you wet. This shit sexy as a muthafucka." He pointed upward a few times and swirled and swiped his fingers around inside. *"I need to feel you for real."*

I pulled his arm out of my jeans. "You said you just wanted to finger me."

He gave me an incredulous glare. "We both damn near grown. People our age been past that."

My expression was blank. I was unsure of what to say. He had a point. I knew many people my age who were having sex already. However, since that day, I've thought of so many things I should have said. Should have done it. And I certainly could have walked out of that room. But I didn't have a handle on my voice back then. I look back with so much regret, which is one reason I don't like to think about that day. I would rather keep it compartmentalized and forgotten, buried deep in my brain.

He stood and began unbuckling his pants and pulled them down along with his boxers. "You got me so hard; I could shatter concrete. And you so wet because you want it." He retrieved a condom from his wallet in the pocket of his jeans. "Besides..." he returned to the bed, pulling my jeans over my hips. "... We at the point of no return now, baby. Can't stop something we done already started."

When it was all over, we both went back to the front. Daijah and her dude were watching Martin reruns.

He slapped hands with his cousin, and I concluded that was their unspoken way of confirming what we had just done.

I sat on the couch, trying to pretend like nothing had happened.

I was confused and angry, mostly with myself. I should have said no.

"Hey, Des, you good?" Daijah asked me.

"Yep," I returned as nonchalantly as I possibly could, through a forced smile.

Meanwhile, I tried to ignore the ache between my legs. He wasn't exactly forceful, but he was certainly not gentle. I took my phone out and busied myself absently scrolling. I decided at that moment that I wasn't going to tell Daijah.

I just didn't know how. Plus, I was embarrassed. And ashamed.

That was the first thing I ever kept from her, and I told her everything.

To this day, I still haven't told her.

I felt guilty for keeping something so significant from her and carried that guilt for a long time. I didn't talk to anyone about it. Daijah was my best friend, and if I couldn't tell her, who else was there? My dad would have murdered that asshole. I hid that away and never spoke of it again.

Ironically, we never went back to the apartment after that. Daijah's dude said his mom's work schedule had changed so he and Daijah hung out in public places like the mall and the movies and shit after that.

And I never saw his cousin again.

The cousin got what he wanted.

twenty-six

DESTINEY

We decided on Torch.

I haven't been here since my birthday weekend. I wanted to let some time go by before I came back, considering everything with Tyler, the owner.

But it was still my favorite hookah place. And I needed my Ragin' Cajun fries fix. I couldn't get them anywhere else.

Indie picked me up, and not long after we got settled in our section, Daijah and her besties, Veronica and Victoria, met us.

We put in orders for some drinks and a few appetizers and got two hookahs. We ordered two new flavors, and I was so juiced to try both of them.

The lounge was jumping with people tonight; the walls vibrated with music and chatter. I was glad we came in when we did. Had we waited just fifteen minutes later, we wouldn't have been able to get a hookah section. I heard our server telling someone there was already a wait.

The five of us were making small talk, and when we heard the distinctive bounce beat followed by Juvenile's intro *"Cash Money Records taking over for the 9-9 into 2000…"* everyone in the lounge went crazy. Including us. "Back That Azz Up" was a banger.

"We're going to dance. Y'all coming?" Daijah asked. She, Roni, and Vic had already stood up, making their way over.

"Yeah, we are! Come on Des!" India grabbed my hand, and we followed them. I usually don't dance on the floor, opting instead to groove to the music from my seat. India can dance her ass off. She and Daijah would usually go dancing, and I'd watch our drinks. But I didn't resist. Not this time. We'd barely put in our order moments before. It would be a while. Plus, this was a somewhat of a special occasion, and my girls turned out to celebrate with me.

I was trying to focus on enjoying myself. And I continued to remind myself that I certainly had a reason to, despite today being an emotional one, with Micah on my mind... heavy. I could dance with them to one song.

We stayed on the dance floor for two songs, then decided to head back, and I was glad. The dance floor was crowded. I was hoping our food and drinks would be out momentarily. I was already hungry, and now I was thirsty. And I wanted to smoke.

The entire lounge was dimly lit, and we were in a single file line as we returned to our section. Daijah was at the front, Roni and Vic were right behind her, and India was in front of me. I grabbed India's hand and followed her, holding up the rear.

We were off the floor and now near the back of the lounge where the hookah sections were. We were almost back to our seats when I heard my name being called. My name is distinct, and not many names sound like mine. So I'm certain I heard it.

Also, there aren't that many Destineys.

I heard it again; it was closer now and coming from behind me.

Shit. Maybe it was Tyler.

I squeezed Indie's hand, and she halted, instantly looking back.

"You okay?"

"Yeah, someone is calling me."

"Tyler?"

"I don't know," I still hadn't turned back to look behind me.

"You scared he's going to do something to you?

"No… I just don't feel like talking to him. But I guess I should get this over with. Clear the air."

"Well, I'm right here. You're good. Where is he? India looked over my head, which was easy for her; she was taller than me, even with my heels on.

I was still facing her and heard the voice again, directly behind me. And it wasn't Tyler.

Since the lounge was dimly lit, I took a moment to register the face standing right in front of me when I turned around.

The face spread into an easy smile. Decorated with two deep ass dimples.

Zeke.

"Destiney. *Wow*. So, it is you! I saw you out there dancing, and I thought I was seeing things." A smooth chuckle left his lips. "You never wanted to dance in front of people."

I shook my head laughing right along with him. "Yeah, I was outnumbered. Got dragged out there."

"Come here, girl. Give me a hug. You look great!"

I dropped India's hand, willingly falling into Zeke's open arms.

And he hugged me like I was a long-lost love he was finally reuniting with after walking thousands of miles.

Through a desert. Barefoot. With no water.

"So do you Zeke. Really." Rapidly shaking my head, I said, "My bad… You remember my best friend India, right?"

"Of course I do. Hey India. How are you?

I'd told India about Zeke. Everything.

And she was always telling *me* about *myself*. Seeing how I left things, everything went in one ear and out the other.

"I'm great. Good to see you Zeke." They gave each other a quick side-hug.

"So, you here with your boyfriend?" Zeke didn't waste any time. "Should I be looking over my shoulder?" He dramatically looked around, feigning fear.

I laughed. "No, I'm not. Just out with my girls."

"So, he's at the house waiting on you." It wasn't a question.

"No man to speak of. I'm single if that's what you're asking."

"Really?" His eyebrows high.

"Yeah. Wouldn't lie about that. Why?"

"I mean, come on Destiney. *You are beautiful,* for starters. Sweet as pie. *My Pie Sweetie.*" I giggled at the nickname he gave me. A silly giggle that turned into a light chuckle and eventually a deep belly laugh.

I hadn't been laughing much. Not lately. And it felt good to laugh again.

I still remember Zeke saying I was his *Pie Sweetie.* Telling me, *"No one was as sweet as me, and that was the only thing fitting since Sweetie Pie was already played out".*

Wow. I totally forgot about that.

"Des, I'm going to sit down," India said as she returned to our section.

"Okay. I'm right behind you." That quickly, I forgot India was standing there. "It was so nice seeing you again, Zeke," I said, starting to follow India.

Zeke grabbed my hand. "Destiney, wait." I looked down at our connection, quickly looking back up at him.

He released my hand as quickly as he had grabbed it. "I apologize. I didn't mean to grab you… so suddenly."

"It's okay." I gave him a warm smile. He was always a gentleman.

"Can I talk to you a while longer? Please."

I thought about that. I guess it was okay. After the way I left him hanging, I felt that I owed him some kind of explanation. "Sure." I turned around, and India was almost back to our table. I caught up with her, telling her I'd be talking to Zeke and I'd be back shortly.

"Let's head this way. It's a little quieter." Zeke led me to one of the bars furthest from the dance floor and closer to the entrance. It was much quieter. And a lot less crowded.

He found us two seats and stepped aside as I moved in front of him to sit down.

"Can I get you anything?" He asked, sitting down and turning to face me.

I shook my head. "No thanks. I have a drink waiting for me."

He nodded, smiling. His dimples were on full display again. I was always a sucker for Zeke's dimples. "Still one-and-done pie sweetie?"

"Yeah," I wore a smile too. "One is still plenty for me."

His smile remained as he looked me over.

Checking me out.

I could tell that's what he was doing. Guys aren't so subtle with that. He had no clue that I was looking him over, too. He wouldn't either, unless I told him.

He was dressed casually in dark washed jeans and a polo shirt. J's on his feet. Still rocking a goatee. He always kept it trimmed and neat. Low cut fade with a little more at the top. He smelled nice too. Fresh like body wash with a tasteful splash of cologne.

"Your locs are *gorgeous*. At your waist now."

"Thank you, Zeke." I last saw Zeke two years ago, and they were long, but they certainly weren't this long. He always loved my locs, too.

He nodded. "You're welcome." Then, "I'm liking your whole get down." He nodded toward me, moving his head down, then up again. "You look amazing."

I was wearing a sage green, one-shoulder body-con dress. It was slightly ruched and stopped just above my knee. My tan peep-toe booties had three-inch heels, giving me some height and a little pep in my step. I felt good about coming out tonight and wanted to look even better. It was sweet to hear Zeke approve. I didn't need it, but just the same, it was nice to hear.

"You look great, too," I told him genuinely.

"Thank you."

"You're very welcome. So," I sighed deeply. "I'm surprised you're being so nice to me. I mean. I didn't exactly say goodbye properly." I'm not even sure why I said that. But it was out there now. No taking it back.

"Honestly Destiney… I let that go. Initially, I figured you needed space. But even after I gave it to you, I didn't hear from you. I kept my number the same. I thought maybe, eventually, you'd call me. But when you didn't, I figured it just wasn't our time." He shrugged. "I thought someday maybe we'd cross paths again. I've searched for you."

My eyes grew wide. My mouth was agape. I quickly closed it, realizing how ridiculous I must have looked. "You searched for me?"

"Yeah. I mean, social media. I found you, but you aren't active there. I let it go, leaving the rest to the universe. Whenever I passed a mural, I thought of you."

Damn.

"Zeke… I…" I shook my head. "Please don't tell me you put your whole life on hold for me."

He chuckled. "What if I said I did?"

I rapidly shook my head at that. "No. That's... Zeke. You're a great guy. You'd make someone so happy."

"Tried that." He shrugged. "It didn't work. But we got a little one out of the deal."

My eyes went up in surprise. *"You're a dad?"*

"I'm a dad. A little girl." He lightly chuckled, nodding.

"That's so sweet. Can I see pictures?"

He pulled out his phone and handed it to me after a few quick swipes. It was a candid shot. The sweetest pair of eyes were filled with so much happiness. No idea how her mom looked, but she definitely favored Zeke. She had his dimples and his copper skin, hers shining like a brand-new penny.

"She's beautiful."

"Thank you."

"What's her name?

"Eden."

"Oh my gosh. That's perfect for her. She's adorable." I handed Zeke his phone back.

"She's almost a year and half. After you, I… seriously, I tried to wait for you. Then I tried to move on." He shook his head. "And it wasn't fair to her—my daughter's mother. I couldn't really give her myself fully because you were in the back of my mind. I had to be honest with her. And myself. It wasn't... I'm not blaming you, Destiney. It just wasn't meant to be. And she's a great mother. A great woman." He sighed lightly. "I'm just doing the single dad thing for now."

I nodded. "I get it. I'm sure you're a great father, Zeke. Eden is so lucky."

He smiled at that.

We chatted for another few moments. Then I told him I needed to get back to my girls. I came here with them and didn't want to abandon them.

Before we parted ways, Zeke asked for my phone number.

And I gave it to him.

He asked if I'd be up for hanging out. Trying again.

I said, sure for some reason.

At that moment, it didn't seem like a big deal. It was nice catching up. I guess I got wrapped up in it all.

But now, I don't know.

India told me how she felt. Right away. As soon as I sat back down. Couldn't even get comfortable before she felt compelled to share how she felt.

"Zeke is cool and all, but I'm team Micah." She shrugged, taking a sip from her straw. "Sorry."

I sighed. My fries were cold. My drink was watery.

"Hey, Des. *Nice of you to join us*. And I'm team Micah too," Daijah said, pulling from the hookah closest to her.

I shook my head.

And meanwhile, Vic and Roni were cracking up.

The twins were solid. Daijah met Roni in beauty college years back, and they were fast friends, even securing an apprenticeship at the same hair salon.

I was cool with Roni from the second I met her. Her twin was just as dope. Daijah calls them both her best friends, but she's a little closer to Roni.

"I hear you've been plain ole miserable, Des. When you gone call that man?" Victoria asked. She was pulling from the other hookah.

Since Vic was sitting immediately to my left, I beckoned for the pipe. I needed to hit this shit and calm my damn nerves.

I took a deep pull. "Vic. Micah hasn't even texted me," I offered. I knew it was bullshit. "I like this one." I took another pull. It was a sweet citrus blend.

"Me too!" Veronica offered. "It's called Ambrosia Fruit Salad."

"Roni, she's trying to change the subject!" Daijah snapped. "Des, you told him to move on. He's respecting your wishes. That isn't fair, and you know it."

"*Girl, really?*" Roni was cracking up.

"How does he even know I'm alive?"

They all peered at me, deadpan.

"He knows you're alive. Stop it." India sneered.

"I'm a complicated person," I whined, shaking my head. "Can I try that one, Indie?" When she silently passed me the pipe, I asked, "Are you mad at me, Indie?" I took a deep pull, closing my eyes. This one was bomb too—a cross between a lemon lime soda and a watermelon jolly rancher.

"Pirate's Cave," Vic supplied.

I took another pull. I liked it a lot but liked the Ambrosia fruit salad a little more. That was a mix of orange, cherry, pineapple, marshmallow, and coconut. I think I have a new favorite.

Opening my eyes, I looked up to find Daijah and India peering at me. They both looked at me for a long time.

"Why are you making this so damn complicated, Des?" That was Indie.

I returned a blank expression. "I don't know."

"Falling in love is a natural thing like *breathing, and pissing*. Resisting it and fighting it like you're doing is not normal! He's not the forbidden fruit or some shit. He loves you back!" Daijah was furious with me. "Don't let this slip through your fingers. You'll never forgive yourself. I won't forgive your crazy ass either." She shook her head and returned to a basket of chips and guacamole.

"I'm not like these other women. I'm complicated. Weird." I sighed, sipping my drink. It tasted like juice since all the ice had melted.

"He doesn't want to change a damn thing about you Des. He loves you just like that. Has he not shown you?" India pressed.

"He has… I just. Maybe I'm stalling. Trying to delay the inevitable. For a woman like me, it wouldn't last. I don't know anything about relationships. I'm still trying to figure my life out. I'm not sophisticated. Micah's older. Established." I looked up, realizing they were all peering back at me again. Daijah and India clearly annoyed.

"The fuck are you even talking about? You are a beautiful queen. Classy, regal, feminine. Men love that. You need to stay out of your head." That was India talking.

"I feel like such a fucking contradiction. He makes me feel safe and open and free to be myself. He loves everything about me. I've never had that before."

"Then let it be Des. Just let it be. *Please let it be*," Daijah sighed, rolling her eyes.

"Don't think about it, just feel it. Love is a natural thing and you're fucking it up worrying," Roni offered taking another pull.

"You deserve happiness. And he does too," Vic said.

"Go get your man sissy," Daijah said through an exasperated sigh.

"*She absolutely will*. I got her from here," Indie said. "The jig is up."

twenty-seven

MICAH

It had been almost two months since the day Destiney broke things off with me.

I hadn't tried to call her, and she hadn't called me either.

I constantly thought of her though, as usual. This time, though, it was from afar. I missed her so much. I wondered if we'd ever have a conversation, for at least the sake of closure.

But I wanted her. I wanted to marry her. And I wanted a child with her.

Only her.

Desperately, I think.

I wanted to tell Destiney that we could explore other paths to parenthood. Blood relations and biology wouldn't make any difference. It wouldn't matter at all.

I thought about my conversation with Mommy right after everything happened. She raised some valid points. I was just conflicted on how I would go about it. And I thought about it. A great deal. It wasn't just as simple as reaching out to Destiney. It had been difficult not to, but I respected her wishes and left her alone.

I decided that if Destiney extended an olive branch and reached across the aisle, I would fight for us. If she opened that door, even slightly. But only then.

In between time, I tried to fall back into my routine. But I couldn't even remember what that was like. Destiney had become such an integral part of my life. I felt incomplete without her.

So, I filled my time with things to keep me busy. To stay distracted. Threw myself into work a little more. I hung out with Mal pretty heavy. And Solomon. And it was mostly working.

I talked to my boy Tyson yesterday. He's good people. We were roommates all four years in college, eventually getting an apartment off campus as upperclassmen.

Ty planned to come to Sac in a couple of weeks, and I looked forward to that. After we graduated, he moved back to San Jose, his hometown. San Jose is about three hours from here.

We've remained in touch over the years. Ty has some family here, and I always try to catch him whenever he comes to visit. I've gone to San Jose to catch a couple 49er's games at Levi's stadium and he's always a great host. Ty did really well for himself. He's an aircraft engineer by profession.

I reminisce about our college days now and then. We had some good times being knuckleheads. But we handled business. Made it out alive. Graduated.

When Ty met Laila, those two were crazy about each other. They clicked immediately, and their relationship blossomed just as beautifully as Ayesha's and mine. The four of us did everything together, always going on double dates.

Then Tyson and Laila got engaged.

Naturally, I followed suit, proposing to Ayesha. And it was a beautiful time until it wasn't.

When I broke things off with Ayesha, it created a delicate situation with Ty and Laila. Ayesha and Laila were friends. Ty was like a brother and one of my closest friends and my very best college friend. When everything was fresh, I was bound to see Ayesha whenever I made an appearance at anything Ty and Laila would be hosting. Oftentimes, I decided not to come at all to preserve the peace. Ty seemed to understand that.

About a year after we graduated, Ty and Laila got married. Their wedding was the last time I saw Ayesha. I hadn't seen her for a few months, and she looked beautiful. She was a bridesmaid. I was a groomsman. Thankfully, they didn't pair us. We kept it respectful, keeping our distance. We didn't speak.

Anyway, about six months ago, Ty and Laila separated. When I talked to him yesterday, he said they would likely be filing. Ty is pretty messed up behind that, and I understand. He mentioned possibly moving up to Sacramento at some point in the future, just for a change in scenery. I guess we'll see.

I'd been out and about most of the day and couldn't wait to get home, wash my ass and relax. I had three games to referee at the YMCA. Lately, I've been picking up additional games just to stay busy. Stay distracted.

Sometimes it didn't seem like the shit was working but...anyway. After leaving the Y, I went to Mal's to help him work on this deck. I was there for a few hours, and Ella fed me when I first arrived. When I left, it was just past five. I made a quick stop and ordered some dinner because I knew I wouldn't have the energy to cook anything once I made it home.

After paying for my order, I headed out to wait in the car for the curbside.

On my way back to the car, my phone vibrated. It was an unsaved phone number, but I recognized it. The same number had called me twice prior, and I hadn't answered. Whoever it was didn't leave a voicemail.

I started to silence the call, but I answered anyway. Maybe I'd finally find out who had been trying to get ahold of me.

"Hello?"

"Micah?"

I stopped abruptly in my tracks. I could never forget the sound of her voice.

Her soft, raspy voice was distinct, and I would always recognize it, regardless of the time passed.

"Ayesha."

"Hey… I know this is a surprise." She chuckled. "Do you have a second?"

Back when things were still fresh, I wondered what I'd say if I ever got the chance to speak to Ayesha again.

But that was before.

I was in a completely different headspace at that point. Today, right now… I was slightly uncomfortable with this; I'd much rather let sleeping dogs lie.

"Uh… yeah, I have a few minutes." I took the remaining steps to my car, then got inside. I placed the phone on the middle console beside me on speaker. Keeping my tone neutral, I said, "What's up? How are you?"

She sighed, and then there was a long pause. "I realize I'm likely the very last person you expected to hear from…" She paused again, and then I heard light whimpers and sniffling.

"Why are you crying?" I asked with care. Gingerly. I hoped everything was alright. When things ended between us, I wished her well, and I genuinely meant that.

She gathered herself then said, "Do you ever think about you and me? What we could have been?"

Wow! My eyes had to be bucked, my eyebrows high on my head. Sure, I had. Plenty of times. But sharing that with her likely wasn't best.

"Ayesha." That was all I could manage.

"Tell me," She pressed. "We had something so beautiful, Micah."

"I had," I revealed after a brief pause, "But that's fruitless for many reasons. Least of all, you're married. You belong to someone, Ayesha."

"Things aren't what they seem."

"How do you mean?"

"Well, for one, my husband and I are separated. I plan to file for divorce soon."

"What?"

"Moved out almost a year ago."

Wow. "I'd offer you sympathy, but somehow I don't think you need it." I used an ounce of sarcasm, but I was serious. Marriage was something I saw as sacred and ordained by God. I didn't speak ill of a person's marriage. Ever. It wasn't my place, and it wasn't my style.

"After things ended with us, I married right away. For all the wrong reasons. Partly out of spite because I was so angry and hurt. To that end, I ignored red flags and figured things would eventually get better. They didn't. They got worse. Much worse."

"Are you talking abuse, Ayesha?"

"Not physically, no. He was controlling and possessive. I couldn't work. My passion was nursing, and children and I never got the opportunity."

Shit. "Well, I'm happy you're free from that."

"Thank you. Me too. It was a dark time. Treacherous. But I overcame that. I have two little girls who mean the world to me. They make life worth living."

"Indeed." I heard my phone chime, and it was a picture of Ayesha with two Mini-Mes standing on either side of her. "My goodness! They are beautiful! It's like your same face three times." I let out a hearty chuckle.

I didn't say so, but Ayesha looked great herself. Still pretty. The years had been kind to her. I couldn't see the pain she'd described. That was a good thing.

She chuckled too, "Those are my babies. I couldn't deny them if I wanted to. Do you have children?"

"No… not yet. I'm the cool uncle, and it's a great gig."

"Of course you are!" I could hear the smile in her voice. After a beat, "For what it's worth, you'll make a great father when the time comes. You were so attentive. Sensitive and loving with me. Affectionate. No one has come close to the way you treated me. Cared for me. I figured out a long time ago the grass wasn't so green." As flattered as I was, I didn't know what to say. "I think back on those days all the time." She continued as an airy chuckle left her, "You were so good to me, Micah. Is there a possibility we could explore things again?"

I sighed, "Ayesha, you killed our child. *A child I wanted so much.* An innocent child I offered to raise all on my own. You made that decision without me. I realize it's your body and your right to choose, but I couldn't get past that."

She was silent. Then, "Micah… there's something you should know. I…I didn't have an abortion."

My breath caught in my throat.

"Wha…how is that possible? You had my baby and didn't tell me? Where are they?!" I pressed frantically.

"No, no. I didn't. I'm saying I never had an abortion because I didn't need to." After a heavy sigh, "I went back and forth on the decision for two weeks. By the time I went in, I was supposed to be twelve weeks along, but the baby had stopped developing at week nine. There was no heartbeat."

"Oh no… Ayesha…"

"Wild." She sighed, "I certainly didn't expect it to affect me the way it did. But I cried like a baby getting that news.

Funny huh? I couldn't even decide if I wanted them and had no clue the decision would be made for me." She chuckled. "Once it was confirmed that the pregnancy was no longer viable, they sent me home with a prescription to prepare my body to pass the pregnancy tissue."

"Wow."

"I had to decide between that or a procedure where they clean everything out. The irony is that's the same way abortions are done. In this case, our baby was long gone."

There was silence for a few beats.

"Were you alone?" I asked gently. So gentle that I hardly recognized my own voice.

"Yes, I was. But… I feel like I got what I deserved. I was so adamant that the life we created was an inconvenience for me that I ate those words when it was all said and done."

"You couldn't have told me this? I would have been there for you."

"It was another one of my bad decisions. You're absolutely right. I should have told you, Micah. And I'm sorry for springing all of this on you now. You didn't deserve the pain I caused you. You deserved the truth a long time ago."

She really had no clue. "I cried for our child just like you did," I shared. "I still think of them. All the time."

"I think of our child too, Micah—all the time. When I had my girls, I thought of them even more. I wondered if she was a daughter who looked like them. Or was it a son who favored you? Super tall and handsome."

We shared a chuckle.

"I am so sorry you were hurting all these years. You didn't deserve the pain I caused. Can you find it in your heart to forgive me?"

"I already forgave you, Ayesha. To move on and heal from that, I needed to forgive you. Now, though, I have a completely different perspective. All things considered," I paused for a moment before continuing, "I can also admit my culpability in the breakdown of our relationship. I should have been more vocal about my feelings. At the very least, I should have told you how that affected me. Who knows… in my being vulnerable with you about it, you may have felt safer in telling me your truth. Back when it all happened, I was angry with you… so angry… turns out I didn't have to be. I thought I'd gotten over it, but now I'm thinking I just compartmentalized it. Pushed it deep down somewhere. Never actually dealt with it properly. Harboring that did so much damage. That damage took root, and it festered. I started to shut down and shut you out… That was ultimately the demise of our relationship. I checked out long before I officially ended it. When I decided to break off our engagement, I should have told you the entire truth as to why I ended things. I was so selfish. And I'm sorry. I felt terrible for hurting you. I hated hurting you, Ayesha."

"Don't do that Micah. We're equally to blame. And you were hurting too. I hurt *you*, Micah. And I'm so sorry. I'm so, so sorry."

"Please don't keep apologizing. It's all in the past. And all is forgiven."

"I can do that."

"Indeed."

"Micah?" Ayesha jested after a few beats of silence.

"Yeah?"

"Everything's on the table, out in the open. Everything. Can we try again?"

Shit. *Could we?*

I mean… I didn't know she lost the baby. "You know…" I paused, "Ayesha… I'm flattered but…"

"Are you married?" She asked abruptly.

"Not married. No."

"But you're seeing someone," She stated.

"I'm not. Not at the moment."

"Tell you what. This is my cell. Maybe think about it. There's a lot to process. Anyway, I'd love to see you. Catch up a little more. Maybe grab some coffee or something." Her soft chuckle cruised through the line. "Our very first date was at a coffee shop. Do you remember?"

"Of course I remember." A small smile made its way across my face. "I can think about it, Ayesha."

"Well." She seemed pleased with that. She laughed again. "I hope to hear from you, Micah."

"Yes, and Ayesha... I'm glad you called me. Thank you for this. I guess I needed this."

"Yeah."

"Well, you take care of yourself and your two beautiful daughters. I'll maybe text you or call you, and we can see about catching up."

"Alright, sure. Have a goodnight."

I hung up and sighed. Talk about a blast from the past.

I needed to talk to someone about this. Ayesha unearthed raw emotions, and they were much too heavy for me. I certainly wasn't going to internalize them. I needed the people I trusted most: my father and my brother. If I couldn't sort through these feelings with them, I would call my therapist for an appointment first thing Monday.

I went inside to grab my food and got back to my car. Before cranking up, I sent a text to the group message Mal and I had with Daddy. It was an emoji that worked as a bat signal—every time we needed to congregate on a serious topic, one of us sent it.

Malachi responded first, per usual.

Brother: Now?

Yes please. I'll be at the blue house in twenty
Brother: Right behind you, baby brother

I started my car and headed toward my parents' home. Their home was my haven and my safe space. I appreciated my tribe every day, especially on days like this.

Twenty minutes later, I walked through the front door of my parent's house and headed straight toward the living room to find Daddy and Mal sitting on the couch. As I entered the living room, they both rose to their feet immediately. Mal embraced me, and Daddy wrapped his arms around us.

No words were spoken, but I knew Daddy was praying. He did that a lot. He had no idea what this was about but had the mind to pray about it.

Prayers didn't always need to be spoken out loud. God is all-knowing. Aware of the situation inside and out. Our job is to bring our burdens to him, leave them there, trust him to handle them, and walk in that authority.

They were both patient as I gathered myself, acting as two pillars, giving me the strength I needed.

I knew exactly where they drew their strength. I knew I could draw some from the same source, and I knew there was an infinite amount of it where that came from.

When I was ready to let go, they released me, and we all took a seat.

And I hesitated because I'd held onto this all these years.

But after taking a deep breath, I got right to it.

"My senior year at Cal Poly, Ayesha and I learned we were expecting."

Daddy and Mal's eyes were wide in surprise, but they said nothing. I sighed. "Ayesha wanted to end the pregnancy, but I didn't. I wanted our child. I even offered to raise it alone.

My understanding was that she decided to terminate. I respected her right to choose, but I just couldn't get over that. Eventually, I ended our engagement." Daddy and Mal nodded in understanding but remained silent. "Well, she reached out to me today. I hadn't spoken with her in years. Haven't seen her either. Turned out… she'd lost our baby. She didn't even need to go through with the procedure. And learning that has me thinking about all these possibilities. Like… had she told me that back then… maybe I wouldn't have shut her out… maybe…maybe…"

"Maybe you'd still be together? Maybe you'd have married her?" That was Daddy.

I sighed. Then I shook my head adamantly. "I wished she'd told me this back then."

"What's going through your mind now? Right now?" Mal asked.

"Destiney." After a heavy pause, I said, "But. Ayesha too. Once she dropped this bomb, I've been consumed with these thoughts of what if and what could have been. Ayesha wants to talk to me again. You know. And I'm not *totally opposed* to talking to her. I don't know… before I was, but that was when I thought she…" I sighed.

"Had that series of events not occurred, you likely wouldn't have met Destiney. Now, imagine that possibility," Daddy said.

I said nothing. But I did consider that possibility and didn't like how I felt.

twenty-eight

DESTINEY

"I love you best, I really do. But you don't seem to know what you want," India told me through a frustrated sigh. She shook her head as she continued stirring the pan on the stove. "Zeke is still fine. But. That's beside the point."

India was over at my place, and we hung out in the kitchen while she cooked us dinner.

"I know, right?" I said, sighing to myself. Yeah. Zeke was F-I-N-E. *Fine*.

We weren't out at Torch super late; I was home before ten. He called me that very night. He texted me first, asking if I made it home safe, and then he called me. We've spoken twice more since then, but I was still unsure of what it all meant.

And… I wasn't thinking I would be calling him back.

We talked for a while that first night and had an incredible conversation. But the two subsequent conversations weren't so stellar. It was like we didn't have much to talk about. It was strange. I don't remember it being that way back when we were seeing each other.

There wasn't much chemistry at all.

He was still very clearly into me.

Zeke is attractive and a gentleman. But that was the extent of it, on my end. The fact of the matter is that I'm not emotionally available.

I can admit that I didn't open myself up with him like I would with Micah.

Micah.

"I know exactly what I want. I want Micah."

"So why are you sulking about it? *Call him!* He misses you just as much as you miss him since you told him to stay away. He obviously respects your wishes. But I guarantee he misses you." India paused long enough to look back at me. I stood against the counter watching her, and we'd been discussing the Micah situation.

A situation I created and managed to piss her off in the process. India insisted we would come up with a game plan. Clearly, this wasn't my strong suit, and I was willing to do anything at this point.

She gestured for me to toss in the cubed potatoes and water, then immediately began stirring them in with the spices. She peeled, boiled, then chopped the potatoes earlier, setting them aside, and now that they were added in, the dish would be ready pretty soon. I couldn't wait. Before adding potato and water, she heated the fresh onion, garlic, curry leaves, turmeric, and a few other spices in a little oil over low heat. "I've heard that men will wait for the women they want. But they won't wait forever." She continued stirring. "Especially with options. We both know Micah has options."

I sighed heavily, mumbling, "Don't I know it."

Indie and I spent the whole day together. We're working on a mural at an Elementary school in Midtown. After we were done for the day, she asked to spend the night, which I readily agreed to. I knew she likely asked to come by to get a little more rest than she would at home. She's still living with her parents, and she told me that sometimes she just needs a break and a little privacy.

Even though we're in our late twenties, India isn't married, so she is expected to still live at home. India is first generation with very traditional immigrant parents who depend on her quite a bit. That's why I kinda sorta felt bad asking her if she wouldn't mind fixing us something. I don't ask her for favors often, but I'm so glad she agreed. She brings me food from home all the time. I love her food.

"What's this called again?" It smelled delicious.

"Aloo Palak."

Yeah, that. It's spinach and potato curry, and it's one of my favorite dishes she makes. She cooks two variations: a dry one and a gravy one. Today, she was making the dry version per my request. I like this one best. Once this is done, she'll make fresh roti to go with it.

India has an Afro-Guyanese mother and an Indo-Guyanese father. She can cook many of their traditional dishes, and many are vegetarian. India is what I call flexitarian. She eats meat, but you'd swear she's a vegetarian. Anytime we eat together, she's strictly plant-based.

"You really should be watching me, Des; then you can make this whenever you want." India joked. "I'm leaving all these spices here. Make use of them."

"Why, so I can burn the place down?" India released a peal of laughter.

Everyone knew I'd burn water. Daijah can cook, but not me.

"It's about time you learned, Best. What are you going to cook for your husband?" I knew Indie was asking in earnest. India was my girl, and I loved her to pieces.

Before I could answer, the doorbell rang.

"That's probably Neeka. I'll be right back." I made my way to the front door.

On the way home from work, we stopped to get a few things India would need from the store. A Boba shop was in the same plaza, so we went to grab a drink and ran into Neeka. I told Neeka she was welcome to join us for dinner.

I opened the door and greeted her excitedly, then went in to hug her.

"Chill, Des. I *just* saw you."

When she stepped over the threshold, I closed the door and noticed Neeka eyeing me skeptically.

"Okay. Girl. Where are you getting your clothes from?"

I looked at her, unassuming but curious as to where this random question came from. "Uh… different places." I shrugged.

"But where, though? What places specifically?"

"All over." Shrugging again, I looked down at myself, then back up at her. "I mean… this, what I'm wearing now I got from a thrift store. I like vintage clothing."

"Makes sense." She hotly informed me. I couldn't get a read on whether that was a good or a bad thing. I could only assume it wasn't good when she didn't follow up by telling me anything positive about my clothes.

Not that I needed her to.

At least I didn't think I did.

Her following words stung like hell, though.

"I'd dress much different than you if I had a body like yours."

My brows knitted as I looked down again at my faded destructed overalls. "What's wrong with the way I dress?"

Neeka laughed lightly. "I mean… You have such a cute figure. You'd look so much more put together if you cared a little more about your appearance."

I thought about what she said for a second.

I didn't need her backhanded compliment, if that's what it was.

I *did* care about how I looked. I liked being comfortable, for starters. I also didn't want to ruin any clothing between painting and bleeding all the time. I didn't owe her an explanation. I did love vintage finds, but thrifting was a great way to make sure I didn't go broke replacing clothes because I'd ruined them with blood stains. On the off chance I wore jeans, they weren't designer. I didn't own anything designer. My everyday wardrobe mainly consisted of black leggings, graphic T-shirts, and some kind of sweater. I'd be wearing it, or it would be around my waist. I was wearing a sweater right now. I was cold a lot, more than the average person. Since I bled so much, I was anemic and on iron supplements. Now, post-surgery, I was hoping to get off of those soon. And *maybe* I will get a new wardrobe.

But it wasn't at the forefront of my mind.

"Just a thought." Neeka absently tossed out.

I was perplexed. Why did she care so much anyway?

I tried not to let Neeka's words ruin my mood, but who was I kidding? I tried not to cry either, but that never worked. As sensitive as I am. My sensitive ass was always crying. Fuck me.

Neeka hung out for a while, and after she left, India and I got ready for bed.

India called her boyfriend and then her parents to check on them. Now, she was in my bathroom, brushing her teeth. We'd already taken showers. I planned to read for a minute but would be knocked out soon. India was a night owl, so she would probably be up for a while longer.

Anyway, I was sitting on my bed while she was in the ensuite, and India told me something peculiar.

"Best, did you notice how quiet Neeka got when we started talking about Tyler?"

"Hmm. Now that you mention it, I did notice that."

Earlier, the subject of Zeke came up again. We talked about Torch and how we'd gone there a few nights ago. I said something about being glad I missed Tyler, and India mentioned that I was bound to run into him eventually if I went back, seeing as he owns the place and all.

India shook her head, "She's fucking him."

"Woah! Indie, you have no facts to back that up."

"Girl, please. This is Neeka we're talking about."

"That's ridiculous."

"Not for her, it's not. She had so much to say, but then the subject switched to Tyler, and suddenly, she was quietly looking around, acting occupied. She doesn't fool me."

I shook my head. Tyler wasn't my man. He could fuck whoever he wanted. So could she. Neeka didn't have be so damn sneaky about it though. We're grown.

"What happened anyway?" India asked. She exited my bathroom and stopped in front of me, firmly putting her hands on her hips.

I knitted my brows. "Your mood took a nosedive as soon as she got here. What happened Best?"

"Nothing happened…. she just…"

India sighed. "She say some slick shit to you, didn't she?"

I nodded silently. My eyes began to well up, and I couldn't stop the tears if they wanted to fall.

India has seen me at some of my lowest moments, on some of my worst days.

And likewise, I've been there for some of hers.

"I could feel your energy was off a little bit. And I was waiting for you to tell me. What happened Best?"

"Is there something wrong with the way I dress?"

She narrowed her eyes. "*No!* Not at all. Are you kidding?" I remained silent and India crossed her arms as she spat, "The fuck Neeka say about the way you dress?!"

"I mean…nothing specific. She just alluded that I didn't dress like she thought I should and that I would look better if I cared more about my appearance."

"I love the way you dress. You have an eclectic personality with the style to match. You mix earthy and bohemian, and the aesthetic suits your spirit."

I gave her a weak smile.

"Don't let Neeka's words bother you. I know they hurt, but they're just words. There is nothing wrong with your style. Always be you, *bravely*. Always. Fuck what Neeka or what anyone else thinks."

She took me into her arms and hugged me.

"Thank you, Indie." I hugged her back. I loved Indie. I wish I were as confident as her. People didn't fuck with India. She was sweet. Probably sweeter than I am but she didn't let people fuck with her.

It's the same with Daijah. People did not try India Rampersaud or Daijah Evans. And they didn't try me either when either of them was with me. Neeka said her whole mouthful while we were in the living room, away from India. Also, Daijah wasn't home.

Girls who would bully me in school learned real quick to leave me alone. Daijah would handle them with the quickness. Especially in high school. Them girls were some bitches, and Daijah took her turn fighting each one up for the challenge. They never messed with me again. The ones who didn't want Daijah's smoke would take the message and move along. Daijah and India are both tall women. I'm short and wondered if that had anything to do with it.

"My pleasure." India sighed, "Freaking Neeka. She's probably jealous you're brave enough to wear what you like. She's so busy trying to maintain that image. All her unnecessarily high-end clothing, perfumes, purses, fancy ass car and all that damn makeup. Then that superior complex." India rolled her eyes hard. "She calls all that trying to bag a husband. She's failing miserably."

I cackled. Damn. India was right about that. It was a fact that Neeka had a great sense of style and fashion if you were into that. Always dressed to the nines. Like always. Hair always impeccable and not a strand out of place. Makeup on fleek. She looked like a runway model.

She had a great career and could afford the finer things. She had an expensive lifestyle. A lovely high-rise apartment in expensive ass downtown Sacramento. And she was pretty outspoken about her desire for marriage. She was constantly speaking of her future husband and seeking him out.

"But she's got her priorities all wrong. Her personality needs some serious work. No one will wife her behaving that way. Not a man with some sense. Why sign up for that? Neeka is the type of woman a man would put in the fun category. She's good for fucking and that's it. She's jealous of you. Best. She wants your freedom. Your carefree personality. And men flock to you and throw themselves at you. She had to hear us talking about Micah and then talking about Zeke, and briefly, we spoke of Tyler. She doesn't have those options. She desperately wants to be someone's wife, but her vibe… I'm done talking about her." India looked at me. "I'm sorry for coming for your friend like that. But she pissed me off coming for you, pretending the shit was a compliment."

"Don't worry about it, Indie."

India wasn't the only one. Daijah didn't care for Neeka. At all.

Not long ago, Daijah told me that when I introduced them, she wasn't even impressed with Neeka. She got a bad vibe from her and couldn't really put her finger on it.

Daijah is better at discerning than I am, so I figured she was onto something. We never told each other to cut friends loose, but I knew what she thought whenever Neeka was around. It had been a while since the four of us had hung out. Daijah adored India and was always glad to see her. Neeka would hang out with India and me, but I rarely invited her to anything Daijah would be at. Also, I only invited Neeka over if I knew Daijah would be over Julian's house. Daijah was saying one time, *"Neeka ain't never getting wifed. Don't nobody want to marry her! **She** wouldn't even marry her!"* India and I were rolling.

I couldn't agree more. Her attitude needs work, but something tells me she couldn't change even if someone paid her. She wasn't sweet, and nothing about her personality was soft or feminine. Anyhow, I wasn't as close to Neeka these days. When we first met, things were cool. Now, I feel on edge anytime she's around.

"Enough about her. It's time for a come-to-Jesus talk. If you mess this up, I'll never speak to you again."

"You wouldn't!"

"Don't try me." India waved her hand dismissively. "Now, let's discuss this plan I've got for you getting your man back." India chirped.

twenty-nine

MICAH

"If Destiney is heavy on your mind, despite all of this, that tells me you're right where you're meant to be. Sleep on it. And then talk to Destiney."

Mal nodded in agreement with Daddy. "Give yourself some time before you make any rash decisions. Either way, I think it's a good idea to have a conversation with Destiney. So you know where her head is. And tell her where yours is. I know you were giving her space, but this is a good reason to give her a call."

When I got home from my parents' house the other night, I lay on my bed thinking things over. And I had a lot to think about.

That day was much more eventful than I could have ever anticipated.

As I lay on my bed, my cell in my hand, I tried to conjure up a text message to send to Destiney.

Hey. I hope you're well. Thinking of you. Truth is, I never stopped thinking of you. If you aren't busy tomorrow, do you mind if we chat?

I hovered over the send button, of what I thought was a suitable message, but I hesitated.

I just couldn't hit send.

Why? I wasn't exactly sure.

Was she even thinking of me anymore? Even just now and then? Lord knows I was still thinking of her. You don't just fall out of that. Or climb the fuck out.

Not after what we've built. I still cared for her. Immensely. I was still very much in love with her.

I thought Destiney would reach out to me at some point. Especially now. But as more time has passed, I've somewhat begun to accept the possibility that she may not be.

I thought about it more that night and decided not to text Destiney after all. Figuring I'd take Daddy's advice and sleep on it. That was likely best, anyway. That way, I had a clear head.

The fact of the matter was that this conversation between Destiney and I needed to happen, waiting for her may not be the best route. But I still wasn't a hundred percent sure. I would see.

***

"Malachi, you been with the same woman twenty fucking years! *And I know you're being faithful.* How you even know what's out here?" Ray sucked his teeth through a smirk.

"I'm more qualified to speak on this shit than you nigga!" Malachi rolled his eyes.

A few days later, I was at Malachi's house watching the game, chillin'. He grilled some tri-tip. Mal makes the *best* tri-tip. Ella made some macaroni and cheese and some homemade rolls to go with it. Also, a green salad I was sure to eat a hearty helping of.

It was almost time to head out; we'd been here for a few hours. Mal's frat brother Jakobi came by. He's the homie and such cool people. He has a son who is the same age as Gabe. They took off a little bit ago, and Gabe headed upstairs.

Now that it was just the three of us, our conversation ended up on Raymond's favorite subject: women.

And something about men not being vulnerable with women and only women being vulnerable with men.

I mentioned that men are often willing to be vulnerable with the women close to them: their mother, sister, aunties, grandmother, maybe a close female friend, and the woman they eventually fall in love with. Of course, there are always exceptions.

That was all I could really add because it turned into a debate between Mal and Ray. I was just here for the entertainment.

A moment ago, they segued again to the different types of women, what women want, and how to satisfy them, not only sexually but in general.

"How? You been married half yo' damn life! Married when you were just barely old enough to buy you a damn beer."

I couldn't help but chuckle at that.

Ray continued, "You been out the game a long ass time. I ain't even mad at that. I have insight as to what's out here in these streets, and you can offer intel on married life."

"Ray, you be lying to these women," Mal said.

"Man, listen, men don't have to lie to women. If a woman likes you enough, she'll start lying to herself. I don't got to lie about shit."

"Nah. Yo ass still be lying." Mal shook his head rapidly, peering at Ray, deadpan. "Anyway," he turned to me, "Check it, I *objectify* my woman. She has everything I need. Women aren't all the same. Learn your woman. Study her like the art she is. Be intentional and curate things to whatever's best for her. Just because you like something doesn't mean she will. Learn what gets her going. You spend enough time with her and pay attention, you'll discover exactly what she needs from you."

"Man..." Ray shook his head and mumbled something under his breath, but Mal kept going.

"When you manage to get to a point where she feels like she can bare her soul, there is not a thing you cannot ask her for. But you must get to the point where she'll open up to you.

Make love with the lights on. *Keep them lights on*. That shit is a beautiful sight. Not only that, but she'll also get comfortable because you're showing her she *can be comfortable*." Malachi glared at Ray for a moment. Finally, he turned to me and said, "Brother, eat the meat and spit out the bones. Regardless of who that shit is coming from." I nodded. Most of this information wouldn't apply to my current situation. But just the same, I could store it in my arsenal for later.

"I'm going to find my wife. I'll be back." Malachi stood and headed toward the stairs.

Ray and I both chuckled, and I took a sip of my drink. We knew exactly what that meant. He was probably about to get a quickie in or something. Malachi stayed, pouncing on Ella. It wasn't any of our business, but he always made it known. Ella seemed to be keeping up with his nasty ass though.

One thing Malachi did was take good care of his wife. Ella was always looking beautiful and vibrant. I recall our conversation around year eight of his and Ella's marriage. He said men at his job constantly complained about their wives for one reason or another. A common one was that they always seemed to be sexually frustrated. Mal said he couldn't relate to that because Ella rarely turned him down. Because of that, he wanted to ensure he always poured into her just as much as she poured into him.

"I owe it all to my wife. She keeps me satisfied. That's why she's so spoiled. Ain't no way in hell I could just take, take, take from her."

Malachi has always been transparent about his marriage with me. They were married young, and I had a front-row seat to all of it, Malachi and I being as close as we are.

I still recall the evening at dinner when he told Daddy he wanted to marry Ella. They were home from college on summer break, and he planned to ask her father for her hand. At the time, Malachi was twenty, and Ella was just nineteen. Relatively young to want marriage so soon by some standards, but here they were fifteen years later and still going strong.

"Marriage is serious business. Ain't nothing to play with." My father's voice was stern. His authoritarian command was in full effect.

"I know that, Daddy."

"Malachi."

"Yes, sir?"

After a long pause, he said, "If you're not done playing games, you leave that sweet girl alone."

Mal had his choice of women as a standout basketball player, and the ladies flocked to Malachi. All I know is everything changed when he and Ella got together. He only had eyes for her seemingly overnight. Ella had no shortage of suitors, either, as striking as she is. But their choice of each other was abundantly clear.

"I love Ella and want to be the man who makes her happy for the rest of her life. I know what I have, and I'm not letting her get away. Furthermore, Ella isn't the type of woman that would last long out here. She's mine." Malachi's tone was adamant and resolute.

Daddy chuckled, nodding his head. "Oh, it's like that?"

Mal and I both chuckled, too.

"Gone get your wife, son."

I'm sure Daddy was confident in Malachi's words. Mal was always determined. Wise beyond his years. Focused. I admired those qualities about Malachi. Anything he set his mind to was a done deal. He was always the type to make what he wanted happen. Irrespective of naysayers, and there were always those. Naturally, many people gave them both the third degree for wanting marriage so soon and so young. But the two of them weren't remotely concerned.

Ray and I took off at the same time. I'd just walked in the door when I got a text from Ayesha.

Ayesha: Hey Micah how was your day?

We'd been texting a little bit.

Well, she mainly texted me. I'd feel bad just leaving her on read, so I would reply. But she was mostly driving the conversations. It wasn't something that gave me the feels like whenever Destiney would text

And we met up. A few days ago, at a café. About a week after, she called me.

Ayesha looked great. Had a few healthy pounds on her. Very pretty. Still.

We fell right back in it seemed. Caught up on so much. She and Laila were still thick as thieves. As it turned out, Ayesha got my number from Ty. She knew we were still in touch and insisted she had something very important to talk to me about. Obviously, Ty gave it to her. I chuckled at that. He wouldn't have done that if I were in a relationship, so no love was lost. And Ty is my boy, but he still could have given me a heads-up.

Anyway, when we met at the café, we talked for hours. We were there so long that breakfast wore off. I felt bad offering to take her across the street for lunch or something, but she needed to get back to her daughters.

I realized pretty quickly that Ayesha was serious about giving things another try—so serious that she was already trying to set up another meeting within the week. I told her I'd let her know once I checked my schedule.

And I walked away from that feeling certain.

Sure, that I didn't feel anything. That spark. *That something.*

It wasn't there.

It just wasn't the same—not that I expected it to be. We are a decade older now. So much has happened in life, but we didn't have any chemistry.

She's still as sweet as I remember. A bit more chill. And so proud of her beautiful little girls. And speaking of, I'll admit I pondered how I would fit into her life now, with them. I'm aware she's a packaged deal. I considered how she'd fit into mine. She already had children, and seemingly, it would be a *feat* fathering children of my own. I mulled over that for a minute.

But no. As far as there being anything between us, it wasn't going to happen.

I planned to let her know—probably this evening. I didn't want to string her along.

And in other news, I still hadn't reached out to Destiney.

She hadn't reached out either.

thirty

DESTINEY

I timidly entered the expansive lobby of the high-rise building. The elementary school India and I were working at was just six blocks from here.

I knew exactly what building Micah worked in. He told me a long time ago.

When we took the gig around the corner, I mentioned it to India. So when we talked over the plans, she suggested the brilliant idea that I come here.

I was sure to come on a day when I knew he'd be in the office because he worked from home part of the time. I glanced at my watch. It was exactly one o'clock, and I knew Micah would be going on his lunch any minute now. He usually had his assistant block out the lunch hour. He had to do that to ensure he actually took a lunch break. Sometimes, he would get so wrapped up in whatever he was doing that he would forget to take it. Once we started talking, he'd gotten so much better about that. I hoped he would continue that even though we weren't talking.

And I hoped this conversation today would change that.

Maybe this wasn't such a bad idea.

On Tuesdays, we had a ninety-minute lunch instead of the normal sixty. This would give me enough time to meet with Micah and talk to him.

Tell him how much I missed him and wanted to be with him.

Tell him that I was in love with him, too. Granted, he still felt the same.

And beg him for another chance.

I stopped at a deli two corners over and got lunch for him. He always went there when we would talk over lunch on FaceTime.

It was a mom-and-pop that had been in business for something like fifty years. It was family-owned and apparently had some of the best sandwiches in town. I knew his order by heart, so when I stopped in, I rambled it off just like it was nothing.

I left the deli and noticed several sandwich shops as I walked toward my destination. There were many restaurants, period, with choices galore. Whatever you were in the mood for. The business district of Downtown Sacramento was bustling. Not quite like New York City, but it's certainly a fast-paced part of town. I had to circle the block a couple of times to find parking. The Golden 1 Center, where the Sacramento Kings played, wasn't far from here either.

I felt sorely out of place as soon as I entered the lobby.

First of all, *everyone* was wearing a suit and tie.

The women were dressed the part, too.

I had on my painting clothes since I left the site and came here directly.

Painting clothes that were stretched, faded, and covered in splotches of random colors. That had me second-guessing this whole thing.

Fortunately, no one seemed to be paying me any mind. I focused ahead.

Gripping the bag containing Micah's sandwich, I took a deep breath and proceeded to the directory adjacent to the elevators. I realized I had left my cell phone in the car when

I got to the deli, but this should be simple enough. I knew the department Micah worked in, but I just couldn't recall what floor.

"Hey, *cutie!* Can I help you find something?"

Cutie was an interesting word choice.

The infliction threw me just a little, too.

I'm a grown woman. It almost sounded like she was referring to a puppy in someone's arms.

Sighing lightly, I looked to the right and up into the eyes of a gorgeous woman.

Thirty something and dressed to the nines in a burgundy dress and stiletto heels. She looked like a damn lawyer or something. Or like she belonged on the morning news. Her smile was perfect, and her hair was styled in a cute French roll. Damn. I hadn't seen one of those since the early two-thousands. She was rocking it, though, and not a hair was out of place.

"I'm Erica, and I'm on the third floor if that's where you're headed." She spoke pleasantly.

"Thanks! I'm Destiney. And I *think* it's the third floor." I nodded. "I left my phone in my car, but I think that's it."

"Who are you looking for? That may help us out."

"Micah Walker."

"*Oh.*" Her demeanor changed instantly. "How do you know, Micah?" She asked curtly. Her bright smiling eyes now shrunk into slits and suddenly she wasn't so friendly anymore.

Nope. Not a trace of her friendliness from seconds before.

I smiled anyway. As best I could, despite this sudden energy shift. "We're... friends," I provided, shrugging casually. I wished I'd said it confidently the second it left my lips. She sniffed out my trepidation and seemed pleased with her discovery—traces of something akin to a snarled expression showing itself.

"*Friends?* Oh! Well, Micah and I are quite acquainted. We have been for years. Funny, he's never mentioned you."

"Acquainted?" Why did I even ask?

"Yes. *Very much so.*"

Okay.

So they're fucking.

"I see," I mumbled, suddenly reconsidering this whole thing. My confidence was shot to hell.

Micah wasn't mine. But. What was I doing?

This wasn't me. I couldn't do this.

I didn't belong here.

The elevator announced its arrival with a loud ding. The doors slid open as a handful of people stepped off into the lobby.

"Going up?" I can take you to his office. "I'm headed there now myself, matter of fact."

"Uh no. That's alright." I turned on my heels and made my way outside.

Who was I kidding? I couldn't compete with her.

I wouldn't compete with her.

She could have Micah. I knew this wasn't a good idea.

I'm not good with these, and they aren't good for me. Here I was trying something new, all for it to blow up in my face. This is the big league, and I'm just a rookie.

I walked back toward my car down the block, passing a homeless man.

"Hey, would you like a sandwich?"

thirty-one

MICAH

"Thank you for the updated analysis on the proposed market value. We'll need to take a closer look at their financials from last quarter to get a better idea of their Proforma. Let's meet next week after you've had a chance to review."

We were swiftly approaching a charter meeting with our mid-West market, and Ellington was instrumental in helping ensure the Fair Market Value and Proforma were completed on time.

"Good stuff. Appreciate you, Boss," Ellington said, saluting me. I chuckled lightly; he always did that.

"I appreciate all of your hard work." I glanced at the time, and it was just after two o'clock.

"Go ahead and get a head start in your evening with your family. Then take another look with fresh eyes tomorrow." Ellington had a beautiful wife and an adorable baby daughter. I was so thrilled for him and the legacy he was building.

"Don't mind if I do!" E chuckled beaming. "Thanks!"

"Have a great evening, Ellington." I did the same salute and ended our Zoom meeting.

I enjoyed working with Ellington.

I had about a decade on him, so he was like a younger brother I was proud to have around.

As my senior Financial Analyst, E was my right hand. He is brilliant and impeccable at what he does. He's also hungry to learn and eager to exhibit his skills. He's grown tremendously over the past two years he's been on my team, and I was glad to have him.

Ellington has continued to exceed my expectations, earning the maximum merit increases and bonuses I'd given him.

I planned to promote him early next year, and I was chomping at the bit to deliver the good news. It was still a couple of months away, but after a final review of our department numbers, I knew we'd have room in the budget to do so. I would see to it that he succeeds anywhere he deserves. I wanted nothing less for anyone on my team. If I had anything to do with it, it would happen.

I emailed my assistant Laurie, requesting that she schedule the follow-up meeting for next week and then told her to log out for the afternoon afterward.

I allowed them both to work from home and only requested that they come into the office when necessary. They were free to do so as long as they could remain productive remotely.

Work-life balance mattered a lot to me. I didn't want anyone who reported to me to get burned out or become too overwhelmed with work, which inevitably had a negative impact on home and family time.

I planned on heading out shortly myself.

Mentally, I was exhausted. I had a pretty hectic day, with meeting after meeting. I still had one more meeting, and then I planned to leave for the day.

I began gathering the paperwork on my desk so that I could take off as soon as my meeting was over.

I couldn't believe it was already two o'clock. I'd worked right through lunch. I sat back in my chair and sighed. I tried not to do that, and usually, I was pretty good about it. Since Destiney and I didn't talk over lunch anymore, it was something I had to be intentional about.

Destiney used to call me every day on FaceTime at one o'clock sharp.

I loved that. And I miss that.

"Knock, knock." I rolled my eyes at the voice I desperately wanted to ignore. And if we were anywhere but here, I most certainly would have. Since that notable conversation, I really hadn't seen much of Erica. I wonder what she wanted now.

"Hello, Erica." I offered, not even looking over at the doorway.

"Hello," She chirped. After a few moments of me saying nothing, she chuckled lightly. "Well, aren't you going to invite me in?"

"Come on in."

"Thanks." She crossed the threshold, and after quick strides, she was right in front of my desk.

"Figured you haven't eaten yet. So, I picked this up for you." She held out a white bag. I recognized the logo. And the smell.

"You didn't have to do that."

"I wanted to."

I rolled my eyes, but subtly enough that she couldn't see. When I didn't reach out to accept the bag, she placed it on my desk.

"It's your favorite."

My eyebrow went up, and I didn't bother hiding that.

"Smoked turkey, pepper jack, and fire-roasted tomatoes on toasted ciabatta."

I sat there. Silently. Giving her a blank stare.

"That's your favorite from *Specialties*, right?" She managed around her plastered smile. It was more like a statement.

It was.

And honestly that sounded delicious right about now. I was starving too.

But I couldn't trust Erica. Not that she'd do anything to my food, but she had an agenda. An ulterior motive. Everything she did concerning me was transactional and I didn't want a damn thing from her. At minimum, she just wanted an excuse to come to my office. I could have saved her the trouble.

Instead of a response, I shook my head rapidly.

"Erica, really you shouldn't have." I picked up the bag and tried giving it back to her.

"It's no big deal, Micah. I insist."

"I brought leftovers." I lied. "Was about to go warm them up now."

"Have this instead, and have your leftovers for dinner."

"No thanks, Erica."

"What am I supposed to do with this sandwich? I already ate."

"Eli will be glad to take it," I said, referring to our security guard. Each floor of the building had its own, and Eli had been with us for a number of years. We blessed him with extra food from catered lunches all the time. He was always grateful to have whatever we offered.

She huffed a frustrated breath, snatching the bag once she realized I wouldn't take the sandwich.

"Fine, I'll give it to Eli then." She snapped.

"Great." I stood and walked around my desk to see her out. "Thanks, Erica. Please close my door behind you if you wouldn't mind."

She took a few steps, then turned to me, and I looked up expectantly.

"Oh yeah…" Erica's top lip curled, and I already didn't like where this was going. "Someone came by for you earlier." Her voice was strangely friendly now. "She only made it to the lobby." Erica offered.

"She?" My brows furrowed. Most of my meetings these days were via Zoom, but I racked my brain trying to figure out who it could have been.

I wasn't expecting anyone.

"Hmm… what was her name?" She tapped her chin as if deep in thought. "*Odyssey?* No." Erica shrugged dismissively. "I forgot her name, but it was something strange like that."

My eyes narrowed.

"She was cute… in an awkward way. Looked like she walked in off the playground or something." Erica cracked up at that as if she'd just heard the funniest thing ever. "Chocolate with locs. Short." Realization hit me, and my blood boiled. "She said she was your friend." She seethed that last part, and I noticed Erica wore a smirk now.

Maintaining my poker face and my cool, I asked, "Destiney came to see me?" I added a pleasant smile for good measure. The first smile she'd seen since she came in here.

Thinking of Destiney did that to me. But I couldn't let on that my mind was in shambles right now. I knew Erica said something nasty to Destiney. And I was frantic at the endless possibilities.

My smile wiped the grin right off her face.

Erica folded her arms. "What kind of friend is she?"

I crossed my own arms. "That isn't your business, Erica."

"Well. I told her we were *quite* acquainted. She seemed surprised. Guess you didn't tell her about us."

"There's nothing to tell."

"You sure about that?"

"Positive."

"I'm sure she'd beg to differ."

Fuck.

"Was there anything more I could do for you, Erica? I'd like to get to lunch now."

"There's plenty you can do for me, Micah. But we can talk about that later. I won't keep you." With that, Erica pranced out of my office and down the hall. I closed my door and couldn't grab my phone quickly enough.

I called Destiney.

When Destiney didn't answer, I called her again. When she didn't answer that call either, I texted her.

Then I called her again.

Then I called her again. And again.

I was beside myself. I needed to talk to Destiney immediately, and knowing Erica, I needed to do some *serious* damage control.

***

"We went on two dates. That's it."

"Have you slept with her?"

I sighed.

"Micah. Just tell me."

I frantically tried to get ahold of Destiney for the rest of the afternoon. Unsuccessfully.

Then, I had to facilitate a meeting I could hardly focus on because my mind was so preoccupied. I worried she'd call me while I was in the middle of my meeting, and I couldn't answer.

Eventually, some hours later, I got her on the phone.

Begrudgingly, she was willing to answer me on FaceTime. I knew I was pushing it, but I had to see her. I needed her to see me. I felt things would land better if she could see the sincerity in my eyes.

"I did sleep with her. *One time*. Worst decision ever."

Destiney nodded. "How long ago?"

"Two years."

"Two years?"

"Yes. It didn't mean anything. Honest to God. But she's still hanging on to that as if there's a possibility of something more."

"Have you given her reason to believe there will be?"

"Absolutely not. I've told her numerous times there won't be. No matter what I tell her, she can't seem to get that through her head."

"That's wild."

We were silent.

More than a few beats went by.

Destiney looked away and never brought her eyes back.

"What are you thinking, Destiney baby? Give it to me straight." I couldn't get a read, and I needed to know. I wanted to fix this, and I wanted us to be okay.

"I'll be honest." She still wouldn't look at me. "I felt jealous. But I remembered I had no right to feel that way. You aren't mine." She said passively.

Her words stung, though it was true.

We weren't officially us. But in my head, we were. Pretty much immediately, Destiney was the only one I wanted. For a while now, she was the only woman in my world.

Initially, she tried to give the impression she was unbothered by the situation, but I called her bluff, in a manner of speaking.

I insisted it was perfectly reasonable for her to be upset at me. Not feeling anything meant she didn't care; we both knew that wasn't the case. I cared immensely, and I felt confident that she did, too.

"Destiney baby. Look at me, please." I gave her a moment, and those big, brilliant eyes were back.

I wanted more than anything to have her in front of me. In my arms. To hold her and reassure her.

"You have *nothing* to feel jealous about."

She sucked her teeth. "I mean. I was intimidated. That woman was just gorgeous. Picturesque. Like a model. I'm not that."

"Well, it's a good thing she isn't who I want. I want you. And you are beautiful, Destiney. And do you know what?" I waited a moment. "I guarantee she was jealous seeing you, even before she knew you were there for me."

Destiney sucked her teeth again. "Oh, please."

"I'm serious." You roll out of bed looking like you do. Naturally beautiful. She looks nice all made up, but she doesn't look that way underneath all that. You're also just as beautiful on the inside. She isn't. Not even a little bit."

"That's nice, Micah. Thank you. Listen. I um… I need to think about this. I'll call you, alright. I promise I'll call you."

I nodded. "Okay. Alright. Please call me, Destiney baby."

She said nothing more and disconnected the call, and I hung my head in defeat.

***

I dozed off but woke up immediately when I heard my phone vibrating on my nightstand. I grabbed it quickly, hoping it was Destiney calling me, but it was Ray.

I already knew he was calling with his usual shenanigans, but I really didn't feel like talking, especially to him. Against my better judgment, I answered his call anyway.

"Whassup?" I let out a breath.

"Cousin?"

"What's good dude?"

"Shit. Thinking 'bout Seals tonight. You trying to slide through?"

Seals was a cigar lounge in West Sacramento. I didn't smoke a cigar, but maybe twice a year, but it was definitely a chill spot. There was always a great vibe, good drinks, and good music.

They had premium cigar options and an extensive drink menu to pair them with, everything from top-shelf whiskey and bourbon to dark, roasted coffee brewed to order. No doubt it would be a good place to hang out and forget about shit for a while.

I didn't even need a whole cigar; a contact high would be good enough with them strong shits.

"Uh yeah… what time you headed that way?"

"About an hour. Can you roll with that?"

"Yep."

"Bet."

After hanging up, I sighed audibly.

I thought about it for another second and changed my mind. I just wasn't feeling up to it.

I called Ray back, and he answered on the first ring.

"Hey, Ray, I'm not really feeling like-"

"*Man! I already know!* You in a funk behind ole girl ain't you?" Ray snapped, cutting me off.

I was stunned into silence.

I didn't appreciate his tone or attitude for one and two. Three, he needed to mind his own damn business.

As if that wasn't enough, he continued, "I been saying that bitch ain't worth all this trouble man. She real cute, but that's it. You stay in yo damn feelings since she been around."

My eyes grew wide. "You know what Ray? Do not fucking call me again!" I ended the call and tossed my cell across my side table.

I was so sick of Ray and his bullshit.

Mal distanced himself from Ray a long time ago, and as I matured, I could see why, though Mal was always civil whenever they were in the same space.

It had literally been years, and Ray didn't even have Mal's number. The two of them would always talk through me. It was mainly from Ray's end, though. Malachi didn't have shit to say to Raymond in the time between them seeing each other.

Ray always seemed jealous of Mal and me for one reason or another. Jealous of us as individuals. Jealous of our relationship with each other. Mal and I were incredibly close and always had one another.

I think Ray envied that as an only child.

Ray's mother wasn't in his life at all, and he envied our relationship with Mommy. Despite the fact that my mother was so kind to Ray and was sure to always love on him, I think he longed for his own mother to love him.

I couldn't blame him.

Then there was my uncle, Ray's father.

He was always gone since he drove long hauls. Uncle Marshall missed so many things concerning Ray, and Daddy picked up much of the slack.

Ray played sports like Mal and me, often on some of our same teams. But Uncle Marshall didn't make time to come to anything. Maybe it wasn't a priority. He missed plenty of championship games because "he had to work."

We never saw the fruits of that labor, though.

For one, Ray was living with us, and two, they had a studio apartment in a shady part of town.

Daddy always said Uncle Marshall could afford a nicer place in the 'burbs, and he must have been tricking off his money.

Who knows.

My phone vibrated. Thinking it was Ray calling me back, I snatched it up and answered quickly.

"Man what? I said don't fucking call me!"

"Yo, baby brother! It's me."

"I'm sorry Mal. I thought you were Ray calling me back." My voice calmed.

"What his simple ass do now?"

I told Mal the latest.

Ray was always trying to find shit to get into and always had some shit to say. I was over it all a long time ago. Maybe this was confirmation that I needed to leave Ray and all his bullshit alone finally.

"Don't pay him no mind, baby brother. He had no business calling your woman a bitch, but Ray don't like to share. His ass was wildin' when Ella first came around. Nigga was beside himself." Mal let out a lazy cackle. "He got over it once he realized Ella wasn't going nowhere."

I shook my head. "I remember."

"He ain't had me for years, and now he's afraid he'll lose you once you settle down. He's feeling threatened, but he can get the fuck over it. And he owes you an apology."

"Right. I told him not to call me. But we'll cross paths eventually."

"Rays ass ain't going nowhere. He'll probably be at the blue house tomorrow trying to eat Daddy's food. Oh! Mommy made lasagna for Daddy to take to the church. Why did Ray go over there and eat off it? Didn't even stop to ask, just helped his greedy ass to it."

"You lyin'!" I shook my head. "Mommy told you that?"

"Hell no! You know Daddy did."

"Fucking unbelievable."

"*Shiiiittt!* I was hot. But Daddy was pissed so you know Ray had to hear his mouth. That's worse than either of us getting on his ass."

We both cackled.

"Mommy probably told Daddy to leave him alone." I surmised. Mommy always seemed protective of Ray whenever Daddy would get on him.

Honestly, I think she felt sorry for him. She was always that way when we were kids and even now.

"She likely had something else she could throw together just as good as her lasagna."

"True."

"What's up though brother?"

"Yeah. Can you meet me at the blue house this weekend? We need to pull some stuff out of the garage for Daddy. I'll have Gabe with me, but it'll be faster if we had two more hands. Ray's ass need to be over there helping too, but I don't want to deal with his mouth."

I laughed again. "Yeah, that's no problem at all. What time?"

"Let's knock it out early. How's nine?"

"I gotchu."

There was a beat of silence. I decided to forgo giving Mal the latest with Destiney and me for the moment. There were still a few uncertain things.

Then Mal said, "Thinking about barbequing. Ella and Gabby are meeting us there after Gabby's soccer game."

"Bet. I can bring some drinks. What's Ella fixing to go with the barbeque?"

"Any requests?"

"Seven-layer dip?" Ella made a seven-layer dip that was so delicious that you didn't even need the chips to go with it. Sometimes, she switched it up and made it with shredded chicken in place of ground beef. I loved both ways.

"Hang on brother… Queen!"

I heard shuffling in the background, then Ella's muffled voice, "Hey."

"You mind making your seven-layer dip for us to take to mommas this weekend?"

"Yeah, I can definitely do that. Gotta get to the store though. I'll need a few things."

"I'll go, don't worry about it baby," Mal said.

"Please tell my sis thank you."

"Micah said thank you."

"You're very welcome, Micah."

Within seconds, I could hear giggles and smacking noises, and that was my cue to hang up.

Nasty asses.

thirty-two

MICAH

"I'm not perfect. I may even let you down. But I'd never do it intentionally, Micah. And I don't want to be on a pedestal." Destiney looked away from me. "I'm not so great with relationships. I don't have the experience, first of all. This is just a lot of pressure, and I don't want to disappoint you." She sighed, then, "I'm rambling at this point."

"Nothing done in good faith will ever disappoint me. I'm not expecting anything. Except what you are ready to give me. I'll receive that with open arms. Nothing more. Especially nothing less. You can expect the same from me too."

"Yeah," Destiney paused for a beat. Giving me her eyes, she said, "I thought you'd already moved on."

"I haven't moved on sweetheart."

I was at the office, and Destiney and I were on FaceTime.

She hadn't called me back last night, so I texted her as soon as I woke up, telling her good morning.

She said good morning back.

Much to my delight, we continued texting throughout the day—just like old times. We didn't miss a beat.

At one o'clock, she asked if I wanted to talk. Instead of texting her back, I immediately called her on FaceTime.

We had an unfiltered conversation. Got caught up on everything that occurred over the past two months.

I told her about Ayesha.

She already knew of Ayesha but not those other details. So, I filled her in on everything, including that I met with

Ayesha. I told her all that and then assured her that that situation was over.

Days ago, before Destiney and I reconnected, I told Ayesha how I felt. I told her as gently as I could that I didn't wish to continue with things. I wished her well. She seemed to take it alright—much different than last time.

Destiney told me she'd spoken to a guy from her past. They hadn't gotten together, but she saw him while she was out with her friends. They had a few subsequent conversations. I worried for a second that she had moved on, but she didn't. She told me that it was over and done with as well.

Her eyes were back on mine now. Her beautiful face filled my screen.

"Do you trust me?" I asked after a beat.

"Yes," she said softly.

Her brilliant eyes bore into me as I spoke earnestly, "Is there any doubt? Or uncertainty...hesitation? Anywhere?" I searched her eyes and continued, "I want you to know if there is, I assure you it won't upset me. We're still building. But I need an opportunity to show you; you can trust me—one hundred percent. You'll always have me. Always. And that you're safe with me. All of you is safe with me. Your mind, spirit... dreams, fears...your body."

"Okay," she declared. She wore a bashful expression and tried to look away.

"Eyes on me, Destiney baby."

"Micah. That was so beautiful. I don't even know what to say. If you haven't noticed, I am a ball of emotions. How would I even follow up after something like that?"

"I'm not even finished."

Her eyes grew in surprise.

Dramatically, I inhaled a deep breath, then opened my mouth, finally saying, "I'll leave it there for now, though." I gave her a silly grin, and she laughed for a while. I did, too, and it felt good—really good.

"Oh my gosh! You're a mess, you know that?" she said after she finally calmed down.

"That I am. A mess over *you*."

"Hmm." Is what she gave me—a sweet, contented smile to match.

Man, I was so sprung off her.

Gone.

And I needed her to be mine.

Fast, quick, and in a hurry. Like yesterday.

I could hardly stand it.

"Can we give this thing a try?" I more so stated than asked.

"What thing?" She knitted her brows, a confused resolve in her voice.

I paused for a moment. Considering the best way to proceed. She made it so easy to be open and transparent with her, but I didn't even know how to formulate my words.

I quickly decided I'd just put it all out there.

"Destiney baby, I want you and you only. A committed relationship. Official. Exclusive. I don't want anyone else to have you. Mind or body. And when you're ready, and you'll have me, I want to marry you."

She held my gaze but was expressionless and silent for several agonizing moments.

"I don't want anyone else to have me either. I only want you to have me," she returned confidently.

I released the breath I was holding. "So, are we really going to do this?"

"I'd love to do this with you."

I smiled real big. "Yeah?"

"Yeah." She gave me a Kool-Aid smile of her own.

And something else. I didn't plan to bring up children again. Ever.

I was fine discussing it with her, but she'd have to bring it up first.

I always saw myself with children in my future, but maybe God had another path for me.

For us.

If she still wanted them. I was unsure of that specific detail, but I didn't want to bring up anything that would trigger her in any way. She had already been through so much, and I was fine leaving well enough alone.

I guess this was one of those things we'd eventually get around to hashing out.

In the meantime, I was glad to have my wife back and so excited that we made things official.

"When are you going home Destiney baby?"

"I can leave right now."

"You sure?"

"Hell yeah."

"I'm leaving now. Coming to get you."

I still had another meeting scheduled, but I could take that at home.

I needed to get to my baby.

Finally.

To be continued…

Destiney and Micah's story concludes in book two *Destiney Fulfilled*.

Thank you for reading! If you enjoyed this story, please consider leaving a review on your platform of choice.

Acknowledgments

I am beyond grateful for the opportunity to share this story and for the courage to put my tongue on the page and write what feels most authentic to the characters and most natural to me. To God be the glory. Always!

This story was a true labor of love, and there are a few very dear people who made it all possible.

JM, your friendship has been a wonderful surprise. My middle child is why we met, as you were his preschool teacher, and you have been a part of our lives ever since. He'll be thirteen this year! Thank you for rocking with me on this journey, holding me accountable, and graciously reading every version of this story. Your encouragement and support have been unwavering. Thank you.

PR, you've been such a gem all these years. I was a brand-new mom when we met. My firstborn was weeks old, and can you believe he'll be fourteen this year? I love that we mark our years of friendship by his age, LOL! I am so blessed to have you! Thank you.

DL, we met in college back in 2015. As a non-traditional undergrad, I was laser-focused on getting my degree and moving on with my life, but I'm so thankful you sat next to me in class that day. I'm even more grateful you were so friendly and conversed with me. You've been a constant presence in my life ever since. Thank you.

My sisters, who beautifully embody the spirit of Destiney's sister, Daijah. I love you and I love our tribe. I'll always be proud of you! Thank you for believing in me and my writing when I was twelve and still believing in me today. Thank you for always showing up for me. I'm so grateful for your encouragement, as it truly helped me finish this story. I couldn't have done this without you!

My babies, I've never grown as much as I have since becoming your mom. Everything I do is for you, and everything I do well is because of you. I love you three with all my heart. Thank you for allowing me to write.

My husband, I can't adequately express how much you mean to me and there aren't enough ways to say thank you. But truly, thank you for being my support. I appreciate you beyond words. This story has taken me on an incredible journey, pushing me beyond what I ever imagined at times. I'm grateful for your constant encouragement along the way. I completed this first draft on our fifteenth wedding anniversary, and I fondly remember you joking about being such a wonderful husband for letting me write instead of taking me out. My love, you are wonderful for many reasons, and I love you fiercely. I always will. Now that we—yes, we—have finally accomplished this, you can take me out anytime, baby!

About the Author

Vivienne Paul is obsessed with a sweet, sappy black love story, and most days—with a cup of tea or glass of wine in hand—you'll find her reading or writing one.
A Northern California native, she's a wife and a mom embracing life's tender moments and its beautiful chaos.
In the time between, she's an occasional artist and amateur chef.
She is currently writing her next book. Follow her for updates on upcoming titles.

IG: vivpaulwrites

vivpaulwrites@gmail.com

www.ingramcontent.com/pod-product-compliance
Lightning Source LLC
Chambersburg PA
CBHW020408110726

47899CB00006B/1905